BLOOD ON THE BAR

Lucas the Atoner book 1

IAIN ROB WRIGHT

SalGad Publishing Group

2389
IAIN ROB WRIGHT
PICTURE FRAME
WANT FREE BOOKS?

An Irishman walks into a bar...

"Ah, would yer ever piss off, ya wee gobshite! Yer giving a fella headache!" Lucas threw his hands up and blew a raspberry as he leapt from his bar stool. The bald-headed youth stood three inches taller than him and sported a nasty-looking battle scar on his scalp, but the most intimidating thing about him was his aftershave—which smelled like a crate-full of cats. He was also as high as a kite and had been making a nuisance of himself for more than twenty minutes now. No one in the pub could hear themselves think. Lucas had finally taken offence when the lad proclaimed he'd lost his job because of 'all the Poles coming over.'

The feckin eejit!

Of all the many things to get on Lucas's wick, racism was among the worst. If people could just embrace their different coloured armpits and funny ways of speaking, the world would be a better place. Tribalism had lost its use the moment the first caveman learned he could hunt more food than he needed and trade it with the funny-looking fella down by the cut for that lovely looking stick he had.

"Watch your mouth, Paddy," said the lad, unsteady on his feet but brimming with testosterone. "You ain't in Belfast now."

Lucas's accent derived from Dublin, but there seemed little to gain by informing the lad. He did make a point, however, of standing toe to toe with the him. "Is there a group of folk you don't loathe, lad? Peculiar, because you're quite the mongrel yourself."

"The hell you talkin' about, Mick?"

"Name's Lucas. Mick must be drinking down another pub with Paddy."

"Come on now, gentlemen!" The landlord leaned over the bar, a red-headed familiar sort of chap about a foot shorter than any man ought to be. With dusky skin and plump oval cheeks, he oddly resembled a mole. Small round spectacles perched on a long nose completed the look. He wagged a chubby finger at them now like a disapproving aunt. "Put the aggro to bed or take it outside. People are trying to relax."

Lucas waved a hand dismissively and told the man not to fret. "The lad and I are just having a wee discourse, guv'na. Did you know his ancestors include Germanic nomads, Romani travelers, and ironically, Polish settlers?"

The lad spat, partly down his own shirt. His pupils rolled about angrily, all over the place. "You want me to plant you right here, mate? I-I ain't no sodding Pole."

Lucas folded his arms and sighed dramatically. "You think genealogy is grounds for violence? Let me assure you, every single person drinking in this fine establishment tonight is a slopping cauldron of ingredients. Far too late in the game for 'purity' to still be a thing. And no, Polish people are not responsible for you losing your job, of that you can be sure."

Despite his defiance—the clenching of his jaw and fists —the lad appeared unsettled. When he spoke again, his tone was less sure. "Y-Yeah? And what would you know about it?"

Lucas reached out and pinched the lad's earlobe, so rapidly the lad stumbled and fingered his ear as if he feared he'd been cut. "Just taking a peek," Lucas explained, holding up his hands innocently. "I can now confirm, with joyful alacrity, that you lost your job because you called in sick two Mondays out of every five, and on the ones you dragged yourself in for, you did so either drunk from the previous night's session, or hungover so impressively that you were asleep on the job. Shame, because the gaffer thought you'd have made a good mechanic. That would have made your parents take notice, aye?"

"W-What? How do you...?"

Lucas shrugged and retrieved his beer from the bar. "I know it because you know it, lad, so stop kidding yourself that anyone else is to blame for your screw-ups. You're an addict. I sympathise, truly, but unlike me, you have to hold down a job. Perhaps you should work on being less of a dryshite?"

The pub's other drinkers were agog, and their chatting ceased. If a tumbleweed had been nearby, it would have rolled across the floorboards then. The mole-like landlord stood back from the bar as if ready to run for the phone, but Lucas remained unconcerned. He was in no mood to play nice. Not tonight.

The lad's eyes darted left and right, as if searching for a

way out—or hidden cameras. "Y-You ain't right in the head, mate. I'd lay you out, but you ain't worth the trouble."

Lucas grunted. "Biggest understatement you'll ever make. Now leave a man to his thinking."

The lad showed he had at least some sense remaining—he stomped away.

A relieved whistle sounded behind the bar and the landlord stepped back up to the pumps. "You had a lucky escape there, pal. Jake don't usually walk away."

Lucas took a deep swig from his pint, then said, "One of us had a lucky escape, aye."

"How did you know all that stuff anyway?" The landlord eyed him dubiously. "Felt like you were about to tell his fortune."

"I like to take an interest. People aren't so difficult to understand when you know what flaps to lift and where to sniff. I've been around long enough to smell a turd pretty quick."

"Huh, fair enough. Want another?" He nodded at Lucas's pint.

"Aye, keep her filled. Don't want to see the bar through the bottom if I can help it."

"Tough day?"

"Tough life, fella. It ain't easy being me, let's just leave it at that. But the thing is, I can't much remember the last few days. There's a black hole where my mind should be—and don't you dare make an Irish joke."

The landlord chuckled and placed a fresh glass beneath the taps, pulling the lever gently. The way he did it without looking showed his time behind the pumps had not been short. The cleanliness of the bar also testified to his tenure. "Well, you weren't blacked-out here, pal, if it helps. I've never seen you until tonight, although you do seem familiar."

"Aye, we drunks all look alike." Lucas took the fresh pint and started on it right away. Crisp and cold. Heaven in a glass.

Ah, sweet beer. Mankind's greatest creation.

He placed the glass back on the bar and glanced at Jake who was brooding over by the pool table with a pair of cronies. They each glared at Lucas with the same bloodshot eyes, but his desire for a scrap had passed, so he returned his attention back to the landlord. "You get much trouble from their ilk?"

The landlord thumbed his spectacles higher up his long nose and raised an eyebrow. "What d'you reckon?"

"I reckon people used to be friendlier. A tavern was a place for men to pat each other on the back after a hard day's graft. Now the kicks don't stop until your teeth are gone and your brains are leaking out through your lugholes."

The landlord plucked another glass from beneath the bar and started polishing it. "What are you? Early forties?"

"Sure," said Lucas. "Let's assume I am."

"Well you talk like an old man. Cheer up and concentrate on your own worries. I know how to run a pub, and this is a nice place." He peered over at Jake and his pals. "Mostly."

And it was no lie. The lounge was poky and dated, with horse brasses hanging from the peeling walls, but it was cosy too—a refuge from the wind, rain, and worries of the world. Shadows danced on the walls, cast from fireplaces at either end, and old cushions and rickety stools radiated a sense of history—generations of drinkers coming and going with time.

"How long you had this place?" he asked.

"Five or six years now. Spent most my life drifting about so thought it was time to put down some roots. Let the drifters come to me."

"Yer not wed?"

The landlord chuckled. "Me? No... Perhaps in another life, but I've never found a woman who will have me. How about you?"

"I've the opposite problem. Women want to have me, but I won't be had."

"A fine problem to have. Enjoy your drink. That'll be three-twenty."

Lucas tossed a blue note and a handful of silver shrapnel on the bar. "For the conversation," he said.

The landlord thanked him and poured himself something red, then moved to serve a drinker at the opposite end of the bar. Lucas appreciated the return to silence, for when Jake had started performing, it had shunted away his thoughts until there'd been no choice but to confront the drugged-up fool. Truthfully, the interruption had done little damage—his mind was a grey sky without a cloud in sight. He'd never had a blackout before, even after a long lifetime of boozing. This was a new experience for him.

Something had happened.

But what?

His most recent memory was of waking up in a pile of rubbish behind this pub. As places went to awake confused, a pub was about the best-case scenario, but he'd prefer to know how he'd got there. He didn't even know the name of this place—and that just seemed outright rude. He wasn't used to feeling lost or confused. That wasn't what he was about. If anybody said anything about Lucas, it would be that he was a fella what always knew the score. Not tonight though. Tonight, he was as lost as mouse tits on a whale.

"Hello, you okay?"

Lucas turned to find a young woman of early twenties standing beside him. She wore a bright smile beneath a small nose, and her crystalline-blue eyes were at odds with her inky-black hair—which her tawny eyebrows betrayed as a dye job. Lucas was an attractive man—when he deigned to be—but he wasn't at his best tonight, so the girl's approach was a mild surprise. He returned her smile, flashing his perfect teeth and enjoying the shiver he sent through the girl. "How are you this fine night, fair lass?"

"I am good, thank you." She possessed an accent. Polish? No... *something else.* "My name is Kveta, but people call me Vetta."

"And I'm guessing you're from the green and pleasant lands of... *Slovakia*? Am I right?"

"Yes! How did you know?"

"I've been there many times, a land of green pastures and ancient woodland, with a half-decent ice hockey team too. The women there possess the same natural beauty as the land, and you are no exception. If you were a landscape, you would be a gentle stream through a field of violets."

The girl blushed, and it made her gentle eyes even more striking against the darkness of her hair. "Your words are very nice, and I also want to say thank you." Her voice shaky and nervous. "Jake is always nasty about us, but you tell him he is wrong. My friends say you are welcome to come drink."

Lucas glanced over at a group of burly men in the

corner. Unlike Jake and co., they didn't glare at him or sneer. Instead, they waved merrily and welcomed him over. "*Cześć*!"

It was difficult to refuse the company of a fine lady and jovial men, so Lucas didn't even try. He told Vetta he'd be delighted to join her, and he went and took a seat with her friends, making fast acquaintances before delighting them all by reciting each of their names perfectly. They were a mix of Polish and Slovakian, with one Romanian for flavour. They spoke English well, though it would not have been a problem if they did not, and they refused to let Lucas buy his drinks all night. They treated him like an old friend, and he chatted with them merrily until turfing out time.

It was shortly after that when things turned nasty.

⊥

LUCAS BADE HIS DRINKING BUDDIES FAREWELL SHORTLY AFTER last call. Most of them lived together in a house within walking distance so they set off on foot, leaving via the pub's front porch. Vetta and the Romanian—Gheorghe was his name—lived in flats elsewhere but were yet to leave, both wanting to stay behind and get another drink. The landlord was having none of it though. "I'm not losing sleep for the likes of you rabble," he said brusquely, before diffusing any offence with a grin.

Lucas could have drunk another ten pints if allowed, still unsettled by his bizarre memory loss, but he didn't argue with the fella. Instead, he reached over the bar and thanked him for his hospitality. "What's the name of this place again, guv'na?"

"The Black Sheep." The landlord wiped his hands off on his shirt and accepted the handshake, wringing Lucas's hand vigorously with a smile.

Lucas was about to return the smile when he was jolted backwards. He snatched his hand away, head spinning.

Burning...

Screaming...

The landlord's plump hand still hovered above the bar, and he seemed a little disorientated as well. "You catch a shock or something, pal?"

"Um, yeah. Got a case of the banshees for a second there. I'm having an odd night."

The landlord frowned. "Maybe you should see a doctor."

Vetta grabbed Lucas by the arm and startled him. "You come?" she said, nodding toward the door.

"We go find more drinking," shouted Gheorgie, staggering about in all directions and colliding with chairs. "*Da*?"

Unsettled, Lucas nodded. "Aye, okay, aye, um yeah, let's take this show on the road. Erm..." he turned to the landlord one last time, trying to make sense of that strange feeling he'd just experienced. "What's your name, guv'na?"

The landlord swallowed and thumbed his glasses. "My name? Oh, it's Julian, pleased to meet you...?"

"Name's Lucas. May the road rise up to meet you, my friend. Um..." His mind spun for a moment, leaving him without words. Why did his head feel so hollow? "G-Good night, guv'na. Yeah. Okay then. Bye."

Lucas stumbled towards the pub's rear exit while Vetta clutched his elbow. Gheorghie had already made it outside, and he put his arm around both of them when they joined him in the alleyway. "Lucas, Lucas. You come to my uncle's restaurant, yes? He make the most amazing meat rolls. Pork, yes? Beautiful. Mwah!" He kissed his fingers. "You come?"

"I shall do me very best, ya wee dote, but right now I think we should call it a night. Any more piss in you, and you'll be pouring pints from your pecker!"

Gheorghie seemed to accept that his sobriety was no longer tenable, so he bid them farewell and proceeded to sing his way unintelligibly into the distance. The night was mild but wet, as it had been raining hard earlier, but that rain was now only a refreshing drizzle on their faces. A full moon pierced the oily-black sky like a shiny silver coin and gave everything an ethereal sheen. Lucas would have called it a fine night if not for the overflowing bins and the cheeky odour of piss. Not to mention he had gaps in his memory. While his jaunty personality was mostly put on, a way to keep people from knowing him truly, tonight it was at complete odds with how he was feeling inside. Despair clung to him, and his attempts to shed it only made it dig its claws deeper.

"I must get taxi," said Vetta, blushing enough to make the subtext obvious, that he should come with her. Lucas could happily waste several hours in the girl's company, but...

"I shall see you off, lass," he said regretfully. There was no other way. Rumpy-pumpy was not what he needed right now. What he needed was answers.

Her face fell, innocent eyes wounded. "Oh. Are you sure?"

Lucas wished he could explain it to her, make her understand why sleeping with him would be such a colossally bad idea, but fairy tales would not salve the girl's ego. All he could do was sugar-coat the truth. "I would love nothing more than to hop in a taxi and expand the boundaries of our relationship, lass. Heaven knows, shameful is my default setting..." He took a moment to steel himself, to double-down on the choice he was making. The way she was looking at him now, so beautiful and mortified at once, made him want to reconsider—but he could not. He couldn't take the risk. He dropped his accent and spoke plainly. She deserved better than the theatrics. "You are too kind a soul to get entangled with the likes of me, Vetta, truly. And, quite honestly, I'm too old for you."

Too old by far.

"Not so old," she muttered. "You are handsome man."

Lucas chuckled. "Aye, I am at that, aren't I? But I'm also a thumbtack. I draw blood, no matter how delicately someone tries to handle me. Your innocence is not something I am willing to remove. I have enough to atone for already."

A slight breeze lifted her inky hair around her face as she peered at him, adding a supernatural flair to her beauty. "My *innocence*?"

Lucas sighed and brushed a strand of that black hair from her face. The brief contact gave him a flash of who she was, and he wanted more. It was like having a mouthful of tender chicken while starving, before having the rest snatched cruelly away. And yet, if he touched her again, his resolve would crumble to dust, and he would fall down a well of poor decisions. He saw a sister in her life, uncovering worms in the soil. He saw a plump mother constantly cooking in a small cottage. He saw no father but felt her longing for one. Yet, there was no resentment or anger. Very little of the thorny brambles he found inside of most people's hearts.

"Innocence is something you have that many do not, Vetta. Now let's see you to that taxi."

She sighed, but despite his rebuff, reached out and took his hand, a gesture he was forced to avoid, leaving her looking even more hurt. He longed to reach out and take her arm and apologise, but that only left him confused. Loneliness was the meat of his existence, but tonight, it felt like a wound raw and bleeding. What was wrong with him? Why did he feel so... *odd.* And why did he care about what this girl thought about him?

As they walked through the alleyway, a *whit-woo* whistled behind them. They turned and saw several shapes emerge from an alcove opposite the pub—three in total—Jake and his two cronies. The *whit-woos* turned into a mocking rendition of *Danny Boy* that was surprisingly tuneful.

Lucas moved Vetta behind him. "Stand back, lass. These chancers are about to do something stupid."

Jake had been the one whistling, but he stopped now and glared at Lucas. "Looks like you pulled, Mick. You got a real hard on for the Poles, dontcha!"

"She's Slovakian," Lucas informed the lad coolly. One of Jake's pals clutched a pool cue and began stoking its length as he leered at Vetta. Lucas made a point of looking the lad in the eyes. "You so much as spit in her direction, and I'll take yer wee bollocks and swap 'em with your eyes."

The lad snickered, but there was also a glint of uncertainty in his eyes.

Jake took a swipe at Lucas, an open-handed slap

designed to humiliate, but it missed by mere inches when Lucas took a step backwards.

"Ooh, you're a fast one!" Jake chuckled—then snarled. "Not fast enough though!"

It beggared belief, but Lucas didn't see the next blow coming. It crunched beneath his chin and whipped his head back. He was more surprised than hurt, but the assault left him off-balance, so when a pool cue suddenly cracked against his skull, the world inexplicably tilted.

"Christ!" came Jake's voice. "That must have hurt!"

Lucas peered up at the moon, lying on his back atop the piss-stained pavement. His vision was blurry. His head throbbed in agony, which shouldn't have been possible. He could count the number of times he'd felt pain on one hand—if it was missing three fingers.

Christ on a bike, what is happening to me?

Lucas moaned, hurt badly and not understanding why. His skull thudded like an over-tightened drum. An odd sensation in his gut made him retch, like he needed to get something out. Why couldn't he find the strength to get up? Things were all wrong. *He* was all wrong.

Jake's mocking laughter turned feral as he stalked after Vetta, and he hollered through the alleyway. "Looks like you won't be getting any Leprechaun spunk up you tonight, sweetheart." He grabbed his crotch and sneered. "Never mind, I'll give you what you want."

Vetta screamed.

Lucas battled to get to his feet, but one of Jake's cronies put the boot in and sent him tumbling over the dirty pavement. He came to rest, gasping, beside the pub's wheelie bins. With his face so close to the ground, he spotted a deep scorch mark in the exact spot where he'd woken earlier, but there was no time to wonder about it now. He grabbed hold of one of the large metal wheelie bins and hoisted himself to his feet. Propped up, he turned just in time to catch the snarling thug coming in for Round 2. Ducking a punch, he threw himself forward, ramming his shoulder into the lad's ribs. Only mildly stunned, the lad rushed back in, but this time, Lucas struck like a snake and rammed two fingers into each eyeball.

The lad dropped to his knees, squealing.

Jake's remaining crony appeared and swung the pool cue from Lucas's left, parting the air with an audible *whoosh*. Lucas was too sluggish to duck in time, but he managed to get an arm up and absorb the blow into his armpit. It knocked the wind out of him, but he held on long enough to tackle the lad into the bin and wrench the pool cue away. Then he cried out as the lad fought back, ramming rights and lefts into his ribs. Eventually, he managed to turn and dodge a punch aimed at his head, giving himself an opening. He straightened his neck and rammed his forehead into the lad's nose. An audible *crunch* and the lad dropped like a lump of coal. Lucas kicked him in the backside for good measure.

"Yer pa must have been a cactus. Because you're a right wee prick!"

It wasn't his best line, but it would have to do. Vetta's screams were calling. Jake had chased her all the way down the alleyway by now, and it sounded like he'd caught her. Clutching his ribs, Lucas hurried as quickly as he could. He found Vetta scrambling through a patch of muddy grass outside a Chinese takeaway, with Jake on top of her. He was trying to flip her onto her back, and even at a distance, and in the darkness, Lucas could see the animal lust on his face.

Jake couldn't stop what he was doing now even if he wanted to. The beast had him. That and a shit-load of Columbia-knows-what.

Lucas roared, and felt exuberant as his fire suddenly returned from wherever it had fled, whooshing back into his body. The weakness that had oddly befallen him was gone. He was himself again.

And in one hell of a pissing bad mood.

"Get off her!" Lucas bellowed. "Get off her before I show you what true violence really is." Jake was obviously surprised to see Lucas back on his feet, and he glanced towards the alleyway for his friends. Lucas snarled. "They can't help you now, lad."

Jake clambered to his feet, allowing Vetta to scramble away on her knees. He seemed to consider his options but decided to rush at Lucas with both hands ready to brawl. As soon as he was close, he threw a punch, an arcing haymaker that could have put an elephant to sleep. Lucas threw a punch of his own, equally dangerous, just as fast.

Their fists collided in mid-air, seasoned conkers cracking together and making the sound of a gunshot. Jake yelled and recoiled, clasping his right hand as if it was on fire. "Y-You broke my goddamn hand, you maniac!"

"Aye! And because I'm having an off night, that's all I'll break. Now sod off before I really get going."

Jake sneered. "I'm going to ki—"

"What? Kill me? Believe me, boy, far greater villains than you have tried. Plenty of heroes too. Yet here I stand." *Barely though it might be.*

Jake swallowed, then looked about sheepishly, before turning and fleeing into the alleyway like a kicked cat.

"Wise move," Lucas muttered to himself. "Eejit!"

Vetta stood nearby, sobbing like a frightened child who had lost her mother, and Lucas did something to which he was unaccustomed. He went and put an arm around her. "Everything will be okay," he said. She was safe.

She was trembling. "H-He was going to-"

"I know what the maggot was planning to do, lass, but he didn't. You're fine. You're okay. Lucas has got you."

Vetta was a child in his arms, and her fear made him ache. He didn't let go until her tears dried up.

It took some time.

⊥

"How did you fight them all off? Those... those *bastards!*" Vetta had recovered from her ordeal and was now angry that Jake had attacked her. The anger was good though, for it meant she wouldn't let fear cow her. She clutched Lucas's right hand now and examined it closely. "You're not even hurt."

"I have tough, old bones," he said, although he felt more fragile than ever. "Takes a lot to cast me down. God himself, one might say."

She frowned, perhaps sensing there were unapparent truths in his words. He chided himself for toying with her, but she didn't seem irritated by it. In fact, every time she looked at him, she seemed fascinated. She broke away from her stare to check her watch, a clunky gold thing, then tapped her finger against the glass. "My taxi will be any minute. You sure I cannot have number? I would like to see you again, Lucas, if only being friends."

He hugged her, growing to enjoy the contact. "You've

already suffered enough of my company, lass. Don't give yourself any more reason to blame me."

She tiptoed and kissed him on the cheek. "Of all people in the world I blame, Lucas, you are not one."

Headlights flooded the road at the bottom of the hill and Vetta wished him goodbye. She glanced back once, but if she did so a second time, he didn't see it because he hurried back into the darkness of the alleyway, wanting to take another look at that scorch mark he had seen. It meant something.

But what?

Jake and his thugs had scarpered, but they shouldn't have posed any threat to Lucas anyway. He was invincible. All powerful. *But not tonight.* Instead, he had taken half a beating and allowed an innocent girl to be assaulted. The fear in Vetta's innocent blue eyes already haunted him.

He reached the spot behind the pub where he had seen the scorch mark and stopped. A blue light hummed above the back door, but there was little else to see by. That the moon was full helped a little, but he had to kneel to get a proper look. The scorch mark was still there, and he was sure it was the exact spot where he'd woken up. What had burned the ground here? Had hellfire accompanied his arrival?

Arrival from where? And why did I end up in an alleyway behind a pub? How bloody much did I have to drink?

But it wasn't a booze blackout. Such things were not a burden to one such as him. No, this was something else. Something that terrified Lucas to his core.

Confused, he reached out a hand, hoping to find further clues around the scorch mark, but before he could investigate further, a massive rush of air buffeted his back and knocked him forwards onto his hands and knees. A single blue feather fluttered down in front of his face and came to rest on the ground. He recognised it immediately, and when he leapt up and whirled around, the brightest of lights blinded him.

A light he knew all too well.

Heavenly Aura.

Not now! Christ on a bike, not now.

"LUCIFER, FALLEN ANGEL OF LIGHT, ADVERSARY AND DECEIVER, FATHER OF LIES AND ABYSSAL LORD, SATAN, DEVIL INCARNATE, AND RIGHTFUL MONARCH OF HELL. I BESEECH YOU."

The light faded, and Lucas faced his kin. "I go by the name Lucas nowadays, Gladri. And you don't need to shout. I have the same hearing you do."

Gladri raised a delicate white eyebrow and gave a hollow interpretation of a smirk. He was beautiful as always—flawless—but it was that flawlessness that made his features so uninteresting. That and the fact he struggled to emulate any single human emotion.

"And you sport a peculiar accent as well," he commented. "Very well, I shall grant you your delusions... *Lucas.*"

"And I shall grant you yours, Gladri, but first d'you want to reign in your glory a bit? You're making a fella feel a tad inferior."

"My apologies!" Gladri retracted his vast blue and red wings like the receding plumage of a posturing peacock. The thick scars on Lucas's shoulder blades twinged with phantom pain as he recalled his own lost appendages. His wings had been magnificent, the blackest of blacks, and of greater span than all but one other angel. Gladri's were minuscule by comparison. He tried not to dwell on the loss. It would only make him angry.

"What can I do for you, brother?" Lucas asked wearily. "It's unlike you to dirty yourself in the realm of men—especially a manky alleyway outside a boozer."

Gladri glanced around and seemed to notice the squalor for the first time. As if to taunt him, a fat rat scurried from one side of the alley to the other. Disdain clung to the angel's face as he spoke. "It is good to see you again, brother, all things considered, but the reason I seek you is not social."

"When is it ever? I was hoping Heaven may have forgotten about me by now. They stopped inviting me to the Christmas party ages ago."

Gladri laughed, but it was an approximation of the sound and thus crudely artificial. "Heaven can hardly afford to forget you, Lucas."

"Oh, come on! I have done no great ill in two millennium!" he shrugged, "Okay, a slip here or there, but not *too* wicked, and that thing with the badger and the marmalade wasn't my fault. Is it not time to finally leave me be? Surely there are more pressing issues for Heaven to deal with?"

Gladri spotted another rat and shuddered. He brushed his platinum tresses behind his ears as if he feared they might drag on the ground. "Do not think me naive, Lucas. You have no desire to be left alone."

"Really? How's that then?"

"If you wanted peace, you would have stayed in Hell, instead of leaving it in disarray. No, you desire Heaven's attention. You seek Father's forgiveness. Ha! The Devil seeks to atone. Is it absurd or poetic?"

Lucas sighed. "How about tragic?"

"Yes! Yes, that is it! Your existence is tragic, brother, and destined to become more so, I fear."

Lucas groaned. *Here it comes! The telling off. The mockery. The contempt.* Lucas was no stranger to Heaven's sanctimony, had even gone to war over it. "Spit it out, Gladri! Either that or let's go find a place still serving beer."

Gladri winced. "Beer? A base substance depriving beings of virtue. You are a disgrace, brother, as much now as you ever were. You act like you wish to be one of them—a human—but it is an *act*, is it not? You do play the part well, admittedly, empathising with their plight, trying to right wrongs... Yes, yes! Fighting the good fight, a reformed villain delivering justice. Ha! Wonderful. But you do not *love* humanity, brother. You seek only to undermine the past. If you simply do enough good, surely you shall be welcomed back into Heaven, a warrior returned. We'll throw a parade and Michael himself shall embrace you." Gladri's glorious face darkened and the joy of reunion seemed to depart. "It is fantasy. A charade. You pursue your own ends under the guise of kindness, and it mocks us all. There is no way back for you... *Lucifer.*"

Lucas felt his temper boiling. Tonight was not a night he would heed a lecture. "I thought God forgives! Isn't that his whole gig?"

"He forgives much, but not all. And not *us*, brother. Not *we*, the first sons and daughters. We subscribe to a higher standard. You know this, for you were once the best of us. It still pains me at how far you've fallen. Michael is still to cease his weeping."

"The dote always was a cry-baby," Lucas muttered. This was the kind of piousness that had led him to turn against Heaven, and he enjoyed hearing it no more now. "You think we subscribe to a higher standard, Gladri? Why? Because of the power we wield? Angels have no power, merely the illusion of it. What can an angel do in Heaven but obey? At least down here there are consequences—choices. Perhaps you're right though, perhaps I *do* have an agenda for helping humanity, but you're wrong about one thing."

Gladri rolled his eyes, a gesture most unbecoming of an angel, and it seemed to make the musky air in the alleyway groan. "And what is that?"

"I love humanity with all my heart. It is the only thing that has given me any joy during my everlasting penance. My brothers abandoned me because of a mistake I made long ago, and still you refuse to forgive me. You cast me into a fiery pit, you took my light..." He inhaled and tried not to let the memories cripple him. "You took my wings, you... you... you feckin' *dryshites*!" He took a moment to gather himself, pinching his nose and focusing on the brittle bone beneath the flesh. When he looked up again, there were tears in his eyes. Even now, the memories devastated him. "And yet, I love you all still. Father too. You say I am Fallen, Gladri, but I love more now than I ever did in Heaven. Love does not exist in duty and obedience. It exists in sacrifice and desire. Without consequence, love amounts to nothing."

Gladri flapped his wings in irritation, sending rubbish and dust hurtling down the alleyway. Two plastic shopping bags rose up and danced together like lovers in the moonlight, and that orphaned blue feather appeared again, swirling upwards into the night like it was en route to the moon. "You are a celestial being, Lucifer, as am I. You are not special. You are not different. One must applaud your rousing speech though, regardless of its delusion. Play a part long enough and you shall become it."

Lucas growled. "It is not an act! I understand humanity more than any brother in Heaven. My rebellion was only unforgivable because those in Heaven lack the ability to see past blind obedience. To not do as commanded is the only sin in Heaven, and it encompasses all. Down here, amongst the weakness of mankind, there are countless sins, yet all can be forgiven. Any soul can atone. Father sees that too, I know it. He would not have cast me down just to punish me. If that were the case, he would have closed Hell off from Earth and left me trapped there forever—but he did not. He tethered Hell and Earth together, and allowed me to mix with mankind, to learn its ways and see the strength he placed in the hearts of every man. I am down here in the dirt because Father intended me to be, so let me get my hands dirty. There's work to do, let me get on with it."

"No, brother, you are here because you broke Father's heart beyond mending, and you have made a nuisance of yourself across the tapestry for too long. Heaven's patience is at an end. It does not please me to render unto you Father's latest judgement, but it is my duty. As you, yourself, once taught me."

Lucas knew when it was time to go, so he prepared to make a run for it, but when he tried to phase away, his body went nowhere—in fact he was frozen stiff. He couldn't move even the smallest finger on either hand, and he had to fight just to get his lips moving. "W-what are you doing, brother?"

Gladri thrust out his delicate hands, summoning blue flames of heavenly fire. His eyes became icy lanterns, and his words cast white smoke into the air. "The sentence is already passed, Lucifer. You may have felt its beginnings already, but I am here to render it whole. From henceforth, you shall walk amongst the lower creatures as one of them."

Lucas fell to his knees, body burning. His chest sucked agonisingly inward—air rushing into virgin lungs. His vision deteriorated rapidly, losing colour and clarity. Hearing dulled. Strength ebbed away. A hollowness fell over him, of which he had never known—even in the lowest pits of Hell.

He felt weak.

Fragile.

Afraid.

Human.

No! No, it can't be!

"Why?" begged Lucas, barely able to lift his heavy head. "Why does Father do this to me? Why can He not forgive?"

Gladri seemed at once amused and regretful, his wings twitching behind him as if he were eager to take flight. "You are an artificer of catastrophe, a wielder of destruction, and Heaven will tolerate your recklessness no longer. Humanity is the thing you claim to covet most, so we shall see how truly you empathise with it. You shall live and die as a man. Perhaps that is the forgiveness you seek, Lucifer."

"My name is *Lucas*!"

"So be it. Farewell, *Lucas*."

Lucas clawed himself along the floor like a baby learning to crawl. Gladri was gone, a small patch of blue flame dwindling where he'd been, and that single blue feather still fluttering in the air. The two plastic bags ceased their dancing and settled on the ground in the middle of the alleyway. Lucas studied them as if they might have answers, but of course there was no sense to be had in any of this.

Cast down again, even lower than before, he finally understood that Father would never forgive him. It had all been for nothing.

His time was coming to an end. There would be no return. No chance to atone.

A shadow emerged from the same alcove Jake and his friends had hidden in earlier. This time it was a woman. "V-Vetta? What are you doing here?"

As much as she looked concerned to find him lying on the ground, she also looked embarrassed, and she lit up the darkness with her glowing red cheeks. "Car at bottom of hill was not taxi. It was someone picking up friend. I not want to wait alone so I hurry after you. I..." She stopped talking, as if worried something bad might happen. When she continued, her voice was half-volume. "Was that an angel you talk to?"

Lucas groaned. "A monster, not an angel."

"But it had *wings*."

He groaned again. "Yeah, okay, fine, it *was* an angel. Can you just help me up, please?"

"Of course." She rushed to his side and got him standing again. His body felt like it was full of oddly shaped bricks. "How do I help?" she asked.

Lucas staggered forwards, taking some steps on his own. "Find me a feckin' drink."

Sobering Thoughts

Vetta rented a poky flat in the bad part of town, and it was filled with only the barest of furniture. She had combated the sparseness by hanging photographs all over the walls. "My family," she explained when she saw him looking at them. "They are in Slovakia. Bratislava, you know?"

Lucas nodded. He had only been looking at the pictures because they'd caught his eye, not because he was interested, so he moved over to the room's worn two-seat sofa and threw himself down in a huff.

A bad night. A bad, bad night. Since leaving the alleyway, his every movement was sluggish and painful, fragile sinews and heavy bones wearing away at each other. He feared death every second as he assumed all humans did, in constant danger of slipping and breaking his papery skull in an instant or dying of a heart attack. There was no way to stop it.

Inevitable.

It meant he approached every single second cautiously.

Vetta dashed into the tiny box that counted for her kitchen and returned with a pint of water, which she handed to him with a shy smile. Since learning the truth about him, she had been tentative and suspicious. One could hardly blame her.

Lucas thanked her for the drink and held the glass in his hands, but he didn't take a sip. Water wasn't his thing. "Do you not have anything stronger?"

Vetta raised an eyebrow and pointed to the glass. "Is vodka."

"A pint?" said Lucas, surprised, but then he shrugged and said, "Yeah, alright then."

"Are you okay?" Vetta asked for the tenth time, as concerned about him as she was suspicious.

Of course he was not okay. In his entire history-spanning existence, this was the least okay Lucas had ever been. The least okay by far.

He put the glass to his lips and swigged, the fire hitting his throat, and he spluttered. "It's good," he said, gasping. "Are you not going to join me?"

"No, thank you. The angel, he call you Lucifer. Are you... are you The Devil? Are you going to hurt me?"

He took another sip of vodka and it went down easier this time now he was expecting the dry burn. "I *was* the Devil," he admitted, "but no, I won't hurt you. I couldn't hurt a kitten if I wanted to."

Vetta was mortified. "You like to hurt kittens?"

"What? No, no, it was just... I was just saying, I'm human now, and not even a very good one at that."

"You're human?" she asked dubiously. "Like me?"

"How much did you hear in that alleyway?"

"I was right behind you when big light come. I hide in

hole next to building. My mama used to tell me that angels could only come to us in dreams, and only if we have good hearts, but that is not true. You knew angel who come?"

Lucas nodded. "Gladri. Sanctimonious sod if ever there was one. He's Chief Bollocks of the Choir of Justice. It's mostly an honorary position—not a lot of crime in Heaven—but he got to indulge himself tonight. It was Gladri who enacted my previous sentence and cast me down from Heaven after I lost a war against my elder brother. He's always been so smug—the angel who sentenced The Devil to Hell—as if he wasn't just following Michael's orders. And don't even get me started on Michael!"

Vetta still seemed worried. "You talk about war in bible between Good and Evil? Michael is good angel. You are..."

"Aye, that would make me the bad angel."

"Are you evil?"

Lucas stared into his glass and sighed. "Yes. And no."

Vetta nodded and seemed to relax. She took a seat on the tatty sofa seat beside him yet perched as far away as she could. There had been a time when mortals had trembled before him, but now they sat nearby with expressions of pity while making chitchat. How had he been reduced to this? How had he not seen it coming? Was he really so weak and stupid? Arrogance had truly been his sin.

"Why did the angel do this to you?" Vetta asked him. Her eyes were baggy and her skin pasty, signs of tiredness and encroaching sobriety, yet despite all that, she was still beautiful. He remembered touching her face and seeing her spirit. There had been no darkness in her at all. Only hope and compassion. He wondered what would happen if he touched her now.

Vetta was staring at him. "Gladri did this to keep me

from interfering," he said. "To keep me from getting involved." He exhaled, finding it difficult to talk and breathe at the same time. It required a rhythm he wasn't used to. "There's a war going on. Multiple wars on multiple fronts, in fact. You humans all think your world is the only one, but there are others—thousands—but only a few left standing."

Vetta chuckled, as if she thought him ridiculous, but then she seemed to remember what she'd witnessed in the last hour and nodded gravely. "What is happening to these... other worlds?"

Lucas grunted. "Don't ask me. I'm just the idiot who tried to lend a hand. God is being attacked, but he doesn't seem to care much about it. So sod Him."

Vetta folded her arms. "No one is strong enough to attack God."

Lucas nodded to the photographs on her wall. "God has a family like everyone else. And just like everyone else, His family is full of dysfunctional gobshites. Some of them are almost as powerful as God, but none of them have his gift for creativity. Only God is able to *create*, the only one able to forge a universe of His own making and fill it with life. But those who sit upon a throne are destined to die upon it. God's kin are jealous of His creation—wanting the power for themselves so that they might create worlds of their own. God has been forced to shut himself away to avoid his kin's avarice. And that there is the answer to the big question mankind has been asking since its infancy. Why doesn't God answer our prayers? Why does he let bad things happen? Why doesn't he put a stop to Logan Paul? Because he can't! Not without endangering existence itself. He's like that Pope in his little bullet-proof buggy thingy, but with less waving and fancy hats."

Vetta frowned dismissively—an expression of hard truths being heard. "I do not understand. Maybe I don't know your words."

Lucas repeated the key points in Slovak, but it didn't help clarify. Vetta seemed as confused as ever. Weary of talking. Lucas lifted his glass and downed half the vodka. It made him shudder and cough, which only added to his irritation, but he enjoyed the warmness it put inside his chest. "Don't worry about it," he told Vetta. "The universe's problems are neither of our concern. I tried to help and look where it got me."

"You not want to be human?"

"Does anybody?"

Vetta gave no answer. Which was an answer.

Lucas felt his thighs tingle, compelling him to straighten his legs. He rubbed at his knees and wondered how long before they stiffened with old age. Would he get arthritis? He swore he could almost feel himself decaying. Was he actually going to die one day? Today? Tomorrow?

"I am tired," said Vetta, breaking the silence. "And frightened. I think I go to bed and put tonight behind me. You should sleep too."

Lucas argued that he didn't sleep, but then realised it might not be true anymore. "Yeah, um, okay. How do you... *do* it?"

Vetta didn't laugh, but the statement obviously amused her. "You do not know this? How to sleep?"

Why would he? He'd never done it before—had never needed to. "It's absurd how humans waste so much of their short lives in bed."

"Now you get to also. Come, I help you sleep." She took his hand and pulled him up off the sofa.

He staggered. "I-I don't feel right."

"You drink half-pint of vodka. Lucas, you are *drunk*."

Paranoia flooded him, and he felt out of control. He'd spent an eternity drinking alcohol, but its effects had always been minimal, nothing more than a pleasant buzz. Now that he was human, it was muddying his senses. He didn't like the feeling.

Vetta led him unsteadily into the bedroom where she switched on a lamp. Unlike the lounge, this room was cluttered and overcrowded with a table sprinkled with make-up and a long mirror taking up one wall. Soft purple linens and pillows covered the bed, but Vetta threw them aside to get to the covers underneath.

She patted the mattress. "Take off your top and trousers and get in."

Lucas did as commanded but received a telling off when he tried to remove his underwear, and a second telling off for leaving on his shoes. So many ridiculous rules. He felt like such a fool. Vetta removed her own clothes until she was wearing nothing but a black bra and lacy knickers. The way she slid beneath the covers, thighs swishing together like that, stirred a lust inside of him—but then he experienced something else, a gushing from his stomach that leapt right up into his eyes.

"W-Why are you crying?" Vetta propped herself up on one elbow and stared at him uneasily. Her pity added yet another emotion to the smorgasbord inside his head. A mortal's pity was an insult. Yet he couldn't help but cry harder.

"How do you do this?" he begged her in a wavering

voice not entirely under his control. "These... *feelings* inside my head. Like worms. Worms in my mind."

"You never feel things before?"

His emotions had always been gradual things, like the gathering of snow, but this... this was like drowning at sea. He couldn't grab any one feeling long enough to pull himself up and get a breath.

He wiped his eyes and looked at Vetta. "I want it to stop."

She stroked his cheek with the back of her hand. "You sleep. Tomorrow is better, I think."

Too fuzzy-headed for anything else, Lucas lay down on the pillow. The covers were frigid, making him flinch, but he soon acclimated. He faced away from Vetta, not wanting her to see the fresh tears rolling down his cheeks, and he focused on the crooked doors of her wardrobes. Eventually a sharp *click* sounded, and the world went dark.

Time went by in silence. How long, he didn't know, but it felt like seconds and minutes all at once.

"This is ridiculous," he eventually said.

Vetta shushed him. "Just close your eyes. Don't think."

It was the exact opposite of what he was doing. His mind was awash with a hundred questions, all clashing against one another like dhows in a storm. Mere hours ago, he had been capable of infinite thought and unparalleled intelligence, now he was confused and feeble-minded. This mess of emotions was torture, and for the first time in his vast existence he, The Devil, was in Hell.

And he was expected to sleep.

Ha!

His huffing and puffing stopped when something touched his back. He shuddered but settled down as he realised it was Vetta caressing his back with her fingernails. The sensation was like nothing he had ever experienced before, a subtle thing that somehow rendered his whole body numb. His bones felt heavy, and his thoughts drifted away as he focused on the caress against his skin, never knowing which way Vetta's nails would glide next.

But then her nails scratched across his scars, the twin set beneath each shoulder blade.

She stopped, and for a moment, they lay there in the dark, silent. Then she spoke. "These were your wings?"

"Yes."

"Is hurt?"

"Every moment since I lost them."

There was another moment of silence. Perhaps Vetta was waiting for him to rebuke her, but when he didn't, she kept on with the questions. "What happened to them?"

Lucas thought back and became sure that he had never spoken of this with a single human being. It was his pain to endure, not something to titillate a lowly human with, but he was human now too, and for some reason, he wanted to share. "Michael took them."

"Your brother."

"Yes. When Daniel and I stormed the throne room of Heaven with what was left of our army, Michael met us. He is the custodian of Heaven in God's absence. He was alone and surrounded by my angels. Despite that, he would not surrender Heaven. He was prepared to die to protect it. We could have cut him down where he stood. Even if he'd taken ten of us, he could not have defeated us all. Yet..." The words dried up in his mouth. The memories felt forbidden, and that he was betraying some secret law by talking of them openly.

"What happen next?" asked Vetta.

Lucas thought about telling her to mind her own business, but he pushed through the feeling and started talking again. "I pictured my glorious victory, of sitting upon Heaven's throne as the new monarch of existence. I had already conquered Heaven, but this was the moment that would be remembered until the end of time. I could not risk Michael being cut down by one of my brothers. In my arrogance, the thought of having my elder brother on his knees before me blinded me to what was important. I ordered my army back and faced Michael one on one, determined to be the one to beat him." Lucas swallowed, and had to force a lump down into his stomach. "But he beat me. My arrogance was my downfall as Michael bested me easily, always the greatest of warriors. On my knees, he asked me to repent. 'Repent,' he said, 'and all will be forgiven. Refuse, and your army will fall to ruin.'"

"You refused," said Vetta, preempting him.

"Yes. I refused, so he hacked off my wings. My army scattered, but when Heaven recovered, they were all hunted down and dismembered too. By refusing mercy for myself, I had forsaken it of them also. We were all cast down without our wings, unable to ever reach Heaven again. My Fallen brothers turned on me. I had promised them a new kingdom, but that kingdom was Hell. And we burned. All of us, we burned."

Vetta said nothing. The silence went on for a long time, and Lucas could hear his own panting breaths. Then he felt her fingertips on his back again, this time running along the edges of his scars. "Go to sleep," she whispered. "Tomorrow will be better."

Lucas tensed, his body taught, but gradually, he

succumbed. He could not fight it, that light tickling sensation overwhelming him like a crashing wave. His eyelids became fuzzy. His mouth went dry. Slowly his body sank into the mattress, and he stopped caring about anything else. He left behind a great burden, his greatest misery shared with another.

⊥

LUCAS COWERED BEFORE A GREAT BEAST THAT HE COULD NOT see clearly. The only detail was its size. Massive. Colossal. Mountainous.

Its huge weight crushed his bones to dust while he screamed.

The beast roared.

Lucas burned. Disintegrated.

"Lucas!"

He opened his eyes, not understanding why they had even been closed, but then remembering he had slept. He was human now. A weak and fragile human being. Father had forsaken him once more.

No!

Vetta stood over him, holding a steaming mug in her hand. She wore purple leggings and a baggy leopard-print t-shirt. The image of her bra and knickers popped unbidden into his mind. Were his thoughts no longer his own? Were unfiltered images destined to pop into his head forever now?

No, not forever. Just until this short, mortal life ends.

His head was throbbing, and his vision blurry, but Vetta's insistence prompted him to take the steaming mug from her. His nostrils detected the dull whiff of coffee, and it made him a little less groggy. He took a tentative sip and it was bitter. He thanked her for it, then apologised for being there. "I'm sorry for all the trouble I've put you through. I'll leave soon."

"Stay," she said. "Is fine. You need help."

The statement was outrageous, but when he tried to think about what to do next, he had no clue. "Perhaps, I'll stay a short while," he relented, realising that he did need help—at least until he got a hold of himself. "Just until I get a plan together."

She nodded, satisfied, then perched on the bed beside him. "Your accent is gone."

"I've lost more than my accent," he muttered. *So much more.*

"Your powers?"

He peered glumly into the swirling brown coffee for a moment then had a thought. "Vetta, take my hand for a moment." She frowned at him, but he persisted, shoving his hand out towards her. "Please. I just want to try something."

Hesitantly, she took his hand in hers and looked at him nervously. Lucas closed his eyes and concentrated, but all he felt was cold. Vetta's skin was icy, the room itself was not particularly warm, but there were no other sensations coming off her. He could not read her soul, or even sense what she'd had for dinner yesterday, no matter how hard he tried.

He slumped back against the pillows. "I've lost all that I was."

"You are no longer The Devil?"

"I haven't been The Devil for a long time, Vetta. Now I'm nothing."

"Last night, I come to you because you are nice man with big smile. I did not know you were something else."

"What's your point?"

"That you are *not* nothing," she said. "Last night in bar, you are good man. Man who spend time laughing and joking with my friends. What has changed?"

"How about the fact I'm impotent, mortal, and," he sniffed himself, "sweaty."

"You have bad dream that make you sweat. I wake you, no problem. And you are not *impotent*." She nodded to the slight rise beneath the sheets.

Lucas blushed and covered himself with an arm. He hadn't meant that kind of impotent and told her so, but then he considered her assertion that he'd been having a bad dream. His mind flashed with images of a great beast crushing his bones to dust, but he could not bring the beast properly into focus. Was it normal for humans to dream such things? Was that sleep? Or was it his memory? Had he seen a glimpse of his lost time?

"I was having a nightmare?" he reconfirmed with her. "What was I doing? How do you know I was dreaming?"

"You thrash. You speak."

"Speak? Speak of what?"

"My English is not perfect, but you say about..." she squinted as if trying hard not to mispronounce the words. "*Red Lord*. You say, 'Red Lord come'. A different name for angel you see last night?"

"No. Gladri's only nickname is tit-head, and *I* gave it to him. Did I say anything else in my sleep? In my dream?"

Vetta got up from the bed and brought over his clothes. "Nothing else. Get up. We have breakfast. Scrambled egg on toast. Mama always told me that good breakfast mean good day."

She left him alone while he got dressed, and when he went out into the lounge, a plate of food was waiting for him on the small side table beside the sofa. Vetta was already eating, plate perched on her knees, so without prompting, Lucas took the food and sat down beside her.

He had always enjoyed drinking more than eating, but now he found the act quite pleasant. The bread was soft in his mouth, and the eggs had a gentle flavour that made him hungry for more. Once he'd finished, he put the plate back on the side table and turned to Vetta. "Thank you for all your help. I'll get out of your hair now."

"Where will you go?"

He shifted back and forth on the sofa awkwardly. "Perhaps back to the pub. Maybe Gladri left something behind. If he did, I might be able to contact him. If not, I'm screwed. I can't survive as a man. I don't even know where to start."

Vetta placed her plate on the floor and wiped her mouth with the back of her hand. After swallowing, she looked at him grumpily. "How old are you?"

Lucas frowned. How old was he? Time was a human construct, so not something he kept particular track of. "I've been alive since the beginning, since before mankind existed. God made angels to protect his creations."

"Then you should know everything," she said. "You should know how to be a man. Have you not watched people?"

Of course he had. He'd spent thousands of years observing mankind and corrupting it, before changing his ways and trying to save it. During that time, he had seen the entirety of human history, but that didn't mean he understood how to cook eggs or make toast. Or earn the money to pay for them. "I can't be like you," he said, crossing his ankles in front of himself for some reason. "I would rather not exist."

For the first time since he'd met her, Vetta pulled a face that was unkind. "Being human is not so bad," she said. "What choice do you have, anyway? Stop complaining. You are man who has lived forever and knows much. Life should be easy."

There was an odd logic to what she said, however much he didn't like it. Lucas did know a lot about mankind—especially the machinations of powerful men—so perhaps he could bend the world to his will with knowledge alone, but when he tried to consider how, he couldn't find his way through the quagmire of his feeble mind.

He shifted uncomfortably on the sofa again and said, "I... I don't know anything. It's all gone."

Vetta frowned. "What do you mean?"

He wasn't sure for a moment. His knowledge wasn't gone. It was just... smaller. Before, he had known everything every little detail of the world before him. He was omniscient. Now, he still knew things, but also *didn't* know things. "My knowledge is spotty," he said, "like my mind isn't capable of holding the knowledge I had as a celestial being. It holds as much as a human brain can—which is extremely finite."

"So, you are still smart?"

"Ask me something."

"Who is American President?"

"Donald Trump. Wait, is that true? Kind of feels like I made it up."

Vetta smiled. "Is true! What is capital of Slovakia?"

"Bratislava."

"Largest animal?"

"On land or sea?"

"Sea?"

"Blue Whale."

"Best... um... Justin Bieber song?"

"That's a trick question!"

She grinned. "Yes! See, you know many things still."

Sickeningly, the simple praise made him smile, but his mood soon settled back to darker thoughts. "It makes no difference," he said. "I was one of the most ancient and powerful beings in the universe. You expect me to live happily as an accountant or a butcher or... something? I can't!"

"You are arrogant!"

He uncrossed his legs and turned on the sofa to face her fully. "I am tens of thousands of years old! You could never understand."

"No, I do not understand," she snapped. "I have only *one* life. One life where I grow up poor and have to work as soon as I am able. One life where I come to UK for better life and to send home money for my mama and sister but get called nasty names and made to be scared. One life where I get to clean tables at fast food shop. One life I get. Unlike you, Lucas, who has lived many. You have lived forever and still you want more."

Lucas squirmed on the sofa, shifting back and forth. The depravity and despair he had witnessed throughout history left him with no illusions of how hard it was to be human, yet it still did not compare to what he was going through. "You are *not* nothing, Vetta," he said, softening a little. "You're a girl kind enough to help The Devil, and that is something special. Life is hard, I know, but there are many worse off than you, believe me. Humanity is a cruel organism. It devours itself, little pieces at a time."

She placed a hand on his knee and gave him a half smile. "You are afraid."

"I fear nothing!" He shot up off the sofa, grabbing at himself awkwardly. "I-I need to leave."

"You go to bar?"

"I don't know what to do or where to go. I just... I just need to go." He jigged about anxiously, unable to keep still.

Vetta met him in the centre of the room. "You should not be alone, Lucas. You are vulnerable."

He clenched his fists and danced from foot to foot. "I am *not* vulnerable. I am not... I am not... Damn it, what the hell is wrong with me? I can't keep still."

Vetta giggled. "You need wee. Toilet is next to kitchen."

He stopped dancing and looked down at himself. "Oh! Okay. Right then, listen to me, Vetta. You will help me do... whatever I need to do in there, and then I am going to the Black Sheep to sort out my other issues. Enough is enough. I'm nobody's butt monkey."

She frowned. "You go fight angel?"

"I will do whatever I have to. I am Lucifer, Lord of Darkness, and rightful monarch of Hell. Now, take me to the toilet. Quickly!"

⊥

"WHAT ARE YOU LOOKING FOR?" VETTA ASKED FOR THE THIRD time. A willing companion, certainly, but not especially helpful. She rooted around the grubby pavement alongside him, kicking aside litter and bits of old brick, but it was aimless searching as he hadn't yet advised her what to look for.

"I'm looking for anything Gladri might have affected," he told her. "If we can find something he touched or influenced, I can perform a ritual and summon him."

"You can summon an angel?"

He nodded.

Vetta lifted the lid on a bin to peer inside, then winced and closed it quickly. "I am thinking this alleyway needs a clean and tidy."

"No such thing as a nice alleyway." Lucas half-expected the scorch mark on the ground to have disappeared, but it was still there on the pavement, even clearer in daylight. He brushed his fingertips over the burn and they came away sooty, smelling of something familiar—iron and sulphur. Iron should have burned him, but as a human it was a mundane substance—present in his very blood.

That he also detected sulphur made it pretty obvious where he'd arrived from.

"You find something?" asked Vetta, clutching a pair of plastic bags as though they might somehow help the situation.

"Iron and sulphur," he said. "I was in Hell."

"You are The Devil. Not so strange."

But it was strange. Strange because he had obviously been there *recently*, during a time he couldn't remember. Then something had brought him *here*. He pointed at the scorch marks so Vetta could see them. "I was either forcefully expelled from Hell or yanked away by something on this side. Iron is the binding component of certain spells and keeps condemned souls confined to their tortures. Sulphur was the base-substance used to create Hell when the universe was formed. Earth was made from hydrogen and carbon, Heaven of silver and gold. Have you found anything Gladri affected yet?"

She shrugged. "I do not remember him touching anything. He arrive, flap wings to make wind, and then stand here until he leave."

It was what Lucas was afraid of. Gladri detested Earth too much to dirty himself by touching it. He pictured the scene from the previous night and tried to re-enact it in his mind, but he knew Vetta was right—other than his wings, Gladri had not moved a muscle.

Yet, perhaps that was enough.

Maybe the answer was right in front of them. "Vetta, where did you find those plastic bags?"

"On floor behind bins." She pointed. "Angel do not touch these though."

"No," said Lucas, "but it doesn't have to be something Gladri *touched*. Those bags hold an echo of his presence. I saw Gladri affect them with his wings when he was flexing his divinity-erection. I can use them."

Vetta smiled and waved the bags about like pom-poms. "This is good?"

"Very good! Well done."

"You are welcome. You do ritual at my flat?"

"No, we do it here. We do it right now."

"Here? Now?"

"Yes!" He took the plastic bags from her and held them out to either side. "I want my powers back right this second."

"How will you make Gladri give them to you?"

He shook the bags, making them *swish*. "I'll need to

think on my feet, but I'm smarter than that self-righteous *lickarse*. Let him try to match wits with me."

"But you're human now."

"Thanks! That little confidence boost is exactly what I needed."

She blushed. "Sorry."

"It's fine. Just stand here, right in front of me." She shuffled her feet and did as he asked. She looked nervous. "Good," he said, repositioning her marginally so that she wasn't standing in gum. "I need you to put both hands on my neck. Our bodies will create a circle."

"A circle?"

"Just an industry term. Now, allow me to say the words. The invocation will pull Gladri before me and hold him in place."

"I am not so sure I want to do this," said Vetta, but she put her hands on his neck and kept them there as asked. Her nails dug into his flesh.

Lucas began to speak the words known only to an illustrious few—words unknown even to most angels—the secret tongue of the High Choir. Images of his dearest brother, Michael, passed through his mind and almost stopped him.

Almost.

Sod Heaven. Sod Michael.

The alleyway whooshed to life—dirt and rubbish rolling across the pavement—wind gathering rapidly and whipping Vetta's hair across her face. She instinctively tried to remove her hands from his neck, but he barked at her to stay in contact. Holding the plastic bags aloft, he focused on them, making them a conduit to that which he sought—Gladri.

Even as a human being, Lucas could feel the power flowing through him—ancient knowledge woken from its slumber. Vetta had been right, his wisdom gave him advantages even as a man. Knowledge was a part of who he was, and no one—Gladri or otherwise—could take that away from him.

He began to sweat. Hands numb. Tongue swelling. His human body was unsuited for wielding power as great and as ancient as this—the words of the Indomitable Prayer—a prayer no angel could ignore. Yet he kept the words flowing, needing to complete the ritual. Soon this would all be over, and he would never again allow himself to fall victim to Heaven's self-righteousness.

Vetta jolted. Her eyes widened, and her jaw bulged. A trickle of blood escaped her lips. She tried to release his neck again, but now it was too late—the spell had tethered them together, woven their bodies into an unbreakable lightning rod. Her eyes rolled back in her head and she moaned. Soon Gladri would inhabit her body, unable to leave until Lucas allowed it. The horror of being entombed within a human vessel would be enough to break the angel's will and force him to undo what he had done. The irony of it was almost too delicious. This was why knowledge always beat power.

You'll need longer than an eternity to outwit me, Gladri, brother. You should have learned that lesson long ago.

Blood spewed from Vetta's mouth as she bit down on her tongue. Her lips quivered, but no words came out. Her body wasn't holding up. The spell was killing her. She just had to hold on a little while longer. Almost there.

Just a little bit longer. Come on, girl.

Lucas shouted in Vetta's face, "Speak to me, Gladri. I know you're in there."

Blood dripped from Vetta's chin, staining her blouse. Her eyes turned black and her jaw cracked wide open, releasing a booming voice from her throat that was not her own. "LUCIFER? IS... IS THAT YOU? I KNEW IT! LAST NIGHT, IT WAS YOU!"

"Yes! I have you at my mercy, Gladri, so do as I demand. Restore me now!"

Vetta trembled. Her blackened eyes bulged in their sockets. Blood erupted from her nose. Her jaw cracked open wider, almost turning her head inside out. "RELEASE ME NOW!" the voice boomed.

Lucas shook Vetta, making her fingernails pierce deeper into the back of his neck. "Restore me!"

Vetta screamed. Lucas couldn't tell if it came from her or from Gladri. "LUCIFER! YOU SHALL PAY. FINALLY, YOU SHALL PAY."

Lucas grinned. He could hear the agony, the pleading. He was close.

Vetta's body bucked, chest heaving in and out in great gasps—dying gasps—but they meant nothing if he got his powers back. Lucas would heal her the second this was over with. He just needed to see this through. Restoring his powers was more important than a single girl's suffering.

A girl who has done nothing but try to help me.

What am I doing?

"Damn it." He released the plastic bags and the spell broke. Vetta's body folded like an ironing board, and he had to ease her to the ground gently before she cracked her skull on the pavement. "Vetta?" he urged. "Vetta, speak to me!"

She was unconscious and showed no signs of waking. Her blood stained his palms, and he stared at them in horror.

How could he do this?

Gladri was right. Deep down, I'm the same selfish monster I've always been.

I'm still The Devil.

"My God!" someone behind Lucas said. "What on earth happened?"

Lucas turned to see the Black Sheep's landlord stepping out of the pub's rear exit. The stumpy man held a bag of rubbish in each hand, but they fell to the floor now as he stared at Vetta in shock. "Please, help her." Lucas begged. "Please!"

The landlord nodded. "You'd better bring her inside."

Hair of the Dog

Lucas carried Vetta in his arms like a rescuer, but he was no such thing. He'd done this to her. A selfish act of a selfish being. Her blood-streaked face summoned more unwelcome emotions inside him, and he wished he could claw them away. He was a monster.

The landlord—*Julian* was it?—asked him what had happened. "*I* happened," said Lucas, hurrying Vetta over to the worn leather sofa by the pool table. She remained stone-still as he lay her down, and if not for the slight rising of her chest he could have mistaken her as dead. Housing Gladri's spirit had seared her insides badly.

The effect of demon possession was a slow, drawn-out degradation—a relentless rotting of the mind and body—but the summoning of an angel was to take in an intense flame. Lucas had known what he was doing but had done it anyway.

"I'll call for help," said Julian, turning to leave. He seemed utterly confused, and he paused to frown at Lucas.

"You're... you... you were both here drinking last night, yes? What on earth were you doing out back?"

"GO!" Lucas bellowed. There was no time for conversation.

Julian fled, muttering under his breath and leaving Lucas alone with Vetta. If he had still possessed his powers, he could have healed her in an instant, but he was powerless, conflicted in ways he'd never before experienced.

The pub's front door swung open and a group of men stomped inside. One of them whistled and shouted. "Bacon sandwich and a pint, please, boss!"

Lucas studied the group for a moment and realised he knew one of them. It was the piece-of-shit who had forced himself on Vetta last night—Jake—but his stomach quickly turned as he realised that he had violated Vetta far worse than this lad had intended to.

Jake noticed Lucas nearby and scowled at him, but then he spotted Vetta—and the blood on her face—which made him recoil. Turning to his three companions, he sounded astonished. "That's the sodding Mick what done me over last night. Wanker nearly broke my hand." He held it up to them and showed the bandage. "What the hell is he doing back here?"

The three other men were not the ones who had accompanied Jake last night, and they appeared confused rather than combative. They were perhaps his former workmates, as they each wore identical black overalls. Jake was in jeans and a jumper, as seemingly unemployed as he'd claimed to be.

One of the men in overalls, a young lad with peachy-blonde hair and a wispy beard, reached into his front pouch-pocket and pulled out a phone. He held it out to

Lucas. "You need to call an ambulance, mate? She don't look good."

"She's not," said Lucas, surprised by the offer of help. "The landlord already went to call help though, thanks."

The lad broke away from his colleagues and came over. "What happened to her?"

Lucas decided the truth wouldn't help him, so he lied. "She had a fit and bit her tongue. That's why there's blood."

"My sister's a nurse. She works at the old people's home across the road. I'll get her to run over until the ambulance comes. She deals with epilepsy all the time." The lad dialled a number on his phone and Lucas thanked him. "No problem. I'm Max."

"Lucas. This is Vetta."

Max made the call and spoke familiarly with a person on the other end. The conversation lasted twenty seconds. "She's on her way," he said, ending the call. "Five minutes."

Lucas gave his thanks again. "The landlord should be back by now," he said. "His name is Julian, right?"

"Yeah. He's owned this place for years."

Lucas relaxed a little, but then Jake approached, which immediately raised his hackles. "What the hell did you do to her?" the lad demanded loudly, actually having the audacity to appear disgusted. "Gave her a night she won't forget, by the looks of it."

Lucas kept his eyes on Vetta, fearing she might slip away if he wasn't watching, but his voice was solely directed at Jake as he spoke. "Step away from me, boy. I won't warn you twice."

"Where's the silly accent gone, Mick? Do you put it on for the ladies? Whatever snags the muff, I suppose."

Lucas leapt up, but Max got in his way. "Just ignore him, man. Your friend needs you."

"This animal attacked us last night!" Lucas glared at Jake over Max's shoulder.

"*You* attacked *me*!" said Jake innocently. "I was walking home, and you thought you'd play the tough guy to impress the Pole tart. God knows what you did to her after that."

Max turned his head and shouted at Jake while still struggling to control Lucas. "Get the hell away, man. You're not helping."

"Fine, no need to tear a ball sack, Max. I'll be at the bar when you're done playing Good Samaritan."

"Just go and get me a pint in. I'll be with you guys in a minute."

"I'll choke the life out of him," Lucas grunted as Jake walked away to join his companions at the bar.

"Jake's an arsehole," said Max. "Don't worry about him. Let's just help your friend."

"She's not my friend. I only met her last night."

Max raised a fuzzy eyebrow. "The way you're trembling, a friend is the least of what she is to you."

Lucas realised that he was, indeed, shaking—and he felt sick. The fury Jake had evoked threatened to spill out of his guts and soak the floor. How could emotions make you nauseas? He placed both hands on Vetta's arm and stroked her clammy flesh with his thumbs, remembering how she had stroked his back last night to help him sleep.

"I did this to her," he said. "She has to be okay."

Max cleared his throat. "Did you mean for it to happen?"

Lucas shook his head. "Of course not."

"Then be guilty about it later. You can apologise after she wakes up."

"*If* she wakes up."

Jake shouted from the bar. "Oi! Julian! Come on, where are ya? The lads have only got thirty minutes for their break."

Lucas tensed, but Max distracted him by talking. "Soon as my sister arrives, I'll go see what's happening with the ambulance, okay, man?"

"You're a good lad, Max."

The lad seemed touched by this, and his eyes flickered with a mixture of emotions. "If we don't help each other, where would we be?"

They sat in silence for the minutes to follow, and it wasn't until the pub's front door swung open once more that either of them moved. Max stood and smiled at the newcomers, while Lucas remained by Vetta's side. Two women hurried over, and one of them had the same peach-coloured hair as Max. The other was older with plain-brown hair and a paunch below her sagging breasts. The wedding ring on her finger and the sensible handbag over her shoulder suggested she lived a life where choice of takeaway was her biggest concern. A woman at ease with herself. Happy.

"This is Annie," said Max, pointing to his sister who gave Lucas a polite smile before focusing on Vetta with concern.

"And I'm Shirley," said the older woman. "I work with Annie."

Annie's lips were thin as she examined Vetta. "What happened to her?"

"A seizure," said Lucas.

"What sort of seizure?"

"Like she was hit by a bus on the inside. Please just help her."

Annie glanced at her brother and exchanged a frustrated grimace. When she turned back to Lucas again, she was chewing the inside of her cheek. "If she has internal injuries, there's nothing to do until the ambulance arrives. The best thing is to keep her still like this. Shirley, can you put a blanket over her, please? She's a little cold."

The older woman pulled a rolled-up blanket out of her cavernous handbag and draped it over Vetta. "Should I try to give her water?"

Annie shook her head. "No, we don't know what's going on inside. Lucas? Think about what you can tell the paramedics when they arrive—the more they know the better—but don't tell them she was hit by a bus on the inside, okay? They need to know where she's hurt and why."

If Lucas shared the real reason Vetta was hurt, no one would believe him. Angel possession wasn't something most doctors would take very seriously.

All the while, she was dying before his eyes.

Lucas stood up, startling everybody.

Max frowned. "Where you going? She needs you."

"I'm going outside to get some air and look for the ambulance." The truth was he intended to summon Gladri again. He would have no hold over the angel without trapping him inside a mortal body, but it was better than doing nothing. Hopefully, Gladri would hear his prayers and take pity on Vetta.

Pity? How he hated the word. But he couldn't rely on doctors helping Vetta. They might not be able to.

Jake was still hollering after Julian when Lucas walked

by, and the urge to ram the lad's head through the bar was hard to resist. Max was right though—it would be unhelpful—so he kept his calm and asked the lad for help instead.

"The ambulance should be here by now, Jake. Can you find Julian and see what's keeping it?"

"I don't take orders from you, Mick."

Lucas had to force his fists not to clench. "Think about what you would have done last night if I hadn't stopped you. Do you have any conscience at all?"

Jake glanced at his colleagues and blushed. When he turned back to Lucas, his expression was hungry, and a little desperate. The guy wanted a fix, and it was making him twitchy. "Fine, I'll go see what's keeping Julian," he said, "but only because it's the decent thing to do. And I want a goddamn bacon sandwich."

Lucas said no more. He continued to the pub's rear exit and reached for the door handle. But there was no handle. He gave the door a shove, but it wouldn't budge, solid as a cliff face. Gritting his teeth, he barged his shoulder against the wood, but succeeded only in hurting himself. Finally, he tried to grip the edge of the frame and peel it open, but no gap existed, not even to thread a hair. With no other resort, he reared back and booted the door with everything he had.

Jake's workmates shouted from the bar. "Hey! What you bloody playing at, mate?"

"The door," said Lucas, rubbing his hurt shoulder and groaning. "It won't open."

The two men approached warily. "You need to calm down, mate," said the larger of the two.

"Just help me get the door open, would you?"

"Stand aside." The smaller man came forward. Thin-bodied, with scruffy black hair greying at the temples. He had a swarthy appearance, as well as tattoos all down each arm. The larger man was a few years younger and sported a bushy brown beard beneath a bald head. He had no visible tattoos, but wide muscular shoulders that had taken obvious work. Both men had name patches sewn onto their chests. The tattooed ruffian was Shaun and the bearded hulk was Simon. Both seemed irritated by the commotion.

Shaun stepped up to the door, but like Lucas, he came away with a sore shoulder moments later. Simon grunted and moved his smaller colleague out of the way. "Can't open a bloody door," he muttered through his thick beard. "I'm surrounded by imbeciles." His comments came back to haunt him when he called it quits thirty-seconds later with sweat on his forehead. "It's welded shut!" he protested.

Lucas shook his head. "You can't weld a wooden door."

"What then? Nails?"

Lucas glanced towards the bar. No sign of Jake's return yet, nor any sign of Julian or an ambulance. What was going on? Where had the landlord got to? What wasn't adding up here? The entire place seemed to be on lock-down.

"I don't know how the door is sealed," Lucas admitted, "but there's somebody I would like to ask about it. Let's find the guv'na."

He marched towards the bar.

┴

LUCAS PRESSED HIS PALMS AGAINST THE BAR AND TRIED TO think, but his throbbing head made it difficult. Somehow, he thought he knew Julian—those mole-like features, dusky skin, long nose. They had met before, he was sure of it.

With only one way to get answers, Lucas slipped behind the bar in search of the man. Passing through a narrow staff door, he found himself in a cramped backroom with an office off to one side and a storeroom on the other. Both the storeroom and the office were empty, but ahead lay a closed door that seemed important somehow. It was to that closed door that Lucas quickly headed, reaching for the wooden knob as soon as he got there.

He flinched as something bit into his hand, and he blinked in confusion. He didn't know if it was the light bulb above his head that was flickering or if it was his own vision. Glancing at his palm, he saw blood, something he had not possessed until becoming human. It was strangely intoxicating, like looking at his own mortality. A small slither coated the doorknob and, as he inspected it further, he saw a tiny iron spike jutting out of it. Why would someone affix an iron spike to a doorknob? Was Julian trying to safeguard this room against demons or angels? Iron was anathema to both, which was why it was so often used in spells and wards.

Carefully, he grasped the knob again, this time around the edges, and pushed open the door. A stale stench permeated the air, and he discovered a long straight corridor ahead. At the end was a pulsing light somewhere between the colour of rust and blood. Nothing about the corridor felt natural. More like standing inside the intestines of a beast.

His flesh tightened around his bones, and he wondered if it was fear he was experiencing. Something was urging him to turn the other way and leave, but he ignored the sensation and forced himself to step forwards. Human or not, he was the ex-king of Hell. Lucifer the Almighty. A being so old he had a thousand names—none of which contained the word scaredy-cat.

Silent as a wraith, he strode down the corridor, deficient human eyesight adjusting slowly to the gloom. There was movement all around him, and he spotted fat spiders the size of hand prints scuttling up and down the walls while ropy snakes slithered around his ankles. There was no place Jake could have gone but down this corridor, yet it made no sense that he wouldn't have turned away in terror at what Lucas was seeing now. The presence of so many venomous creatures suggested something wicked lay at the end of this corridor.

Lucas called out.

He got a reply immediately. "Oh God, help me! Help me!"

Lucas hurried. He wasn't God, but he was the best Jake would get. The light pulsing at the end of the corridor blinded him as he got closer, but once he passed beyond it, his vision corrected, and he found himself standing inside a shrine room. Iron pillars held up the corners of the small room and a bone alter stood off to one side. It was a shrine dedicated to The Devil.

To him.

Christ on a bike!

Jake hung upside down from an inverted cross, a crown of thorns encircling his scalp. Blood flowed from wounds on his hands and feet that were pierced by thick iron bolts. Despite his agony, Jake was alert and crying out for help. His terrified eyes locked onto Lucas, and he babbled hysterically. Lucas shushed him and promised to help, but before he could do anything, Julian emerged from the shadows and startled him. The man's dark eyes loomed behind his spectacles.

"Why would a serpent help the mice it feeds on?"

Lucas glared. "Who are you, Julian? Why are you doing this?"

The question drew a grimace from the man. "You don't remember? The world altered course the day we met. I was a pawn, and you the chess master. For centuries, I have been trying to bring you before me, but Hell has apparently been vacant its king—which is why your arrival was such a surprise. I recognised you last night, but I couldn't quite accept it, not until you drew me into that girl right before you. It has been a long time, Satan, but finally you fall into my lap. This Devil's Trap was meant for you, but there's no rush now that I have you."

Lucas recoiled. "It was *you* I summoned into Vetta? But you're human! How could I have drawn you?" He pictured the scorch marks in the alleyway outside. Sulphur and iron. Was this the man who had yanked him out of Hell? Lucas, as The Devil, could only be summoned from Heaven or Hell, but he had not stepped foot in either place for an age.

Until recently.

Why did I go back?

Julian snorted. "You seem at a loss, Satan?"

"I *am* at a loss," he admitted. Totally lost. He felt like a pebble skipped across a great lake, hurtling towards the unknown.

Julian clasped his hands together like a priest about to give Mass. He seemed calm and relaxed—smugly satisfied. "What has become of you, Satan? The last time we met, you were a dagger in humanity's intestines, drawing out the filth and bile, a nightmare made flesh. A—"

"Times change!" Lucas cut him off. "I abdicated Hell's throne long ago to seek another path. What do you want with me?"

Julian frowned, giving away a key fact. As much as he knew of Lucas—including his true identity—this was apparently news to him. Lucas had still been The Devil as far as Julian had known, and he flapped his gums for several seconds while he digested the information, apparently not knowing what to say. "Y-You abdicated the most powerful position in existence, second only to God himself? Why? Why would you do that?"

Lucas shrugged. "Too much overtime. Tell me who you are and let us be done with this nonsense."

Jake squirmed on the cross, blood still streaming down his body. "Get me down from here! Please!"

"In a minute," Lucas snapped. "The grown-ups are talking. Julian is about to tell me who he is, and what he's playing at."

Julian wagged a pudgy finger back-and-forth like a pendulum. "No, no, no. I shall reveal nothing. That you have forgotten me is insult enough, but you and I have unfinished business, Satan. Your deliverance shall buy my entry into paradise."

With a weak grin, Lucas gained some satisfaction by telling the man he was too late. "I'm human now, Julian. And believe me when I tell you, you can't bargain your way into Heaven."

"Ha! I want no part of Heaven. And your serpent lies will not save you."

"Didn't anybody ever warn you about summoning The

Devil? It never ends well." Lucas launched himself at Julian, but his movements were sluggish and inaccurate—human—and the man stepped aside easily. He tried to strike again but missed every time.

Julian cackled. "Come now, creature. Do battle earnestly. I've waited a long time for this."

Lucas swung both arms, one after another, but again, every time, he missed. His breath escaped in strangled puffs. "W-Who are you? What do you want? Tell me!"

"Help me!" Jake cried, blood pouring from him.

Julian stepped in front of the inverted crucifix but kept his eyes on Lucas. "It is true then? You are no longer what you were? You are just a man?"

Lucas doubled over, panting and clutching his knees, but he forced himself to stand tall. "I haven't been The Devil for two thousand years, you fool. Now tell me who you are. What do you want with me?"

Julian wasn't a large man by any measure, but he seemed to get smaller now, shoulders slumping. "All my plans are ruined," he muttered to himself. "Without a celestial soul, you are nothing to me."

"Yeah, thanks! Tell me who you are, and we'll sort things out like gentlemen."

Julian stared at his own hands, breathing deeply, almost panting. At first, it appeared he was thinking, but then Lucas realised the man had a rage growing inside him. Julian's eyes turned to black oil as he glared at Lucas and his voice boomed.

"Sort things out like gentlemen? I am the wretch whose soul you damned for all eternity. I am the patriot you made a monster. And I am the righteous steel that shall shed your life's blood, Satan."

The venom in Julian's words stunned Lucas into silence. It possessed the kind of hatred cultivated over a great length of time and with unwavering focus. He was so taken aback by the ferocity that he was slow to react when Julian produced a hooked dagger and plunged it into Jake's intestines. The lad's screams lasted mere seconds before his guts pulled out onto the floor and blood gushed down his inverted body and soaked his face and chest.

Julian turned back to Lucas and sneered. "I damn you, Satan. As you once damned me."

Lucas leapt for the man again, but Julian blinked away —not in a cloud of smoke or a burst of raindrops, but a simple cessation of existence. Lucas found himself clutching at air.

What nightmare is this?

Jake was bleeding out fast, eyes wide and disbelieving, guts piling on the floor. Lucas could do little for him now, save from cutting him down from the cross and letting him die on his back.

With no way of doing things gently, Lucas yanked the iron nails fastening the lad's hands and feet and let Jake crumple to the ground. More reeking intestines unspooled and Lucas winced in sympathy. A terrible way to go—even for a thug like Jake.

From on his back, the lad gasped for air, but his insides had slipped out, and he could do nothing but grow blue in the face. Despite despising the lad, Lucas put a hand against his cheek and tried to ease his passing.

Jake couldn't speak, but he edged a trembling hand towards his hip. Lucas told him not to move, that it would only take longer, but the lad didn't listen. He kept on reaching, sliding his hand into the pocket of his jeans. After several clumsy attempts, he plucked out a wallet, but immediately fumbled it.

Lucas caught the wallet and raised it. "You want something inside? I'll get it for you."

Jake nodded, the fear fading from his eyes. Not long now.

Lucas searched the wallet, ignoring bank cards and gym memberships, assuming the lad wanted something else. But what? What was he meant to be looking for?

Jake's bloody hand jerked, and he smeared a bloody fingerprint against the wallet's upper edge. Realising what the lad was indicating, Lucas nodded and thumbed open the hidden fold. Inside, he found a single item—a small passport photograph of a young girl, fair-haired and innocent. A sweet child. She resembled Jake.

Jake pawed at Lucas again, prompting him to shove the photo into his palm. Jake lifted the photograph in front of his face so he could see it, and a smile shoved away his grimace. How could people be so monstrous and so human at the same time? It was a puzzle that had perplexed Lucas for thousands of years.

He glared up at the ceiling and cursed. Father could do nothing to help Jake, or anyone else in need, but when did this madness end? When would He finally come out of hiding and do something to roll back the chaos? Mankind was on the brink, so surely now was the time to act. Time to take a risk.

Come out, Father. Please.

Damn you, come out!

Lucas slumped forwards, tears sliding down his cheeks. He placed both hands on Jake's chest and waited for the lad to die. May his sins be forgiven.

"It doesn't hurt anymore," Jake muttered, eyes gazing up at the ceiling.

"Think about your daughter, Jake," said Lucas softly. "You'll be watching over her soon." A lie.

Jake didn't seem to hear him. "I'm okay. I'm okay."

"What?" Lucas removed his hands from Jake's chest and shuffled back on his knees, barely believing what he saw. It couldn't be. Couldn't be.

"It's a miracle," said Jake, patting at his torso. Blood soaked his torn t-shirt, but the flesh underneath was healthy and pink. His wrists and ankles were no longer pierced. His intestines were back in place. Even the battle-scar on his shaven head was gone.

A miracle.

Lucas lifted his hands and stared at his palms. Blood wept from wide gashes stretching from his thumbs to his pinkie fingers, but before his eyes, the wounds closed up and disappeared. He had laid hands upon Jake and healed him. Drawn away his wounds.

Jake sat up gingerly, the stupidest of grins on his face. "You saved my life, man!"

"Y-You're welcome," said Lucas, trying to smile, but instead, he passed out on the floor.

┴

MAX HURRIED TO HELP LUCAS AS HE STUMBLED OUT FROM behind the bar. While he and Jake were both unsteady, Jake was more giddy than weak and could walk on his own. Lucas, however, could barely place one foot in front of the other.

Max took his arm and guided him towards the sofa. "What happened?"

"I'm fine. Just... help me over to Vetta." As delicate as he was, Lucas didn't want to be fussed over, but he needed to see Vetta right now. Annie was still supervising her, checking for a response, and Shirley was rubbing her arms to pass on some heat.

"How is she?" Lucas demanded, shoving Max away and staggering over to the sofa.

"She's not doing good," said Annie. "Where's that damned ambulance?"

"It's not coming," he said.

Anna frowned, but Lucas moved passed her and got down beside Vetta. She was barely breathing now. Gladri's presence—or had it really been Julian's?—had obliterated her. She was slipping away fast, and no one in the world could prevent it.

Except, perhaps, for him. He had healed Jake from certain death. Maybe he could heal Vetta too. He placed his hands on her, one against her forehead and one against her chest. Her skin was icy cold, blood like snow in her veins. The guilt over what he had done increased, but he used it to focus his concentration, trying to mimic what he had done with Jake.

Healing that shithead had been an accident, but it had woken something inside of him. He might be human, but it appeared he was not completely without power. Something flowed inside of him, and when he healed Jake, he had grasped hold of that power momentarily. Now he needed to grab it again. With both hands.

Annie unfolded her arms and folded them again, just so she could make a display of huffing. "We need to get her some proper help," she complained. "I think she's *hypothermic.* If we don't get her to a hospital soon..."

Lucas gritted his teeth, sweat beading on his brow as he concentrated. All he felt was the iciness of Vetta's skin.

Where was that power he had latched onto earlier? Why wasn't she getting better? Why was nothing happening?

She is not going to die. I will not let her die. Damn it!

"Come on, man," said Max, putting a hand on Lucas's shoulder. "I know you blame yourself for this, but you need to listen to my sister. She needs proper help."

"Shut up!"

"Hey, man. You need to chill out."

Jake inserted himself and shoved Max away. "He can heal people, man. I was all torn up to shit, and he put me back together just by touching me. Julian is a serial killer or something—a total nutcase. We need to get the police down here."

"And that bloody ambulance," said Annie, hands moving down to her hips. "This girl needs help right now!"

"I'll call for one," said Shirley, fishing a clunky phone from the depths of her handbag. Used tissues and a roll of Polo mints fell out in her wake.

Lucas leapt up and hissed at them. "Everybody be quiet! Damn it, why isn't it working? How did I do it before?"

Annie gawked at him. "You really thought you could fix her just by touching her? Are you mad?"

Lucas turned his glare at Jake, making the lad wither slightly. "Why did it work on *you* and not *her*? She should be the one healed, not you."

"Hey," said Jake, although he gave no further reply.

Annie turned to her brother, fuming. "Max, what the hell did you drag me into? These people are insane."

"You want to know what's insane?" asked Lucas, exposing his teeth like an animal—an unprompted gesture that came without command. "You want the truth? Okay, fine, how about you're standing before one of the most ancient beings in all existence? One of the most powerful creatures in all of human history and beyond."

"He's lost the plot," said Simon. He was leaning on the bar and rubbing at his beard.

"I have *not* lost the plot," Lucas shouted over. "I have lost everything else, but not that. I used to go by the name Lucifer, King of Hell, and before that I was one of The Three. Now I'm a pathetic human being like the rest of you. Yet, even despite that, I laid hands on this lowlife earlier and pulled him back from death." He pointed accusingly at Jake, but then let his arm drop and sighed. "Looks like it was a one off."

"L-Lucas?"

He whirled around and dropped to his knees. Beside the sofa, he gasped. "Vetta, you're okay?"

She looked anything but okay, yet she was awake at least. Lying on the sofa, her skin was almost blue. Her lips appeared gritty and dry. "I... I don't know what happened," she whispered. "I feel cold."

"I'm so sorry, Vetta. I'm so sorry." He winced as he realised it was probably the first apology he'd ever given a human being. He got up from his knees and turned to the others so he could tell them that Julian was not what he seemed. Jake backed him up for most of it, but at the end, Annie gave a derisory laugh, and marched over to the pub's front porch. She attempted several times to open the door but ended up kicking it in frustration just like Lucas had earlier, followed by both Shaun and Simon.

"No one is getting out of here," Lucas told them all. "The pub is sealed. Julian has unfinished business with me and he's not about to let me walk away. I'll try to deal with him alone if I can, but the rest of you should stay put and be careful."

Jake was unravelling the bandage from around his hand —perhaps that was healed too now—but he paused to raise an eyebrow at Lucas. "You really don't know what Julian wants? He seemed pretty pissed off at you."

Lucas scratched at his head, trying to pull something loose. "There's something about him I recall, but every time I try to snatch at the memory, it floats away like a crumb in the ocean. Last night, I shook his hand, and I got a... some kind of flashback. I saw fire and burning. I had a dream about the same thing this morning before I woke up."

"This is all just a game," said Annie, tapping her foot and glowering over by the porch. "Stop listening to his bullshit."

Max was staring at Jake with a slightly slack-jawed expression. "Y-Your scar," he muttered. " It's gone!"

Jake touched his forehead, then shrugged. "Told you he fixed me."

Vetta sat up and tried to get to her feet. She succeeded, although she did so stiffly and in obvious pain. Unlike Jake, she was not seemingly better than new. Lucas took her arm, and she allowed him to steady her.

"I see angel last night," she said huskily. "You should believe things Lucas tells you. He is magic."

Lucas cringed. "Let's not bandy the M word around, shall we? And I'm not what I was when you first met me. I don't want you getting hurt again, Vetta. What happened to you was my fault. I thought... I thought I was summoning Gladri, but I think it was Julian who came. He was nearby, so the spell latched on to him instead. It makes no sense because he seemed human, and the spell can only snare a creature from Heaven or Hell."

"What the hell are you talking about?" said Annie.

"He's saying that what happened to Vetta was his fault." Shirley was clutching her handbag and frowning. "Because he used her body for a spell or some such nonsense."

Vetta stared at Lucas. "Is... Is this true?"

Lucas nodded. "Yes."

Vetta stumbled, aghast. Lucas couldn't bear looking at her while she processed what he had just told her, so he turned away to face the others.

"I am a wicked creature, no point denying it. People used to call me The Devil, The Defiler, The Morning Star, Satan, and a hundred other things, none of them good. Humanity fled from me in terror for thousands of years, and evil men made unholy bargains with me that changed the course of history. My advice to you all is to stay out of my way and let me deal with this situation. Understood?"

While Jake and Vetta might have believed his words, he could tell the others didn't. They thought he was mad, but that didn't matter. Mad or evil, they just needed to fear him enough to keep out of his way. He would deal with this mess.

But first, he needed a pint. He couldn't face this mess sober.

Happy Hour

Simon folded his meaty arms as he spoke, looking more like a doorman than a mechanic. "We're supposed to believe you're The Devil, are we? Come on, mate, don't treat us like mugs."

Shaun agreed, running his fingers through his slick black-grey hair and looking a little panicky. "I swear, I'm not usually a grass, but I'm going straight to the Old Bill as soon as I get out of here. Trapping us in here is kidnap, and I'm starting to have an anxiety attack. My heart is going a mile a minute."

Simon put a thick arm around his friend and gave him a reassuring squeeze.

"Believe what you want," said Lucas, supping the pint he'd just pulled himself.

Annie actually growled, making a sound not dissimilar from a cornered mastiff. "What have you dragged us into, you moron?"

"If you all leave me to bloody well think, I might come up with an answer," was his only reply.

"Just give him a break," protested Jake.

Simon slapped his large hands flat on the bar, making everybody flinch. "What happened to you back there? You went in hating this guy, and you came out singing his praises. When me and Shaun went searching for you, we found nothing but a dingy office and a storeroom. Where the hell did the two of you get to? What am I missing here?"

"Maybe there's a secret room," said Shaun, chest heaving in and out. Maybe the guy actually *was* having an anxiety attack.

"It was a magic hallway," said Jake seriously.

"Are you bloody serious?" said Max. "What prank are you two playing? How did you cover up your scar, Jake? Something is fishy here, and I don't like fish."

"He healed me," said Jake, tapping at his head. "I've had that scar since I fell off my bike as a kid. Now, it's as though it was never there!"

"It's make-up," protested Max.

"No, it's not. Come have a feel."

Lucas ignored them all, their words becoming white noise. He had meant it when he'd said he intended to deal with things on his own. They just needed to shut up and let him think.

His eyes went to Vetta, sitting in the corner on her own, and it reminded him of how toxic his influence was. The last thing he wanted was to drag anyone deeper into this situation than they already were. The problem was that his feeble mind wouldn't provide him with any understanding of this bizarre situation. Supping a pint was usually how he did his best thinking, yet Julian's identity remained a mystery no matter how many times he stared into his glass.

He was pretty sure the man was human, yet he had been imbued with great power. Was Julian a master or a servant?

Why can't I remember him? What did I do?

An electronic scream made everyone in the bar jolt. Their attention switched to Max who had moved over to the pool table. He looked embarrassed and held his mobile phone in the air for them all to see. "Thought I'd try calling for help again," he explained, "but my phone is a bit floopy."

"I don't have any signal on mine," said Annie grumpily.

"Me either," echoed Shirley, holding up that clunky plastic handset big enough to swat an eagle.

"You won't get a signal," Lucas muttered without looking their way. "You've been removed from the network, trust me."

"Okay," said Simon, smashing both hands against the bar again. This time he dropped off his stool and marched towards Lucas. "I've had enough of this shite. Start giving straight answers, or I'm going to kick the crap out of you."

Jake yelled from the pool table where he was bouncing the cue ball around off the cushions. "He's tougher than he looks, Si. Be careful."

Simon sneered over at him. "What pills did this guy make you swallow back there to make you start defending him? Didn't you get into a ruck with him last night? What changed."

Jake shrugged. "Water under the bridge, innit?"

"I suggest you listen to the lad," said Lucas, slipping off his own stool to face the larger man. "Be very careful about what you decide to do next."

Simon didn't heed the threat. He grabbed Lucas by the

lapels and yanked him forwards. "Get this place unlocked right now, mate, or you and me are going to have problems."

"What are you going to do?" Lucas asked wearily, not yet bothering to fight himself free of the man's powerful grasp. "Not like we can take it outside, is it? Besides, I'm not the one who sealed this place. So back off!" He whipped his right arm around Simon's left and used his free hand to palm-strike the man in the centre of his chest. It sent him backwards, slightly winded, but didn't do enough to deter him.

This time, instead of trying to grab Lucas, Simon swept his legs with a vicious kick. Lucas thudded to the ground hard, smacking the back of his skull against the floorboards. The blow sent his vision spinning and he struggled to get back up. Simon loomed over him like a viking, boulder-fists raised and ready to unleash Odin's fury. Max and Shaun appeared just in time to keep the big man from delivering a full-on beat down.

"Let me at him," Simon bellowed. "I want to know what the hell is going on!"

"Easy," said Shaun. "He's not worth doing time over."

Vetta moved towards the bar. Her expression had darkened, like a change had occurred in her. "What is happening is that we are innocent victims caught in middle of Lucas's bullshit. He is being punished."

"Punished for what?" said Shaun, looking mortified by all the violence. "Being the freaking Devil?"

"Yes!" said Vetta. "Last night, I see angel. It take away Lucas's powers. It make him a man."

Jake frowned. "When did this happen?"

Vetta glared. "It happen after you try to hurt me. Lucas saved me from you, Jake. You are monster that needs prison."

Everyone looked at Jake, but he gave no rebuttal. Instead, he looked ashamed and turned away. There was also a slight hint of confusion to his expression, like he genuinely didn't know what she was talking about.

Lucas watched from on his back until Annie came over and helped him to his feet. He had to clutch the bar to stay upright on his wobbly legs, but it was still better than the floor.

Simon grunted, ready to go again, but Lucas kept him in place by raising a hand in surrender. "Whoa there, big guy! It wasn't too long ago I would have dismantled you with a fart, but it appears I'm less capable nowadays, so just... take it easy, okay?"

Simon folded his meaty arms and seemed partially satisfied by the plea, but to make a point, he grabbed Lucas's pint and took a swig from it. A petty move perhaps, but pretty emasculating if Lucas was to admit it.

"Look," said Lucas, hoisting himself back onto his bar stool and leaning on the bar to keep from falling down again. "Can we at least keep things civil? It's hard enough to think as it is *without* people beating me up."

"Then start talking," demanded Annie. She may have helped him to his feet, but she clearly wasn't on his side. She stood right next to him now and glared in his face.

Lucas let his head slump forward. "You people don't believe I'm The Devil, fine, but can you deny I healed Vetta right before your eyes?"

Simon shrugged. "I don't know her any more than I do

you. You could both be a pair of scam artists for all we know."

"I am not this thing," said Vetta. "I am not scammer artist."

"What would be our angle?" Lucas asked incredulously. "What could we hope to fleece from a bunch of confused labourers on their lunch break?"

"Hey," said Shaun. "I'm a mechanic—it's a skilled job."

"And we're both registered nurses," said Shirley, gesturing towards Annie.

"I'm just making the point," explained Lucas, "that you're not exactly a bunch of gullible sheiks. If Vetta and I were running some kind of scam, there are better targets."

"But you *are* responsible for whatever is going on," said Annie. "We're stuck in here because of you, right? Whether you intended it or not."

Lucas nodded. As little as he knew, that much was certain. "Yeah, sorry."

Annie went on, growing angrier even though her words became more conciliatory. "Vetta was at death's door before you put your hands on her, I'm certain of it. I would have known if she was faking it. Somehow you fixed her, but I have no idea how that's possible."

"Because he can heal people," said Jake. "I keep telling you all!"

"He is a magic man," added Vetta, although she stated it as a condemnation.

Simon sneered. "The Devil, you mean?"

"I believe Lucas," said Shirley, putting her bag on the table and pulling out some chewing gum and handing out strips to the group.

Lucas gawped at the woman. "You believe me? You believe I am what I say I am?"

The woman shook her head. "Not that you're The Devil, no, but I believe you're not the one doing this to us. Me and my Eric used to drink here all the time, years ago when the old owners had the place—two young girls, Kate and Laura. I don't know if they were dykes, or just friends, but they were a lovely pair and ran a good bar. There was no reason they would have left so suddenly like they did. It's always bothered me."

Max frowned. "What are you talking about? Julian's always run the Black Sheep, long as I remember."

"And how long is that, Max? You're what... twenty-one, twenty-two?"

"Twenty," said Annie, answering for her brother.

"Exactly," said Shirley, hoisting her handbag onto her shoulder as if she planned on leaving soon. "I've lived on this estate twenty years. The Black Sheep's changed hands more than once, but Kate and Laura had it longest."

"And they just disappeared?" asked Annie. "With no warning?"

"Yep! The pub closed with no notice whatsoever and was shuttered for months. Then, one sunny afternoon, I was walking by with some shopping, and the place was all lit up again, doors and windows wide open, smoke coming from the chimney. I went inside and found Julian stood behind the bar—said he'd bought the place, that Kate and Laura had moved abroad. Sounded iffy at the time, but who was I to stick my nose in? I thought maybe he'd black-mailed them on account of them being dykes or something, but I wasn't about to get involved. It wasn't until the local vicar went missing six months later that I really began to get suspicious about Julian."

"The local vicar?" said Max, intrigued like a child listening to a spooky campfire story.

Shirley shrugged. "Malcolm was his name. Gave sermons at St. Peter's on the corner. He and Julian used to hold all kinds of philosophical debates across the bar, and they both seemed to enjoy it, but one night, Malcolm got a little too drunk and started shouting about how he had discovered the truth about Julian. There was a bouncer back in them days called Carl, and he tossed Malcolm out on his arse. No one ever heard from him again."

"Shirley, you've never told me this," said Annie.

"The estate was a different place back then. You didn't have Facebook or mobile phones. Sometimes you just stopped seeing people about. You assumed they moved away or were having problems. Haven't given it a thought in years, but now, here we are, trapped with Julian nowhere to be seen. I've always had a bad feeling about that guy. My Eric never liked him either. We stopped drinking here after a while."

Once Shirley got talking, she was quite the authority, and her story had piqued Lucas's interest. "Do you have any idea what the vicar was talking about the night you saw him arguing with Julian?"

"No idea whatsoever. By that point he was the oldest piss-head in the pub. No one paid him much mind."

Simon was gripping the bar and shaking his head like he was going to kick off. When he spoke, it sounded like a bull snorting. "This is getting us nowhere. How do we get out? I've tried both exits and they might as well be made of titanium. I've tried the windows and they don't even rattle.

There's not even..." His words trailed off, and he went back to brooding.

Shaun, who was standing beside Simon, pulled a face. "What were you about to say, Si? Is there something you haven't told me?"

Simon scratched his beard, reticent to elaborate. "I, um, tried waiting at the window for someone to walk by and see us, but it's like a ghost town out there. The chippy is open, but I can't see a soul behind the counter. The supermarket on the corner is empty too. It's lunchtime, and there's not a soul walking by."

Lucas left his stool and went over to the long window at the front of the pub. The sky outside was grey, the weather non-existent. As Simon had said, the small shopping centre was deserted. The five or six shops all had their doors open and lights on, but no one came out and no one entered.

"Ever see *the Langoliers*?" said Max, kneeling on the sofa beside Lucas.

Annie frowned next to him. "That movie about the people on the plane and that annoying kid? What does that-"

"It's based on a Stephen King novella," explained Max. "A bunch of people slip out of time and exist in an empty world. This is starting to feel a little like that."

"This isn't like that," said Lucas, putting things together in his mind, "but it's not far off, I suppose. I don't know *how* exactly, but I think Julian has pulled us out of reality and isolated us. The doors won't open because they're not really doors. We're stuck inside a cage, and even if we make it outside we will find ourselves no better off. In fact, we'd probably be in an even worse predicament. The only way to solve this is to get a hold of Julian and find out what he wants from us."

"What he wants from *you*," corrected Shaun. "He has a grudge against you, not us. I don't see why he won't just let the rest of us go."

Lucas sighed, but had no recourse except to agree. "You all have the right to be angry at me," he glanced at Vetta, wounded when she looked away, "but I promise I'll try to fix this. You just have to trust me."

Annie cackled. "Ha! Sure, let's trust The Devil."

"Yeah, well, laugh it up, because I'm the best you've got."

⊥

LUCAS STOOD IN THE MESSY BACK-OFFICE WONDERING WHERE to start. He'd expected things to be staged, but it appeared to be an actual working office, with genuine accounts and a lock-box full of petty-cash. He even found a chocolate bar in the top drawer of a desk. Whoever Julian was, he seemed to actually be running a pub—one that was losing money by the looks of things. But surely that had nothing to do with this? Had Lucas affected Julian's business in some way? Was that what this was about? It seemed unlikely, but men could be needlessly petty. Julian was some kind of powerful warlock, possibly even a demon or a pathwalker, so it seemed trivial to be running a pub, but there was a reason for everything.

What was the man's true agenda?

Someone walked into the room behind Lucas; it was Vetta. She struggled to meet his gaze when he smiled at her. "Thank you for healing me," she said in a quiet voice, then turned to leave again. It seemed like she had come to talk, but then found herself without anything to say. She was beating a hasty retreat.

"I wouldn't have had to if I hadn't first..." He closed his eyes and fought a tightness in his throat. "Vetta, I'm so sorry for what I did to you. Being human is new to me. I acted before I knew what I was doing."

She glanced back and managed to meet his eye. "You did not know what would happen?"

"No, I..." *Don't lie to her.* "I knew what I was doing. I knew."

She turned away. He couldn't tell if it was disgust, anger, or something else making it impossible for her to look at him. "I wish to help," she muttered.

"No, Vetta. Stay away from me. I've hurt you enough."

"Yes, and it is not over. We are all trapped here because of you. I will not do nothing. I will not be powerless."

Lucas looked at her, tried to read what she was thinking. "I just don't want you to get hurt."

She folded her arms and locked her jaw even as she spoke. "When I was little girl, my papa used to let me help him around our little farm. I would help feed pigs and chickens, and plant tomatoes in ground. One morning, he take me to fix big wall around tractor shed, while my mama take my sister into town. He tell me to stand back, because wall is dangerous. He need to knock down and put in new bricks. I stand back and mix cement, and when I am doing this, I do not see snake in the grass. We do not have many snakes in Slovakia, but there was one right behind me. It slither onto my leg, and I scream. I am little girl and I scream like child. This frighten my papa. It frighten him so much he lose his balance and fall against wall. Bricks, they land on him, big pile, and he scream. I run over, and his head is bleeding. I see teeth broken in mouth. He is trying to speak but cannot. He is turning blue. I try to move bricks, but..." There were tears in her eyes. "I am just a little girl. They are too heavy to move. I cannot take them from my papa, and they crush his chest. He cannot breath. He die. My mama and sister are poor now because my papa is gone and cannot work farm, because I was stupid girl who could not lift bricks. Stupid girl who scream at snake."

She met his gaze then, and Lucas understood what she was saying to him. She couldn't be a powerless bystander. She needed to take charge of what would happen to her next. She rolled up the bottom of her top and pulled down her jeans. On her hip was a tattoo of an adder. "This remind me not to be scared of snakes."

Lucas sighed. He had no right to show her horrors and then expect her to close her eyes. She was part of this now. "I need to know who Julian is," he told her. "Can you help me search this office?"

Vetta smiled and they got to work, sifting through piles of papers and ring-binders on the shelves. It looked like they wouldn't find anything useful, but then Vetta discovered a safe behind an oil painting of a purple-flowered tree. She stood back and looked at the safe. "You think money inside, or something else?"

"I don't see a way of finding out, unless you know how to crack a safe?"

Vetta frowned. "You cannot open with powers?"

"I'm as human as you are, Vetta. More or less."

"You heal me," she argued. "You cannot open metal box?"

He decided she might have a point. He had lost his angelic powers, yes, but evidentially not all of them. What still remained? What could he do? Feeling idiotic, he placed both palms against the safe like he had when he'd healed Vetta and Jake. This time, he didn't want to heal. He wanted to destroy.

He felt something. A tingling in his fingertips. Vetta watched him anxiously, and he pictured her beaming as he burst open the safe, as if impressing her would somehow repair her opinion of him. A stupid thought. Why were human minds so prone to fantasy? Why did he care what this girl thought of him?

"Nothing is happening," Vetta eventually said, looking at him as if she was missing something.

Lucas removed his hands from the safe and grunted. "I can't do it. I thought for a second I could, but I can't."

"Then we must try something else." She felt around the edges of the safe but kept her eyes on him. "You say this place is no longer part of reality, so why not the safe be open?"

"Because it's still a safe. I can't crack steel."

Vetta scowled at him like she was about to kick him in the backside. "Do magic! Like when you put Julian inside my body. You did magic then, do magic now!"

Shame rushed to the front of Lucas's mind and made him look down at the worn carpet they were standing on. She was right; he needed to try harder. He might not have the innate power he once did, but he still had some of his knowledge. Did he possess, somewhere in his mind, a spell that could get a safe open?

Maybe.

Probably.

Yes!

"We need to get the others," he said. "I have an idea."

┴

It was a tight squeeze, assembling everybody inside the office, and they had to back right up against the wall. Simon, being the largest of the bunch, had to scrunch up like a crisp packet. "What is this achieving?" he asked grumpily as he bumped up against the desk. "I thought you wanted the lot of us to keep out of your way."

"I changed my mind," said Lucas. "We're going to do a little magic trick instead. Let's call it... *Open Sesame*."

"You want to get this safe open?" asked Shaun, frowning. With his tattoos and slick-backed hair, he looked like the type of guy who might have some experience in getting safes open, but it wasn't to be for he gave no offer of help. "You have a stick of dynamite you're not telling us about?"

The next question came from Max. "What do you hope to find inside?"

Lucas shrugged. "More answers than we have right now. I think I can unlock it with your help."

"You mean like when Vetta tried to help you?" said Annie. "That worked out really well for her."

Vetta started fidgeting with her top. She wouldn't look Lucas in the eye again. "Last magic trick hurt me very bad. I not want to do another."

Asking Vetta to help was contemptible, but what other option did Lucas have? There was no whiff of a solution except for, possibly, getting whatever was inside this safe. "None of you will get hurt," he told them. "I promise. My word means nothing to anyone here," he glanced at Vetta, "and it's downright tarnished for some, but I won't put any of you in unnecessary danger. I think I have a way to open this safe, but I can't do it without the rest of you."

"Who cares what's in the safe?" said Simon. "It's probably just papers."

"We need to know who Julian is," said Lucas. "Whatever is inside might provide answers."

"And money," said Shaun. "If there's money, I want some."

Everyone gave a chuckle.

"I say go for it," said Jake. "What other ideas do we have?"

Max shrugged, seeming to suggest he was on board. Vetta stared at the floor, but she muttered her assent. They all wanted to get out of this pub.

"I want to get to Bingo tonight," said Shirley. "There's a rollover jackpot, and if my Eric goes and wins it without me, the bugger will do a flit."

"Shall we get this over with?" said Simon, wincing as his hip crunched up against the desk. "I'm feeling claustrophobic."

"Okay," said Lucas, feeling something bordering on positive as he contemplated finding some answers. It was a long shot, but at least it was something. "You won't like this," he said, "but we all need to hold hands. Magic needs a circuit, just like electricity, or it will drain away. Once we have the power inside of us, we need to keep it contained."

Simon rolled his eyes. "What the hell, man?"

"Just humour me," said Lucas.

Simon grunted, but he took Shaun and Annie's hands either side of him without further complaint. The rest paired up as well, and together they made a ragged circle. Lucas caught Vetta staring at him, but she looked away as soon as he made eye-contact. Jake was grinning like he expected to be entertained, but everyone else just looked awkward and depressed.

"We're going to perform a simple unbinding spell," Lucas informed them. "Egyptian priests used it to seal and unseal tombs. I'm pretty sure I remember the words, but while I speak them, I need you all to focus on the safe. I need you to *will* it open. I shall channel your demands and get them to the relevant authorities."

Simon pulled a face. "And who might that be?"

"If I told you Thoth, would it mean much?"

Everyone stared at him blank-faced, and it made Lucas chuckle. It was good feeling like an authority again. "Thoth was an angel the Ancient Egyptians worshipped as a god. He gave hieroglyphics to mankind and allowed them the discovery of writing. Guy always was a swot."

Max's eyes widened. "You knew an Egyptian God?"

"Thoth is one of my brothers. Not a god though, just an angel. They used to worship me under the name Set. Those were the good old days. We had us some great orgies beside the Nile. Anyway, shall we begin?"

He waited for everyone to shush, and then spoke the ancient words, pleasing himself at how fluently they came to him. A dead language not spoken in thousands of years, yet it was crystal clear in his mind.

Until it wasn't.

The words deserted him halfway out of his mouth. He mumbled, trying to get back on track, but...

Vetta glanced at him. "What is wrong?"

"I... I'm struggling to remember the last part of the unbinding. I-I don't—"

The safe popped open, making them all—including Lucas—yelp.

"You did it!" said Jake. "Amazing!"

But he hadn't done it, had he? There was more to the spell; he was sure of it. His memory had ended a few phrases short of completion. In fact, he couldn't even remember the words he had just spoken. The knowledge slipped away from him, curling up like the edges of a dying leaf. Gone. He was getting dumber.

The safe had opened though, and that was what he'd wanted, wasn't it? Was there any reason to question the methods if the results were as intended? "Is everyone okay?" he asked the group, worried something had gone wrong.

"I did not feel anything," said Vetta, looking relieved.

"Me either," said Simon, pulling his hands free of the others. "I can't actually believe it worked. We really did that? We opened the safe by holding hands and concentrating? Well stone me!"

"I told you I wouldn't hurt anyone," said Lucas, looking at Vetta. "It was a simple spell from a time when spells were ordinary."

"What's inside the safe?" said Shaun excitedly. His tattooed arms were already reaching inside it.

Lucas moved the man aside so he could take a look himself. The safe's interior was a gaping black hole, dissected in the middle by a slim metal shelf. Nothing appeared to be inside, and he was about to curse at having gone through an ordeal for nothing, before he noticed the glint of an object nestled towards the back.

Reaching inside, he went to grab it, but quickly pulled his hand back. A surge ran up his arm, a coldness that whispered in his ear to *run*. Another stupid emotion, another senseless human component of an inadequate mind. Fear.

Chiding himself for being so ridiculous, Lucas snatched the object out of the safe and examined it at once. He knew immediately what it was.

“Is that a nail?” asked Max. “It looks old.”

“It is,” said Lucas, “Over two thousand years old.”

Bitter Spirits

The sun drifted down behind the sandy walls of Jerusalem and bathed the world in amber. The beggar climbed the hill leisurely, kicking aside human skulls and rotting refuse. This was not an ascent to fresh air and scenic views, for this summit offered only despair and misery. The crowds drew away in the opposite direction, hurrying down the hill to their homes. Peasants might relish the spectacle of death by day, but by night, they shunned it for their warm beds and family meals.

Dawdling, the beggar passed by Roman militia and city officials finishing up for the day, but nobody on the hill noticed him. No one acknowledged the presence of a sickly old vagrant in a city stuffed with them—no one except for one man.

The condemned man hung from the central of three crosses, and he actually smiled as the beggar traipsed towards him. His long brown hair was filthy and caked in dried blood—his forehead equally so. A Roman spear lay in the mud beneath the man's dangling feet, responsible for the deep gouge beneath his ribs. A crown of thorns rested upon his head, and a crude banner nailed to the top of the cross declared him 'King of the Jews.' Right now, the man was anything but regal.

"Hello, beggar," greeted the man in a dry, thirsty voice. "I'm afraid I have nothing for you right now."

The beggar laughed unexpectedly and chided himself for it. "You hang naked and shamed, yet offer jokes?"

"Are jokes ever unwelcome? Is humour not a mechanism for joy? A thing most needed in my current state, wouldn't you agree?"

"I would think anger more befitting your situation. You have been betrayed and put to death."

The man sighed, pain and weariness on his face but not the hopelessness one would expect. "I am alive, and for that I am grateful."

"You have mere moments."

"And I will not waste them on anger or sadness. Such things will not ease my passage to Heaven, nor keep me here on Earth."

The beggar sneered. "Heaven? A cesspool worse than this."

"And what is so bad about this place, beggar? Is it not full of wonders?"

"Wonders? You've been persecuted by those you sought to save, and you speak of wonders? Your time here has been meaningless. Nothing shall change. Mankind is offal spoiling in the sun."

It started to rain, droplets splashing on the man's cheeks and cutting lines through the dirt there. He closed his eyes, seeming to enjoy the feel of it. "Man is a passionate and complex animal, and a furious battle rages within each human heart, but while war is never pleasant, it can end in only one outcome."

The beggar wiped drizzle from his eyes, irritated. "And what, pray, is that outcome?"

"Peace. War may only end in *peace*."

The beggar took two steps forward, bare feet sinking into the bloody sand. "Or destruction."

"To quench a flame is not to kill fire. God's spirit cannot be extinguished. It will forever reignite, even when fully dampened. If ruination and rebirth is the intended path for humanity, then so be it. All things die. There is no failure in it."

The beggar was close enough now to smell the man's approaching death—a sickly, sweet odour that men instinctively feared. He found it intoxicating. "Then what is the point of it all?" he demanded. "Why live only to die?"

"To ask such a question is to miss the point of it all."

The beggar growled. How dare this man speak to him as if he were a confused child? Hanging from this cross, the man was less than nothing—less than the beetles feasting on his flesh. "You think yourself wise, *King of the Jews*, but all I see is a dying peasant, betrayed and broken."

"All I see before me is a lost soul posing as a beggar."

"I have no time for riddles."

The man sighed as if frustrated. "Why do you come to me this night, cousin? Do you wish to revel in my final agonies? Such things are petty and beneath you, old one. Have you not witnessed enough death in your vast existence?"

A thief strung up on one of the rear crucifixes flinched, not yet dead, but the beggar ignored the movement and stared into the eyes of the man who had just said something quite unexpected. "You know what I am?"

"I know *who* you are. We have met once before in the desert. I saw through you then as I see through you now. I feel your pain. It reveals your entire history."

The beggar spat in the mud. "One such as I does not feel pain. I am archangel, one of The Three."

"You are an angel no more, cousin. You are lost and weary, bearing a cross of your own. It must be lonely, knowing so much among those who know so little, *Lucifer*."

Lucifer lost his focus for a second. His facade faltered, and his bare feet turned to hooves in the bloody sand. "Why did Father put you here? What is your aim?"

"Perhaps I am here for *you*, cousin, so that you may ask me a question."

Lucifer snarled, darkness bubbling to the surface through his eyes. "What question?"

The dying man's eyes fluttered. His body was failing fast, flesh pale and wounds no longer bleeding. When he spoke again, his words were strained. "What question do you yearn to ask most? I fear I have time to hear only one."

"I have nothing to ask of an insect. You are merely Father's latest discarded creation. He loves you as much as He loves me."

"A great deal indeed then. You claim not to want answers, Lucifer, yet questions are all you have. Your mind swims with them. Ask and find yourself answered. But do so quickly, my time is at an end."

"I am not one of your meek flock, enamoured by the cloying spices of your tongue."

"No, cousin, you are not. You are magnificent."

The beggar wavered, confused by the direction of the

conversation. "I am The Devil, defiler of all for which you stand. This world is my playground, and I fill it with hate and suffering. Just this very morning, I whispered in a widow's ear to kill her child. I filled her head with terror that she would fail to provide for the young girl and killing her quickly would be the kinder option. I am not magnificent, I am wicked beyond all compare."

"You are Lucifer, eldest and most beautiful of Heaven, the incarnation of innocence."

"*Innocence*! How can you call me innocent? I *devour* innocence."

"Innocence is merely the search for answers, cousin. God made you to be inquisitive, to question and to *want*. He created mankind the same way. The thing you claim to hate most is more akin to you than your own brothers. Mankind seeks answers like you do. That is why I am here on this cross. I am just a question mankind is asking of God."

"I seek no answers. I know all."

"You know nothing. So ask!"

"I want nothing from you, *Jesus*."

"Yet here before me you stand."

"To watch you suffer! I engineered your downfall, *son of God*. Ha! You agonise because of me. I relish your pain."

"Then why do you weep, cousin?"

Lucifer touched his cheeks in shock. An angel could not shed tears, and yet...

Jesus smiled down at him with pity, his compassion a force comparable to the wind. "Your heart brims with fear and pain, Lucifer. Discard it and discover what remains."

"I am The Devil."

"Until you choose not to be."

"It is not a choice! Father did this to me."

"*You* did this to you, Lucifer. You made decisions that held consequences, and you must shoulder them."

Lucifer stomped forward on cloven hooves. He grabbed the iron nail fastening Jesus's left wrist to the cross and twisted it cruelly, but Jesus only smiled.

It made Lucifer angry. So angry he felt like he might explode and consume the earth in the fires of his rage. "I hate you!" he bellowed, causing a wind to whip atop the hill. Dark clouds blotted out the sky. "Heaven has no authority over me. My brothers are weak. God is impotent. You are *nothing.*"

"As are you, cousin. You discarded your authority in search of something else. There is no shame in it."

"I am King of Hell. I warred with God Himself."

"The son always hurts the father, and the father hurts the son. It is so."

"Father cast me down for all eternity. He fears me."

Jesus shook his head slightly, an expression of even deeper pity. "Eternity doesn't have to be forever."

Lucifer smashed a clawed fist into Jesus's gentle face, crushing his nose. "You speak more riddles!"

Jesus spat blood but didn't cease his gentle smiling. "Sometimes the riddle is in the mind of the listener. Ask your question quickly, cousin. It must be now!"

"End this nonsense! I despise you, *Jesus.*"

"Yes, let it out! What else do you hate, cousin?"

It was raining heavily now, and Lucifer sneered through it all. "I hate my brothers who turned their backs on me. I hate this earth with its mindless cattle and endless stink. I hate it all. I hate that I was cast down for refusing to bow down to these insects. I hate Father for asking me to."

Jesus nodded. "More. There is more hate in you. Give it to me, cousin. Let me take it with me."

There was a flood inside Lucifer, emotions gushing forth and breaking dams he didn't even know were in place. "I hate... I hate... I hate that I acted so rashly and hurt my kin. I hate myself for being so misguided. I hate... *myself*... I..." He realised he had fallen to his knees in the mud, prostrate beneath Jesus's dangling feet. "I hate what I did to Father. Why did I do it? Why did I ever let in so much anger? Why?"

Jesus's eyes closed. "Ask your true question, cousin. It is time."

From on his knees, Lucifer looked up at Jesus and asked something he never thought he would. He asked, "Can I ever be forgiven?"

Jesus smiled.

┼

"YOU *KNEW* JESUS?" THE EXPRESSION ON ANNIE'S FACE WAS partway between amusement and bafflement.

Lucas nodded. "I did."

"The messiah? The son of God?"

"He just went by *Jesus* back then. But yes!"

"So, so, so, this nail," she said, pointing at the slither of metal now sitting on the centre of the bar. "This was one of the nails used to pin Jesus to the cross?"

"Jesus," muttered Max.

Lucas grunted. "Yes! *Jesus* Christ."

"No," said Max. "I just mean, *Jesus*, that's crazy."

Annie prodded the nail on the bar with her index finger as though she feared it might bite her. It was an ugly thing

—aged iron hammered into an uneven spike with a square head formed of one end. It had been driven into the space between Jesus's left ulna and radius bones. A crude, yet precise torture.

"So, Julian..." said Vetta, squinting with consideration, "is Jesus?"

Lucas wished he knew the answer. Julian looked and behaved nothing like that man he had met on that cross in Jerusalem—but people change. *Even* The Devil had changed. And yet... "I don't think Julian is Jesus," he said. "That doesn't feel right."

"Then who?" Max scratched his head like a confused monkey. With his wispy blonde hair he looked a lot like an infant. "I thought you were going to get answers. Now all we have is more questions."

"Questions are good. Questions mean we're still in the game. Answers are final."

"You're talking in riddles," said Simon angrily.

Shirley nodded. "Yeah, this is getting a bit much for me too."

Lucas sighed. The nail on the bar took him back to a time long ago. A worse time. A better time. A time when he hadn't tormented himself every second about what he *was* and what he had done. There had been a joyful abandon in being God's Adversary, in being The Devil.

Some secret part of him had always yearned to revert back, like a middle-aged family man lamenting on his glory days. Tormenting mankind was a game he had been unrivalled at. His wickedness had been glorious. He missed it. But he had given it all up, the thing that had defined him for thousands of years, suppressed so that he could become one of the *good guys.*

And where had it got him?

Up shit creek with a paddle wedged up my arse!

Lucas moved away from the bar, sickened by the sight of the nail—sickened by what had become of him since the last time he'd seen it. *Damn you, Gladri. There will be a reckoning for this, I vow to you.*

"You okay?" asked Max. While the others remained at the bar in silence, he broke away and followed Lucas over to the pool table. Lucas plucked a pool cue from the rack and started belting the white ball off the cushions. *Whap-whap-whap.*

Max picked up a cue as well, as if he wanted to play, but Lucas ignored him.

Whap-whap-whap.

"Hey, man. Just cool it, okay? We'll figure this out. Hey, man...? Come on!"

Lucas smashed the cue ball harder. *WHAP!* It hit the cushion and ricocheted into the air. Max had to duck, and when he stood back up, Lucas was snarling in his face. "What do you know about anything, kid? I've existed for eons. I fear nothing. I know all. So get away from me before I flay the flesh from your puny body!"

Max looked shocked at first, then hurt, but his expression eventually settled on something else—something that seemed almost mocking. Instead of going away, he started talking.

"There was this lad I was friends with at school, right? Greg, his name was. Used to act tough all the time. Bullied just about everyone, even me, his friend. Told us his dad was an SAS soldier and that his whole family took Karate lessons. Everyone in school was afraid of him. He was tough."

"Nice story," said Lucas. "Go tell it to someone else."

"He was tough," repeated Max, "until somebody put him to the test. A new kid joined our school. His name was Ross, and he'd come from a tower block in Kings Heath. From the get-go, Ross wasn't willing to put up with any of Greg's bullshit—he called him on it straight away. And of course, Greg had been top dog too long to let that stand and still keep his cred, so he had no choice but to face Ross."

"Who kicked his arse," said Lucas. "Your story lacks originality."

"Yeah," said Max. "Ross kicked the ever-living shit out of Greg. Left him sobbing on the ground. The entire school just walked away and left him there in the middle of the car park. No one was ever afraid of Greg again."

"The end," said Lucas, rolling his eyes.

"No," said Max. "The beginning. Everyone left Greg lying there on the ground, except for me. I stayed. I helped him up and got him home, and that's when he finally stopped with the bullshit. He admitted how his dad was never home, and his mom was a drunk who said she hated him and wished he were dead. He told me how alone he was. How scared he was."

Lucas slammed the pool cue down on the table. "What's your goddamn point, Max?"

"That the guy who acts toughest is the most afraid. Greg and I are still friends to this day. He joined the Army after school and became a paratrooper, just like he used to fantasise about his dad being. He's a genuinely tough SOB now and dedicated to protecting others. No more bullshit. No more bullying." Max looked down and smiled as he reminisced, and it seemed pretty clear that this was a true story.

When he looked up at Lucas again, his eyes were steely and determined. "Words and actions are two separate things, Lucas. I know you're afraid, probably more than any of us, because you have so much more to lose."

Lucas reclaimed the cue and considered snapping it to relieve more of his anger. "I've *already* lost everything," he growled.

"You could let it strengthen you—like Greg did."

Lucas wanted to punch Max right in his sweet, understanding face, yet somehow his anger slipped away, and he only felt exhausted. "You're a good lad, Max, but please just give me some spa..." He trailed off, spotting movement in the corner of his eye. The cue ball that had leapt from the table earlier was now rolling across the floorboards towards the pub's front door.

Max noticed it too. "Huh, guess the floors in this place aren't plum. I'll go fetch it."

Lucas didn't object, despite the odd feeling at the back of his mind that told him something wasn't quite right. He watched the lad stroll over to retrieve the ball, then glanced at the others still huddled around the bar. They were staring at the old nail, so intently they hadn't noticed Lucas and Max arguing. On the wall behind the bar, the spirits rattled. The spirits inside the bottles sloshed to one side, as if gravity had suddenly turned sideways.

Something was wrong.

Lucas turned his focus back to Max just as the lad knelt by the front door to pick up the elusive cue ball. But it rolled away from him, forcing him to creep after it until it clunked against the door inside the front porch. The sudden, sharp noise got everyone's attention, and those at the bar turned their heads.

Lucas put down the pool cue. "Max! Listen to me. Get away from that d-"

The door burst open and a colossal gust of wind forced its way inside the pub. At the opposite end of the room, the rear door burst open as well, and the interior became a wind tunnel, chairs and tables sliding and shifting across the floorboards. Shaun stumbled off his stool and collided with Shirley. Max stumbled backwards, hit full-on by the gust. The crack of his head on the floorboards was ghastly —even over the sound of the howling wind.

"What the fuck is going on?" shouted Simon, clutching the bar to keep from falling. "Get that door closed!"

"We've been desperate to get it open," said Shirley, scurrying about on her hands and knees.

Annie screamed. "Max is hurt."

Lucas clutched the pool table and pulled himself along it, fighting to get to the door to close it. Max lay on his side, trying to sit up, but the wind kept pushing him back down. Annie crawled along the bar to get to him, her blonde hair blowing everywhere.

The wind stopped. Just like that, it ceased.

A gin bottle fell from the wall behind the bar and smashed on the ground. Everyone yelped, but then there was nothing but silence. What just happened?

"You did it," said Shirley, looking at Lucas. "You broke the spell on the pub. We can leave."

Both doors were open, but what had caused the seal to break?

He shook his head. Something wasn't right here. "Nobody move!"

Annie scrambled over to her brother. "What are you

talking about? We can finally get the hell out of here. Someone, get that door before it closes."

"No," said Lucas. "Stop! Everybody stop."

But Annie had made up her mind. She grabbed her brother and yanked him to his feet while he was still dazed. "This was one hell of a weird afternoon," he said, stumbling along with her hand on his back. "Just wait until I tell Dad."

Annie halted and turned her brother to face her. "What are you talking about, Max? Dad's dead." She grabbed him and stared into his eyes. "Damn it! You have a concussion."

"I'm fine," said Max. "I just got a bit confused for a second. Dad is really…? Yeah, I remember. He was—" Something from outside the door snatched Max and yanked him into the porch. It cut off his words and left him too startled to scream, and he only just managed to get a hand out in time to grab the edge of the doorway. He clung on for dear life, something unseen tugging at both his legs.

Annie screamed. "Oh God, Max!"

Lucas hurried to help. Together, he and Annie grabbed Max's arm to pull him back inside, but the force pulling him out was too strong. The tendons in his fingers bulged around the door frame. His face grew purple. He couldn't hold on for long. What the hell had him?

The others hurried to help, but there was little they could do to insert themselves. Lucas and Annie were still wrestling to get Max back inside, but it wasn't doing any good, and there was only enough space in the porch for them.

"Help me!" Max cried. "Please!"

Lucas shoved Annie aside so he could get a better grip

by himself. "Hold on, kid," he urged, pulling with all he had. "Just. Hold. On!"

Max looked at Lucas pleadingly, eyes bulging with terror. He had been yanked clean off his feet by whatever unseen force had him, and inch by inch he was slipping away. Lucas could not keep hold of him. One of Max's fingernails tore away as his hand slipped further down the wood.

Jake arrived and thrust a pool cue out through the doorway. A vicious *crunch*, and the cue was ripped out of his hand. Something outside growled malevolently. The lights in the pub flickered.

Simon raced forwards next and grabbed Max by the back of his neck with both meaty hands. Max cried out, but his terror turned to a pitiful mewing. His eyes searched desperately for his sister until he spotted her sobbing over by the bar. They shared a moment, terrified eyes meeting across the room. Max opened his mouth. "Annie!"

The creature outside roared.

Lucas and Simon flew backwards into Jake, and the three men crumpled to the ground. Max fell on top of Lucas, free from the force trying to yank him outside.

Lucas shook the boy urgently. "Max? Max, are you okay? Max?"

Max stared at Lucas with wide, hemorrhaged eyes. Blood ran from his mouth.

Annie raced over in a panic, but when she reached her brother, she screamed. And screamed and screamed.

Lucas possessed Max's top half, but the lad's legs were slithering out of the doorway, dragging behind a creature now standing half inside the pub. The abomination skittered about on elongated arms and legs, akin to a spider but with a long, twisted neck supporting a contorted human face. Long, greasy black hair hung from its skull and weeping sores covered its flesh. The creature had once been human. Now it was a demon.

Shaun stood frozen in the middle of the room, hands trembling by his sides. He was sobbing openly. "W-What the hell is that thing?"

Lucas scooted backwards on his butt, getting away from Max's blood-spewing corpse. His eyes were transfixed by the creature in the doorway. "We're so screwed," he muttered. "We're so screwed."

┴

THE CREATURE SKITTERED OUT OF THE DOORWAY, LEAVING everyone in the pub horrified. Lucas got up and hurried over to the doorway to make sure the thing was truly leaving. He struggled to believe his eyes as he watched its retreat. The creature clutched Max's legs against its fat abdomen with a spindly arm while it pounded the ground with its other sinuous limbs. It was heading down the hill towards the deserted shops—a spider leaving with its prey.

"This is so messed up," said Jake, joining Lucas at the doorway. He was sweating, and his lower lip trembled. "What is *happening*?"

"Are we dead?" asked Vetta. She was propped against the pool table, taking deep breathes like she might throw up. "This is Hell, yes?"

"This isn't Hell," Lucas told her. "It's something else. We're still trapped." Julian had snatched them from reality and placed them inside a cage of his making, but why?

What did I do to this guy?

"This is all your fault, you bastard!"

Lucas turned in time to catch Annie charging at him. "You killed my brother!" He didn't fight back as she collided with him, even though her fists against his chest hurt like buggery. He just waited until Vetta and Shirley pulled her away.

Lucas tasted blood in his mouth as he spoke. "I don't know who Julian is, or why he's doing this."

Annie spat at him. "It's your fault."

He nodded. "You're right."

Simon was pulling at his beard, like it was the only way he could keep his hands from making fists. "You've dragged us all into your mess, and now you're covered in Max's blood. What the hell *is* that thing outside?"

"Aswang," said Lucas—the word thick in his mouth.

Simon jutted out his hairy chin. "What you call me?"

"I didn't call *you* anything. That creature outside is an *aswang*." Nothing from Lucas's days in Hell stayed with him quite as much as the aswangs. They were truly abhorrent creatures—monsters, even in Hell. "They have other names, but that's the one that comes to mind."

Vetta stepped in front of Lucas as if she feared Simon might attack him. "What is *aswang*?" she asked.

Lucas's mind conjured memories of Hell, the landscape teeming with abominations, some human, others barely even flesh. He remembered the aswangs more than any of them.

"Aswangs are formed from the tortured souls of suicide victims," he explained. "People who hoped to escape their pain by ending their lives. Instead, they found themselves damned, sentenced to relive their most painful regrets forever, ruminating on the most painful moments of their lives over and over again in exquisite detail. Eventually, the unbearable weight of their suffering forces them down onto all fours where they lose all trace of what made them human. I know their suffering because it was I who passed their sentence."

Annie shook her head in revulsion. "You sentenced them when you were king of Hell?"

"A long time ago now, but yes. I am responsible for the creature that took Max."

Annie stomped over to the bar, obviously trying to hide her tears. Lucas wished he could say something that would make things better for her, but he knew there was nothing. He'd seen enough weeping widows and orphaned children to know words could not erase pain.

"What do we do next?" asked Shaun, rubbing his sinewy arms as if he was cold. His tattoos looked alive as they bunched up and shifted beneath his skin. Truthfully, it was neither hot nor chilly. The room lacked temperature in either direction.

Lucas pointed to the deserted shops outside the window. "We go outside. There's no other way."

Shirley gasped. "What? Go out there with that thing skittering about? Are you insane?"

"I wish I were, but we have to go outside and kill that thing. This fabricated reality is tethered to it."

"I thought Julian was behind everything," said Shirley. She had retrieved her handbag and had it clutched against her chest.

Lucas rubbed at his temples, feeling sweat in his side-burns. "Julian is behind everything, but he would have needed to implore a higher power to cast the kind of magic this would require. By summoning an aswang, he opened a conduit to hell to syphon its dark energies. He's using that energy to drag us out of reality. Right now, we're in a space between Hell and Earth. A bit like the meat between two pieces of bread. A kind of purgatory."

Shaun groaned. "Some place between Hell and Earth? That doesn't sound good—or in any way believable."

Rather than continue to fret, Lucas tried to focus on the positives, on the things they could actually tackle. "If we kill the aswang, we'll untether ourselves and fall back in line with reality. I doubt we were ever supposed to see the creature, but when we did the unbinding spell on the safe, we accidentally unsealed the pub as well. I forgot the final words of the incantation that would have focused the spell only on the safe, but because I didn't say them, the spell spread out and unbound the doors too. It was a lucky error, I suppose."

"Lucky?" said Simon. "Luck is the last thing any of us have right now. Max is dead, you prick."

"I still can't believe it, man," said Jake, leaning over the bar and rubbing his forehead. "I've known Max since we were kids. He helped me when my... I just can't believe he's gone." He looked at Lucas and frowned. "Why are you here, man? I mean, you were at the pub drinking last night like any ordinary geezer, but you're not an ordinary geezer, are you? What is The Devil doing hanging out in a Birmingham pub?"

"*Ex*-Devil," Lucas corrected. "And where else would I be? You choose to spend your nights down the boozer, so why can't I? Why does a person go to a pub, Jake?"

Jake shrugged. "Company, I suppose."

"Exactly. A pub is a place where you can go for company, and yet still be alone. It's lonely living forever, let me tell you, but it's pointless forging friendships. Human beings come and go in a heartbeat, while time stretches on forever for an immortal. I spend my time in pubs so I'm not alone, but also because I never have to get to know anyone beyond a friendly conversation or the odd joke or two. It's the best life an immortal can hope for. Not that I qualify anymore."

"You sound like a nutter, mate," said Simon.

Jake sighed. "Vetta said she saw an angel last night. Is that true?"

"Yes," said Vetta. "I see."

"Gladri," said Lucas. "An angel in the service of Heaven. It was he who turned me human last night."

Shirley sniffed. "Why did he do that?"

"Because I've been interfering."

"In what?"

"A war. God has been under attack since before he made the very first man and woman. In fact, he created mankind in order to protect Heaven from assault. There are those who seek to take His power, so He instilled it into humanity—into every human soul—rather than keeping it all in one place. Next, He created a near-endless stream of worlds, ensuring the spread of His power far and wide. But for the last few thousand years those worlds have been systematically wiped out by sadistic forces, and with each dead Earth, more of God's power returns to Him, where his enemies can try to take it."

Annie groaned at the bar. Shaun was sitting beside her and made the same noise. Simon was standing and folded his meaty forearms while he remained silent. Vetta appeared thoughtful. Jake pulled a face. "Wow!"

"Yeah," said Lucas. "Wow. God's enemies want his

power to create a new universe of their own, one they can rule however they want. So, God sealed himself away in a secret place where nothing could get at him. His barriers are maintained by the power he placed into mankind, so as it weakens with each dying world, God becomes more vulnerable. If humanity is extinguished, God will be vulnerable, defenceless against the avarice of his kin."

Annie cackled from the bar. "Bullshit. What a load of..." Her volume lowered, as if she couldn't be bothered to finish her sentence. Or maybe she was coming around to the idea that she was in deep shit whether she believed it or not.

Lucas ignored her. "I know it sounds mad, but it's because you're too close to things. I've been watching on the big screen, and the ending doesn't look like it's going to be a happy one. I've been trying to even the odds in mankind's favour, but it seems like Heaven prefers me muzzled. Gladri is the guy they call for that kind of thing."

"He's a Heavenly pest controller?" Simon grunted sarcastically.

"Gladri's a justicar. He passes God's laws and judgements. He and I were close... once."

"He hurt you," said Vetta, seeming to read his mind.

Lucas sighed. Yes, Gladri had hurt him, but it was just one nick amongst a thousand deep, gangrenous wounds. A mere graze compared to the agonies Lucas had inflicted on others—like the fate of the aswangs.

"Look," he said, "you don't need any more back story, so let's just focus on that creature outside. Kill the aswang and you all get to go home. I will disappear from your lives forever, you have my *word*!"

"Amen," said Annie. Shaun lifted his head out of his arms and nodded in agreement.

"It won't be that easy for some of us," said Shirley, who was now sitting on the sofa and rubbing at her armpit. "It won't bring back Annie's brother."

"Or will it?" Jake raised both eyebrows and looked at Lucas. The lad seemed excited. "You healed me when I was dying. If we break the spell, or whatever, you can bring Max back, right?"

Lucas watched Annie's ears prick up, and he considered lying to give her hope—but he couldn't do that. "No," he admitted. "Max is gone. I'm sorry."

"Where do Max go now?" asked Vetta. "He go to Hell and become monster like thing that kill him?"

"No! Of one thing I can be certain, it's that Max is going nowhere but *up*. I may be just a man now, but I've been alive long enough to recognise a good soul when I see one. Max is in Heaven as we speak, of that you can be sure." He glanced at Annie and hoped it would at least be *something* for her to hold on to.

A silence descended, but they would need to get moving soon. Lucas plucked a pool cue from the rack and weighted it up in his hands. "Grab anything you can," he said. "Pool cues, spirit bottles, stabby things. Anything we can use to hurt the aswang. It's scary, I know, but trust me, that thing bleeds."

"We all do," said Shirley, somewhat ominously. She reached into her bag and pulled out a long green packet. "Anybody want a mint?"

Next Round

Vetta was fretting. She stood in front of the window, staring out at the grey landscape below. "I really don't think we should go out there," she said. "There must be better way, no?"

Lucas wished there was, but Julian had wanted them trapped inside the pub, so heading outside would throw a spanner in the works, and that could surely only work in their favour. Lucas being human had ruined whatever Julian's original plan had been, but it wouldn't be long before he had another in place.

The group assembled behind Lucas, clutching pool cues as weapons. He felt as though he should say something inspiring, a general leading his troops into battle, but no words came to him, and they didn't feel like his troops. They hated him, eyes glaring at his back. He'd been alive since the dawn of time, yet one single day of being human had exhausted him to despair. Everything was so *intense*.

"Let's go," he said finally. "Stay together, and whack anything that smells bad."

They stepped outside, and immediately, Lucas felt the air change—gravity itself becoming somehow different. It was colder too. While the pub had possessed no detectable temperature, outside it was crisp and frigid.

"It feels wrong out here," said Vetta, making the same observation as him.

"Yeah," said Jake. "It's freezing. And I feel… I dunno."

"Heavy," Simon answered for him. "I feel sluggish. Like I just spent an hour on an exercise bike and now I can't walk right."

"It feels wrong," Vetta said again. "Wrong."

Lucas nodded. "This place is a hernia in reality, a bulge outside of normality. We need to be careful. I don't think Julian ever planned for us to leave the pub, but now that we have, he'll rethink things. Hopefully he'll make a mistake."

Shaun looked around warily. "Why doesn't he just let us go? What is he hoping to achieve?"

Lucas remembered Julian referring to him as a 'token' and his death being intended as some sort of payment. But to *whom*? Who did Julian serve if not himself? And why did he possess one of the nails used to crucify Jesus? Lucas reached into his pocket and clutched the chunk of iron now, checking it was still where he'd put it. It was, and it somehow felt important not to lose it.

They headed down the small decline in front of the pub and approached the shops opposite. The chippy was closest, its heavy glass and aluminium fire-door hanging wide open. The counter inside lay abandoned, so the group went in cautiously and spread out warily around it. Jake wasted no time in moving behind the counter and rooting around the cupboards. Simon and Shaun went to investigate the back area, but reported finding nothing except machines for cutting potatoes and adding batter. Lucas knew many things, but he couldn't see how either machine would help their current situation.

"Score!" shouted Jake, grabbing something from underneath the counter and clonking it down next to the cash register. It was a large glass jar with murky water and bobbing items inside. "Gherkins," he explained. "I love these, and I'm starving." He twisted off the lid and dipped his fingers into the vinegar, snatching out a pickle as if it were a dozing green fish. He bit into it like a savage, which was why it was so surprising when he spat it out onto the counter a moment later. "*Gross*!"

Shirley rushed over and patted him on the back, assuming he was choking. "What is it, love?"

"Tastes like shit. Tastes like..."

"Ash," said Lucas, pointing at the half-eaten mouthful on the counter. The green skin and juice were dissolving, turning to a grey powder. "It's not a pickle."

"Sure as hell looked like one," said Jake, wiping his mouth with the back of his hand.

"It's a trick?" asked Shirley. "Are you okay, Jake?"

"Yeah, I just wasn't expecting it." He nudged the jar of pickles away from him on the counter.

Lucas tried to explain things. "This place is formed from a pact with an aswang. It's as much a part of Hell as it is Earth, and you cannot gain sustenance in Hell. Any food or water you try to eat will turn to ash in your mouth. If you try to get warm, you'll only get colder."

Annie rolled her eyes at the back of the group. "You're telling us we're in Hell?"

"No, we're in a place *influenced* by Hell. It's like being influenced by a planet's gravity once you get too close.

We've been pulled in enough for Hell's rules to apply, but some of Earth's too. It's not all bad—Hell is a place I know well."

"You being The Devil and all," said Annie.

"Let's just keep looking, shall we? We need to find that aswang."

Mentioning the creature stopped their conversation, and they followed Lucas silently out of the chip shop and back onto the featureless grey pavement. Lucas peered up the small hill back at the pub and considered retreating back inside. The orange glow from its windows was warm and inviting, and the beer inside was real. It wouldn't turn to ash. He theorised that the pub was the anchor between this fabricated reality and the one they belonged in, therefore the pub was closer to Earth than Hell, which is why the normal rules of existence still applied inside—more or less.

So why the hell did I drag us out of there?

Because we have no other choice. We have to get ourselves out of this oven before the door slams shut.

Next up was a small supermarket. Its double-doors were shut, but when Lucas pushed on them, they opened easily—if a little heavily. He glanced back to make sure the others were still with him. They were breathing a little heavily, but they followed him inside without complaint.

Jake picked up a handful of chocolate bars from a basket right inside the entrance, then let them fall through his fingers. "So, none of this food is edible? That sucks so hard, man. My stomach is kicking off, innit?"

"Mine too," said Shaun, tucking his pool cue under his armpit so that he could rub his belly.

"All part of the VIP Hell experience," said Lucas, feeling

pretty famished himself. Hunger was another new feeling that he didn't care for. "Everything and everyone in Hell is desperate for nourishment, but unable to ever get any. Damned souls suffer every neglect imaginable, but it's all in your mind. Try not to think of your hunger, or anything else you might be feeling, because it will only get worse."

Shirley plucked a pack of samosas from a nearby chiller cabinet. Her mouth seemed like it was about to drool. "It'll get worse?" she said. "The hunger?"

Lucas admitted he wasn't entirely sure. "In Hell, your hunger would get worse and worse until it drove you insane —but this isn't Hell. Hopefully, all you're experiencing is a taster."

"Nice choice of words," Annie muttered. "Seeing as we can't eat anything and will probably all starve to death."

Simon scratched his beard, which made an impressively loud rustling sound. It got their attention, so he decided to speak. "Suppose we should get busy then, before we start eyeing up each other's legs?"

Annie huffed, and then set off down the aisle. It was hard for her to be around them—or maybe just Lucas— and she was clearly struggling to hold it together. The others followed after her, but Lucas kept to the rear.

Simon hurried and caught up with Annie, which was good, because if Lucas had to choose one person to put in the firing line, it would be the large bearded man. Simon was unflinchingly macho, which meant his fear would be buried deep enough that he barely realised it was there. The man was prone to anger and aggression before panic and anxiety yet, despite that, Lucas was fairly certain Simon was a good man. A man who would fight to protect the others if—*when*—things turned ugly.

If a question mark hung over any of the group, it was Jake. The lad had been a thug last night, yet he seemed different now. Since Julian had crucified him and spilled his guts on the floor, and Lucas had subsequently healed him, Jake had become enthusiastic and helpful. Maybe even *pleasant.* Could the change be more than just a near-death experience?

Lucas studied the lad from behind, trying to get a read on him. Jake was searching the aisles with intent, prodding at shelves with the thick end of his pool cue, and glancing at the others in the group from time to time. Was he checking that they were okay? Was he worried about them? For obvious reasons, Vetta kept her distance from Jake, and he seemed to respect that, but every now and then he would give her a guilty glance. A glance that seemed to express remorse.

"Are you okay?" Lucas asked Vetta quietly as he moved beside her. She turned to him and he saw how pale she was —sickly even. Her ordeal had been severe, and she hadn't been given time to recover. Had Lucas truly healed her? Or was she still damaged? She managed to smile, but it lacked the warmth of the woman he had met last night.

"I am good," she said evenly. "Frightened, but... I go on."

"I'm sorry about all this." *God, that sounds so ridiculous*. "I wish I could take it all back."

"You can't though!" she snapped, then seemed to regret the outburst, her face softening as quickly as it had hardened. "But perhaps you can make amends. That is word, yes?"

He smiled weakly. "Amends, yes. I shall try very hard to make amends."

Just like I have for the last two-thousand-and-odd years. And I'm more screwed than I've ever been.

The lights flickered overhead, making the empty supermarket feel like the setting for an apocalypse movie. Everyone yelped, getting more and more on edge. Where had the aswang scuttled off to? Was it watching them?

"It's all just games," said Lucas, shaking his head. "Everything about this place will try to unnerve you."

Vetta saw something and screamed. She leapt against Lucas and pointed down the aisle. "Is that game? That thing is game?"

Lucas eased her towards Simon, who put an arm around her protectively. Lying in the aisle ahead, some slug-like beast slithered towards them.

Lucas approached the thing cautiously, trying to make it out in the dim light. The lights continued to flicker overhead. The monster was human. Bleeding and broken, but human. Someone Lucas recognised. Not at first, but once the broken face peered up at him with those dark-brown eyes and bushy eyebrows, the man's identity was unmistakable. "G-Gheorgie?"

The Romanian reached out a hand that was missing all its fingers. His lower lip was torn down the middle and flapped down in two pieces like the collar on a dress shirt. The only part of Gheorghie that hadn't experienced massive trauma were his eyes. The human, pleading eyes of the amiable young man Lucas had shared many drinks with last night. How had he ended up this way?

Lucas knelt on the floor and took Gheorghie into his arms, adding his blood to the stains already on his shirt. One more innocent soul tortured because of him. Gladri had called him an artificer of catastrophe, and it was true. "I'm sorry, Gheorgie,"

"What are you doing?" Simon demanded. He had his pool cue raised like a baseball bat. "Get away from that thing."

"I know him," Lucas shouted back to them. "He's a... a friend of Vetta's."

Vetta started. "Who?"

"It's Gheorgie but stay back! Let me help him."

Vetta cried out to Gheorgie, but she came no closer. Simon kept his arm around her while she sobbed, and Lucas turned his attention back to her tortured friend. There was no question what had to be done.

Lucas had to heal Gheorgie.

He closed his eyes and placed his hands on the man's ruined face, wincing at the floating, shattered cheekbones beneath the skin. The power came more easily this time. Having fumbled blindly for it the last two times, this time he knew exactly where to grab and found the power right where he expected it to be. He pushed it around Gheorgie, trying to draw away the man's pain and injury. Slowly, miraculously, the young man's grievous wounds started knitting together, blood retreating back into his veins, bones snapping back into place. His anguished eyes sparkled with renewed life. His pitiful moans became exultant gasps.

Lucas's eyes rolled back in his head and he tumbled away from Gheorgie, drained and disorientated, but he lay on his back happily. Gheorgie rose gingerly to his feet—fully healed—and exultant sounds spilled from Vetta. He had given her a miracle—his third of the day—and perhaps it went some way towards making amends.

But then it all went very wrong.

⊥

VETTA RAN TO GHEORGIE AND THREW HER ARMS AROUND him. The man was understandably confused, peering around like a newborn kitten. "W-what happened?"

"We're in trouble," said Vetta. "You were hurt, Gheorghie, but you are okay now. Lucas made you better."

Shirley was staring at Lucas with an impressed look on her face. "You could win Britain's Got Talent with that."

"Aye, maybe that's what I'll do when all this is over. I'll need to make a living somehow."

Shirley tried helping Lucas to his feet, but she succeeded only in getting him into a sitting position. He was happy enough taking a short rest, and he watched happily as Gheorgie and Vetta reunited. The Romanian's clothing was torn and bloody, but he seemed fine underneath. He laughed and smiled. "I leave my wallet at pub," he said. "I come back to get and then..."

"Julian is an evil magician or something," said Jake. "He must have jumped you when you came back on your own."

Gheorghie frowned at Jake, either surprised at what he said or the fact he was not shouting racist obscenities at him. There was a slender trail of blood dripping down his right ankle, but no one seemed to notice, including Gheorghie himself.

Lucas frowned. *What the?*

The trail of blood increased into a cascade. Vetta flinched when it washed over her shoes, and she leapt back from Gheorgie in fright. Gheorgie's face turned ashen. His mouth opened in mute horror, but he spoke no words. His terrified eyes said everything.

Lucas tried to get up, but he was still weak. Simon grabbed Vetta and pulled her away from what was happening. They all retreated several feet as Gheorgie shook before them in the centre of the aisle. His eyes bulged, and he looked at them imploringly. "W-what is happening to me? V-Vetta?"

Vetta moaned, but everyone else fell silent. Gheorgie started to bleed from his eyes, and then from everywhere else, skin slicing apart like it was being cut by invisible knives. His elbows snapped the wrong way, forearms pointing backwards. His neck contorted inhumanly. Finally, his knees buckled, and he collapsed onto his stomach, once more dragging himself along like an oozing slug. His dark-brown eyes dulled with pain, and they focused on Lucas accusingly.

"What's happening to him?" cried Vetta. "Please help him!"

"He's damned," said Lucas. "Julian must have given Gheorgie as a sacrifice to bind the aswang. His soul is no longer his own. His suffering is like a battery powering this place."

Vetta screamed at Lucas. "Make him better! Heal him again!"

Lucas battled to get up on his feet, and once he succeeded, he leaned against the nearby shelving to keep from falling back down. "You want me to put him through that all over again? I can't heal him, Vetta. This place... I just *can't*."

Vetta yanked her hair in despair. "We have to do something. We can, we should, I.... The *pub*! Yes! We can take Gheorghie to the pub. It is different there, yes?"

Lucas was pretty sure it wouldn't make any difference. Gheorghie wasn't just hurt, he was damned. "I'm sorry, Vetta. Gheorgie has been dead since this whole thing began. That thing on the ground is not a living creature, it's a tormented soul—just like the aswang. There's only one thing we can do for him now. Give him release from this place so that he might go on to the next."

Lucas expected Vetta to protest, but instead, she went over to Gheorgie and got down on her knees beside him, placing a hand against one of his ruined cheeks. "How do we do this thing?" she asked, addressing Lucas behind her.

Lucas stepped towards her. "Let me."

"No, I will stay."

It was her call. "Okay, but I'm not sure this will work. Gheorghie shouldn't be in this place. It's not a final resting place for a soul. If we take *care* of him, he should... *ascend.* Or descend."

"He will go up. I know this." Vetta looked into Gheorgie's eyes, tears spilling from her own. "I understand, but I cannot do this thing."

Lucas didn't expect her to. He placed his hands on Gheorgie's face and smothered him, blocking his nose and mouth. Gheorgie trembled, but he didn't fight, limbs and bones too broken to even try. It didn't take long, and within a couple of minutes, Gheorgie's brown eyes stared off into space. Vetta sobbed quietly.

It was done. *Best of luck to you, Gheorghie.*

Lucas stood up, feeling strange. It was unexpected when he bent down and vomited into a chest of frozen pizzas. Did being human ever stop being such a colossal pain? What was he feeling now? Guilt? No...

Grief!

He didn't care for it.

Annie slumped against the chiller cabinet, looking like she, herself might vomit. She asked a question of Lucas. "He's in a better place now, yes?"

Lucas nodded. "I think so. I hope so."

"What if you did that to the rest of us?" Annie then asked, seemingly thinking of something. Her brow was furrowed, and she had a finger against the dimple in her chin.

Jake was the first to react. "What you on about, Annie?"

She no longer appeared angry, only tired. "This place is Hell," she said. "Or close enough. I don't want to die here and end up like... that thing."

"That was Vetta's *friend*," said Jake, once again displaying his newfound compassion.

Annie sighed. "I know! I'm sorry, Vetta, but he's in a better place now, right? He's the lucky one."

Vetta didn't disagree, but she did look away to hide her tears. Lucas rubbed his temples and straightened up. "Let me understand this, you want me to kill you like I did Gheorgie?"

"Yes."

Shirley gasped. "Annie!"

"What?"

"You're suggesting suicide," said Lucas. "Whether by my hand or your own, you are making the decision to die."

"And we already know what happens to suicide victims in hell," said Jake, shaking his head sadly. "They go to Hell and become monsters."

"He's right," said Lucas. "The sentence I passed on suicide victims is still in place. Kill yourself and you'll end up as an aswang eventually. You'll be punished."

Annie regained some of her anger. "You think suicide is a crime? How about you blame the messed-up world that makes people feel like they have no other way out? We're just toys to God, aren't we? Just wind us up and watch us suffer and punish anyone who refuses to perform."

"I wish I had the answers you want," said Lucas. "I don't always understand God myself, but there's more to things than you understand. Just trust me that suicide is not the answer. There's another way."

Annie turned and folded her arms while the others stood by aimlessly. Lucas needed a moment to think. He needed to tell them all what to do next. But first, he needed to know himself.

A can of baked beans fell off the shelf. Followed by another.

And then another.

Soon they began to fall like hailstones.

"What the hell?" Shaun picked up one of the cans and examined it. As he did so, the shelves on either side of him began to rattle.

Lucas clenched his fists. "Everyone, get ready."

"For what?" asked Simon, readying his pool cue. They all still had one, except for Lucas who had put his down when he tried to help Gheorghie. "What's about to go down?"

Something shrieked above their heads. The aswang leapt from the top of the shelves and landed on Shaun, pinning him to the ground.

As Lucas had predicted, Simon raced to the rescue first,

swinging his pool cue and smashing it over the aswang's horrendous skull. The monster roared ferociously, and swatted Simon with one of its hind legs, sending the big man hurtling into the refrigerators.

Shaun used the distraction to clamber out from underneath the creature and get to safety. He was blabbering like he'd lost his mind.

Annie launched the next attack, using her pool cue like a spear and thrusting it at the aswang's face. She missed its eyes and struck its neck. It was enough to make the aswang shy away in pain, but as it withdrew, it whipped out a sinewy arm that almost took Annie's head off. She ducked just in time, and then Shirley pulled her out of harm's way.

Jake and Lucas came forwards together, Jake swinging his pool cue, but Lucas, unarmed, leaping onto the aswang's back. Jake's pool cue snapped against the creature's bony shoulder, but he held onto the stub and planted it in the aswang's left eye.

The aswang reared up, bellowing in agony. Jake had hurt it.

Good on you, lad.

Simon clambered off the floor and attacked again, clobbering the aswang with his heavy fists. Even Vetta came forward and got in a cheeky wallop with her pool cue. Together, they beat the creature from all sides, forcing it down onto its belly. Shaun actually leapt up and connected with a flying-kick before hurrying back into safety.

They were winning.

The aswang was half-blind and disorientated, spindly arms and legs thrashing. One of its limbs struck Lucas under his chin and buckled his knees. He hit the ground hard and found it difficult to know which way was up, so he had no choice but to watch from his back as the aswang struck at his companions.

It managed to kick Jake in his ribs, and then Simon in the knee. The big man toppled out of the action, clutching at himself in pain. Jake was badly winded and struggling to stay standing.

That left only Vetta, Shaun, and Annie.

Vetta swung her pool cue but lost it as it jarred against the aswang's shoulder. Unarmed now, the monster was able to lash out and grab her by the wrist. She yelped and tried to break free, but it held onto her too tightly. Drool slathered from the beast's hungry jaws.

Shaun stood watching, close enough to do something, but frozen in terror. His pool cue had dropped to the ground, and his hands were trembling by his sides. Vetta reached out to him, but he didn't react.

Lucas shouted from the floor. "Shaun, help her!"

Shaun still stood frozen like a startled deer.

"Help her, goddammit!"

Shaun broke out of his stupor. He glanced at Lucas, then at Vetta. Finally, he turned and fled, racing towards the supermarket's entrance and slipping outside.

"No!" Lucas roared. "Get back here!"

Vetta screamed in agony as the aswang wrenched on her arm. It opened its jaws wide and pulled her closer, preparing to bite down on her face. Lucas clambered towards her, but it was too late. No way would he reach her in time. He was powerless.

Totally powerless.

Vetta closed her eyes.

Annie appeared. She leapt at the aswang with her pool cue and rammed it tip-first into the creature's jaws. Startled, the aswang forgot about eating Vetta, but did not release her. Instead, it held her off to one side so it could face Annie.

Undeterred, Annie continued her attack, beating at the aswang with her fists now that her pool cue was wedged in its jaws. It bit down on the wood and spat the pieces into the air. Annie dodged aside as the aswang then turned its sharp fangs on her, but she yelped as one of its long legs clobbered her in the temple. She skidded across the tiles, bleeding from a wound on her forehead.

The aswang turned its attention back towards Vetta, still held in place by one of its claws. It glared at her with its remaining eye, foul goo dripping from the socket of the other. Its mouth cracked wide open, like the hinged jaws of a salivating python.

Vetta screamed. Once again about to be devoured.

"Go to HELL!" Annie sprung up from the floor, groggy from the fierce blow to her head, but too furious to care. She rushed at the aswang again, this time leaping onto its back. "You killed my brother!" she roared. "Die, you fucking monster!"

The aswang released Vetta altogether now, and she finally clambered to safety. Lucas grabbed her in his arms.

The aswang now fought to get Annie off its back. Lucas let go of Vetta and tried to help Annie, but he couldn't get past the wild flailing of the aswang's limbs. Annie battered it in the head, turning her fists bloody, but she was gradually slipping from its back, losing her balance on the bucking beast. Her hands were getting tangled in its oily black hair.

Lucas called out, "Annie! Be careful!"

The aswang flipped her off onto the floor. She tried to

get right back up, but it was already too late. A spindly arm thrust down at her and pierced her chest, pinning her to the ground. Blood erupted from between her lips, but still she refused to surrender. She pushed herself up onto one elbow and spat blood in the creature's remaining eye—blinding it fully. It was her final act, immediately after, her head hit the tiles with a heavy *clack!*

Simon recovered and dragged Jake to his feet. Lucas gathered Vetta and Shirley into a huddle. All of them were battle shocked, weak and wounded, and it took a moment before Lucas could get a hold of himself and shout at them all to run.

"Run!"

┴

"I'M HEADING BACK TO THE PUB," SAID SIMON, ALREADY limping in that direction. They had hurried out of the supermarket and closed the doors behind them. "It's where Shaun probably went."

Lucas snarled. "That coward!"

Vetta put a hand on Lucas's shoulder. "He was just afraid."

How many men had let this girl down, yet still she refused to let it jade her?

"Fine," he said, deciding it would be self-righteous to argue with her when she was ready to forgive. "We'll regroup at the pub, but we still need to kill that aswang. We should attack while it's injured. We should catch our breath and go back in there."

Shirley cackled with laughter. "Are you blinking serious? We threw everything we had at that thing, and it still came out the winner."

"Jake blinded it," Lucas argued. "We had it on the ropes."

Simon smashed his fist against his palm and grunted. "I want a better plan than 'whack the monster with pool cues.' We can think of something back at the pub."

The pub was still lit up, contrasting the featureless grey sky above it. Simon probably had the right idea, but Lucas was so used to making the rules that he found it hard to consider anyone else might have a point. But so far, his attempts to end the situation had left a brother and sister dead. His only solace was that they might be together again.

God bless them.

Lucas relented, and the group rushed back up the hill. Halfway up, the wounded aswang emerged from the supermarket and wailed mournfully. The sound was so piercing that they had to cover their ears, but the creature hadn't seemed to notice their retreat, and its wailing was not directed at them. Perhaps it was calling to Julian. Would the man finally show himself?

They kept hurrying up the hill, but they grew weary against the unnatural weight outside the pub. Shirley's oldest legs wobbled erratically, and Simon had to grab her beneath the arm to keep her going straight. Lucas held Vetta's hand but didn't remember grabbing it—perhaps she had grabbed his.

"It's behind us," Jake shouted as he glanced back down the hill at the aswang.

"Don't look," said Lucas. "It's not focused on us right now."

Simon moved to the front with Shirley. He was the nimblest of them all despite being the largest, and his wide back oscillated as his shoulders and arms pumped back and forth like truck pistons. Jake looked like he should be the sprinter of the group with his lithe body, but he was huffing and puffing worse than any of them. Lucas was starting to struggle too. And they were only getter more tired.

Behind them, the aswang continued to wail.

Simon cried out from up ahead. Shirley collided with his back and let out her own shout—although hers was only of surprise. The big man had been startled by something, and now he was back-pedalling.

The pub was alive with movement. The ground had burst open and thick vines now whipped the air. They crept up the pub's brickwork and twisted together into a thick mesh, encircling the entire building. Wicked thorns jutted out in a thousand directions.

Lucas forced everyone into a crouch. The aswang still lingered outside the supermarket, but now they had nowhere to retreat if it saw them and gave chase. The pub was sealed once more—this time from the outside.

Simon cursed as a vine leapt up beneath his feet and slashed his forearm. He stepped aside and put the bleeding wound to his mouth. Shirley yelped as a creeper tried to encircle her foot. Jake pulled her away just in time.

Behind them, the aswang stopped its wailing.

Lucas looked back. What he saw now led him to stumble in shock.

"Please, Father, no!"

A dozen aswangs scuttled from the rooftops and alleyways between the shops and congregated around their wounded brethren. They seemed to fuss over it, concerned. Family.

"You said there would be only *one*," said Shirley, rubbing her eyes as if to check she wasn't hallucinating. "You said this place was tied to a single one of those monsters."

"I was wrong," said Lucas. "I was completely wrong."

"We need to get out of the open," said Simon. "Before those things see us."

Jake pointed. "The alleyway. Around the back of the pub. Come on!"

Lucas nodded. "Everybody, move!"

A chorus of aswangs howled behind them.

Last Call

The rear of the pub was entangled by vines, and it made the alleyway feel even more claustrophobic. Aside from that, the narrow access was the same as Lucas remembered it—litter-strewn and filthy. He slumped against the wheelie bins next to the scorch mark that still blotted the pavement. This reality was an exact duplicate of the real one. Julian's power continued to impress him. And terrify him.

"There were a dozen of those things at least," said Shirley, perched on a low brick wall and rolling down her pop socks so that she could knead her calves.

"We couldn't even kill *one* of them," said Jake. He was glancing up and down like a sentry, constantly checking the coast was clear. "Let alone a dozen."

"No chance," added Simon, sucking at the wound on his forearm again. "If that's what we have to do to leave this place, then we should just follow Annie's advice and top ourselves."

"That will just send us to Hell," said Jake. "Which would be even worse than this."

"Hell is made-up," said Shirley, but when she looked at Lucas she seemed to reconsider. "Well, that's what I thought, until today. Those things will tear me apart whatever I believe, so why delay things?"

Vetta looked to Lucas. "What do we do?"

"I have no idea! Maybe it's time you stopped asking me for advice. Where has it got you?"

"So, you give up?" she said. "You have no ideas to help us? You make me sad, Lucas. Gheorghie was your friend too!"

"No, he wasn't. I barely…" Lucas grunted. For the first time, he found Vetta a little irritating. He owed her a debt, no question, but that didn't mean she could keep expecting him to fix everything with a shake of his cock. "Look, my idea was to kill the aswang. We failed, and the situation is even worse than I realised. There's nothing else I can do or say. Julian is the one with all the power here. We're just a bunch of ants beneath his magnifying glass."

"Who is he?" demanded Simon, kicking a bin in a rage. It toppled over and spilled its contents making everyone flinch. They all looked towards the alleyway's entrance, but no aswangs appeared. For now.

"Shhhhh." Vetta glared at Simon. "Calm down before you bring monsters."

Simon kept still, but it looked like a struggle for him not to kick something else. "I'm just sick of hearing Julian's name," he grunted. "If he's such a bad ass, he should show himself and fight like a man instead of sending a bunch of his rabid pets after us."

"Some bloody pets!" said Shirley. "A pack of sodding demons."

Simon folded his thick arms and grumbled. "Whatever."

Jake patted the big man on the shoulders. "This is messed up, Si, but just keep it together. We'll figure this out."

Lucas had enough. It was time to address something which had been nagging at him for a while. "What the hell is with you?"

Jake frowned. "Who? Me?"

"Yes, you! Last night you were a low-life thug. You tried to *rape* Vetta!"

Jake recoiled, almost like he'd been hit. "I *what*?"

"You tried to rape me!" said Vetta firmly, face contorted with anger. She had understandably been tense about the situation, but now that it was out in the open, she struggled to contain herself. "Don't you dare deny it. Don't you DARE!"

Simon looked at Jake and shook his head in disgust. "You want locking up, Jake. Long time coming, if you ask me."

"I... I don't know what you're talking about!" Jake went to Vetta with his hands out, but Lucas stepped in his way. The lad got the message and took a step back. "I'm sorry," he said. "For whatever I did. You mentioned something earlier, but I assumed I just started a ruck like usual. I had no idea I... Oh fuck! Fuck, fuck, fuck!"

"You're claiming amnesia?" said Lucas. He would have laughed if it were not so pathetic. Some people were so screwed up that they had to lie for their own mental well-being, convincing themselves they were innocent of their own atrocities. Some of the worst human beings were the ones convinced they were the best.

Jake held his head in his hands like he might have a breakdown. "I-I remember getting into a scuffle with you at the bar, Lucas, and m-my hand..." He held it up to show them, although it appeared perfectly normal now. "It stopped hurting when you fixed me, but it was bad before."

"My pleasure," said Lucas. "I obviously didn't fix whatever brain damage you have, if you honestly don't remember trying to force yourself on Vetta last night."

Simon huffed. "Probably not even the first time he's done something like this considering the state he gets himself in most nights. I was glad when he got the sack. Thought I'd seen the last of him, but then the idiot turns up at lunchtime like we're all still going to be buddies."

Jake looked like he was going to cry.

Lucas turned to Simon. "What do you mean? About the state Jake gets himself in?"

"The powder," said Simon, thumbing his nose. "Whatever the kids are calling it these days. I've lost count of the times I've seen Jake smacked up on coke. Kid's one bad trip away from the knick, or death. Lucky to have held down the job as long as he did, but then the idiot crashes an eighty-grand Range Rover trying to get it up onto the ramp. We were all glad to see him gone after that. Even Max, who used to stand up for him more than anyone."

"I... I had no idea," said Jake. "I thought you were my mates."

Simon shrugged and looked away.

Lucas studied Jake, trying to work out if what he was seeing was an act. The lad seemed truly mortified. "You really don't remember?"

Jake shook his head. "I swear."

"You lie!" said Vetta.

"I swear! I don't remember."

"Doesn't make it okay," said Shirley.

"No," said Lucas. "It doesn't."

Jake's eyes were teary, but he gave Vetta an earnest stare. "I'm so sorry. I've been an addict since I was fourteen. My uncle Robert got me into it. He used to babysit me after school while mum and dad worked evenings at their restaurant. Uncle Rob was in the Army, but when he came back, he never got another job. He just became a screw-up. Used to sell gear to make ends meet, and... shit, why am I even telling you this? I'm sorry. You're right: I'm scum. Most nights I don't even know what planet I'm on, but what I tried to do to you, Vetta. I... what can I say? I'm an addict. If this is Hell, it's where I deserve to be."

Lucas realised something, a bubble popping in his brain and releasing a thought. "You're an addict? That's why you're different! When I healed you in the backroom of the pub, I healed your addiction too, just like that scar on your forehead."

Jake touched his forehead. "Yeah, I had it since I has six years old. I was learning to ride my bike, but my dad took his eye off me to take a call. I went crashing against the brick wall of our garage."

"Whatever mess the drugs made of your brain has been put right," Lucas surmised. "You've been high since you were fourteen, but now your body is as pure as if you'd never touched so much as an aspirin."

Simon pulled a face. "You *detoxed* him?"

Lucas shrugged. "Kind of. I also put right all the damage that cocaine does to a fourteen-year-old brain."

"It still does not make it okay," said Vetta. She had her arms folded in a defensive posture, making it clear she felt her attacker was being absolved before her very eyes. That wasn't right at all, so Lucas went to her and put a hand on her shoulder.

"The kid so much as looks at you wrong," he whispered, "and I'll tear out his eyes. You're the victim here, Vetta, okay? No one is losing sight of that."

"I'm sorry," said Jake. "I really am. I'll admit to everything if we get out of this alive. You can tell the police on me."

Lucas put up a hand to quiet the lad. He'd done enough apologising and more wouldn't achieve anything. "Look, Jake, I believe you may not be quite the remorseless animal I pegged you as, but you still have a lot to answer for. Let's just focus on the present for now though."

Jake nodded. Vetta tapped her foot, but she nodded too —after a moment's resistance.

Lucas ran his hands through his hair and tried to get his mind straight. "Okay, so... does anybody have any other addictions I can cure? Warts I can remove? Come on, I'm not doing much else."

Everyone chuckled. The dank air became a little lighter in the alleyway.

"I haven't been able to grow hair on my head since I was twenty-six," said Simon, laughing. He patted his smooth dome like one of the *Three Stooges*.

"Is that what you're trying to make up for with that magnificent beard?" asked Shirley, slapping her thighs.

Jake seemed ashamed to laugh after what he had been accused of, but he gave a small quip of his own. "The smell of paint makes me heave; is that fixable?"

"I'll see what I can do," said Lucas. "Maybe just keep away from paint!"

"My breath in the morning could kill a horse," said Shirley, covering her mouth to keep from cackling too loud.

"How about an aswang?" Simon asked, fighting to keep his own guffaws contained.

Vetta smiled now as well, getting over the previous conversation. "Sometimes," she said, "I get very bad period pain."

The laughter stopped. Simon cleared his throat and rubbed his hands together. "Um, okay, right, shall we get back to dying then? Is our best option still to try and kill one of those things?"

"I don't think that will work," said Lucas. "Even if this place was tethered to one of the aswangs, we have no way of telling which one it is."

"Maybe it'll be wearing a crown," said Jake weakly.

"There's only one crown in Hell," said Lucas, "And it doesn't belong to an aswang. We have to find a way to get Julian's attention. I have to find out what he wants. This can't all be about nothing. There's something he's hoping to gain from keeping us here."

"No shit!" said Jake. "The guy's been running the pub for years, so something must have pushed him over the edge to start murdering his customers."

"*I* pushed him over the edge," said Lucas. "But I don't know why. I think he's been trying to cast a summoning spell on me for a very long time, but it didn't work because I wasn't in Hell to be summoned. Then, for some reason I can't remember, I went back there recently. I went back to Hell, and Julian's spell finally kicked in and snared me. It brought me here." He pointed at the scorch marks on the pavement. “Something must have affected the spell though, because I landed out here by the bins instead of the shrine inside that Julian had constructed to contain me. There was iron on the doors and in the four corners of the room. It was a Devil’s Trap.”

Jake seemed surprised. “So, summoning The Devil actually works?”

“It was easier back when I was answering calls, but yes you can summon celestial beings if you have a pinpoint on their location or something connected to them.”

“Like the plastic bags,” said Vetta. “You used them to call Gladri.”

Lucas nodded. “Yes, like the... Like the plastic bags! If we can find them again, I can try to call Gladri for help.”

Simon raised an eyebrow. “Would he even help us?”

“He’s not my biggest fan, but none of you should be here—you’re innocent. As an angel, Gladri would see that as an injustice. Julian is messing with forces that don’t concern him, and Heaven won’t ignore it. Search this alleyway for two white carrier bags.”

“Seriously?” Simon asked. “Like, just normal shopping bags?”

“Yes!”

Everyone got to work. The bin Simon had kicked over made things difficult, adding additional litter to their search, but they walked together in a line, covering maximum ground. Fortunately, there was no wind, which meant the litter at least stayed where it was. The alleyway was long but narrow enough that they shouldn’t miss anything. If the plastic bags were still here, they would find them.

“Reminds me of prison,” said Simon as he sorted

through bits of rubbish on his knees.

Shirley stared at him. "You were in *prison*? What d'you do?"

"Killed a guy."

Everyone stopped and looked at Simon. Simon guffawed and shook his head. "I'm pulling your leg. I used to go on the rob. Tried to break into some offices to snag printers and stuff, but the place had a silent alarm. This was, oh, twenty-years ago. I'm a different man today. Thought Shaun was, too, which is what makes it so hard he abandoned the rest of us like he did. He really let me down."

Shirley frowned at the big man. "You a pair of bummers or something?"

"If you're asking are Shaun and I homosexuals, then the answer is no. We're just good mates. Neither of us has had much luck with women, so we kind of ended up together. He has a few stretches in the knick under his belt as well, so we've kind of helped keep each other on the straight and narrow. We got a flat together about six years ago when it was clear neither of us would settle down and do the family thing. Better than growing old alone."

"Is nice," said Vetta. "Would be nice to live with friend."

Shirley shrugged. "You sound like two queers without the sex."

"You have a problem with it?" Lucas asked the older woman, hoping she wasn't going to cause an issue that they didn't need right now.

"Yes," she said firmly, glaring at Simon. "They're living together as friends while I'm stuck with my bloody husband. Ha! If I could bunk up with one of the girls from bingo, I would have put Eric out on his arse years ago!"

There was a moment's awkward silence while they tried to get a read on Shirley, but then the titters started as it became clear the older woman was having fun with them. Shirley increased their amusement with another quip. "Least I have an excuse for a non-sexual relationship—I was stupid enough to say, 'I do,' Ha!"

"Come on," said Lucas, smirking. "Let's get back to work and find those carrier bags before a pack of monsters comes and eats our faces."

They laughed some more, then continued their search.

But they didn't find anything.

┴

LITTLE SENSE OF TIME EXISTED IN THE ALLEYWAY, WHICH WAS why they could have been searching an hour for all Lucas knew. They had found nothing. They were getting fed up. Tense.

"I'm still starving," said Shirley. "I would kill for a big, fat greasy cod and chips."

Jake groaned. "Ah shit, Shirley. Don't talk about food." He licked his lips. "I would go for a curry down the Spice Mill. You know that place down Gavin Hill?"

"I would have a big fat steak," said Simon, rubbing his tummy. "Cook it myself."

"Big surprise there," said Jake, squeezing the man's biceps.

"I would have my mama's *Zemiakové placky*," said Vetta dreamily.

Shirley scoffed. "What on earth is that?"

Vetta frowned as she apparently worked out an explanation in English. "It is... potato pancakes, yes? Lots of garlic, dough, spices. My mama make it all the time back home. It was my papa's favourite. Remind me of being little girl." She looked sad. "I miss home."

Jake nodded thoughtfully. "You ever planning on going back, Vetta?"

"Why? Because people like me should go back from where we come?"

"No, no, I didn't mean it like that, I swear. I just think it must be lonely, that's all. Being away from your family. I... can imagine."

Vetta let her shoulders drop out of their guarded stance, but she seemed a little teary as she spoke. "Lonely, yes. I want to go home long time now. I come to UK to escape unhappy memories and to send home money, but I think it was mistake. I am not wanted here, and I feel alone. I miss my mama and my little sister. I think now I will not see them again. Never did I think I would die here, in a place that is not my home."

The conversation faded, and they resumed searching, but only half-heartedly. "It's useless," said Simon eventually, saying what they were all thinking. "I can't find these bags of yours, Lucas."

"I don't think they're here," Lucas was forced to admit. "Damn it. At the moment, all we have is a big pile of rubbish." He leaned against the wall and felt a pinch against his leg. He pulled the object out of his pocket and held it in his palm. "Oh, and one of the nails used to crucify Christ. A novelty item at best."

"It has to be of *some* use," said Jake. "Why else would Julian keep it in a safe?"

"I don't know."

"You still don't think Julian is Jesus?" asked Shirley. "He does look a little... *Arabic.*"

"I don't know who he is," said Lucas, squinting. "But I'm getting there."

Vetta tapped him on the arm. "What *do* you know then? *Think*, Lucas."

A noise sounded at one end of the alley, the end closest to the shopping centre. It was a bin tumbling onto its side and spilling its contents. This time, Simon hadn't kicked it over.

Shirley yelped. "Oh God! It's one of those things."

"Time for round two," said Jake, stepping into the middle of the alleyway with his fists clenched. What he hoped to achieve was anybody's guess.

Another bin clattered onto the floor, this time at the other end of the alley. The shadow of an aswang shifted against the wall before the creature then revealed itself, snarling and hissing in their direction.

"They're coming from both ends," said Simon. "We're penned in."

"Stay together!" Lucas made everyone back up into a tight group.

The aswangs skittered towards them, closing in fast. They grunted and growled, more like dogs than the humans they'd once been—the humans they'd been before Lucas had passed their sentence.

No, that wasn't me. That was Lucifer. I'm trying to make things better.

Doesn't mean I'm not guilty.

The aswangs stalked the group from both sides, seeming to savour their terrified prey. Simon backed up against Lucas. "God, these things are ugly."

"Monsters," said Vetta. "Real monsters."

"Ah, I dunno," said Jake. "I kinda fancy this one."

Shirley groaned. "You *deserve* to get eaten."

"Stay together," Lucas warned. "Don't let them drag you away."

The aswangs snarled and gnashed their crooked teeth. Drool slopped from their uneven jaws, and their eyes burned with hatred and hunger. Hatred for everything. Hunger for flesh.

"It's been really horrible meeting you, Lucas," said Simon, sounding entirely earnest.

Lucas flinched as one of the beasts hissed at him. "I know. Sorry about that, big guy."

"Let's go down swinging," said Shirley. "Wish I knew where I'd left my handbag. It would have given these things a mighty good whack."

"You don't need it," said Jake. "Show us what you got, girl."

"I haven't been a *girl* in three decades, son, but I can show you what a middle-aged care-worker can do."

"I can't wait," said Jake.

"Get ready," said Lucas.

The aswangs attacked. This time they intended to finish their meal.

┴

The aswangs worked together, attacking in unison from both sides. Simon faced the first, grabbing it by the head and keeping it at bay. Its jaws clacked together, trying to bite him, and its greasy black hair tangled around his wrists.

On the other side of the group, Jake kicked his legs like a bucking horse to keep the second creature back. Lucas tried to be in both places at once. "Stay together," he shouted, kicking at the aswang battling with Simon. "Don't let them pull you away."

"I think this one wants to dance," said Jake.

"You should buy her a drink first," said Shirley.

Jake chuckled. "If I do, it won't be at the Black Sheep."

Shirley spat at the aswang attacking Jake. "Get out of it, you bloody mutt!"

They held their ground, backs together, keeping the aswangs from singling anyone out. It worked for a while, but they had no way of fighting back, only playing defence —and they were getting tired. Their movements were heavy.

Simon lost his grip on the wildly thrashing aswang, hands slipping further and further towards its mouth. "Shite, I can't hold this bitch much longer!"

Jake was faring better, although his kicks seemed only to make his aswang angry. Each time he bucked, he risked his foot ending up in the monster's thrashing jaws.

Lucas decided Simon was most in need of help, so he leapt at the aswang's flank while the big man wrestled with its head. With no idea beyond simply launching himself, Lucas beat at the creature's back and shoulders desperately as hard as he could.

He'd forgotten he'd been clutching the iron nail, so it was a surprise when the chunk of metal sank into the aswang's back.

Blood spurted—a thick black ooze—and the aswang screeched in agony. It tried backing away, but Simon held on to its head tightly, redoubling his grip and cinching in a tight side-headlock.

Lucas stared at the nail in his hand and then, without thinking, struck again—this time harder—embedding it deep into the creature's neck. A torrent of black blood gushed into the air, covering Simon and Lucas. Simon flinched and let go of the aswang, which wheeled away in a panic, wounded and... *smoking.* A plume of stringent fumes spiralled from its open back wounds.

"You hurt it!" Shirley shouted triumphantly. "You sliced its tyres!"

"Help me!"

Lucas turned to see Jake losing his balance as he threw another kick. The lad spilled onto his side, and the aswang pounced immediately, clamping down on his ankle with its razor-sharp jaws.

Vetta was nearest, and she grabbed the aswang around the neck, trying to yank it away from Jake. Lucas ran to help, iron nail held before him like a stubby sword. He drove it into the top of the aswang's skull, and the thing dropped like a lead weight.

A few feet away, the other aswang was still wounded, bleeding and smoking from its back. Then, it too, dropped to the ground and went still.

Both creatures were dead. The iron nail had killed them.

Jake extricated his ankle from the dead aswang's jaws and scrambled backwards. Blood pooled beneath his foot and didn't seem like it was stopping. Simon slumped up against some bins to catch his breath, sweat pouring from his bald head and glistening in his beard. They were battered, but alive.

"They are both dead?" asked Vetta, glancing back and forth between the two slumped aswangs. "How?"

Lucas held up the iron nail. "I should have thought of it sooner. Creatures from Hell can't abide iron. God created it to place in the blood of human beings as a ward to prevent demon possession. It's become less effective over time, but a demon still cannot directly touch iron. I don't think that's what killed the aswangs though."

Shirley frowned. "What then?"

"Jesus Christ's blood. It was on this nail, and maybe it still is. This nail is literally coated in God's essence. It's like Excalibur as far as demons are concerned—if Excalibur was nine-inches long and slightly crooked."

Jake laughed from his back. "When did you see me with my pants off? Ha, ha, *argh*! Shit, man, my ankle is messed up. Can you heal me again, Lucas?"

"I'm not sure." He headed over to take a look. The ankle looked bad, not just torn open, but crushed. The fragile bones inside were splintered from the crushing weight of the aswang's jaws. Lucas placed his hands on the wound and concentrated, but he knew right away that nothing was happening.

"It still hurts," said Jake, wincing.

"I'm sorry, lad. I can't help you. Whatever power I have, it doesn't work properly out here. Even if I fixed you, it wouldn't hold. You saw what happened to Gheorgie."

"We need to get back inside the pub," said Vetta. "Your powers would work in there, yes?"

Lucas nodded. "They did before. Outside is too close to Hell, but the pub is different." He looked at the thick, thorny vines still wrapped around the building. "But I don't think we'll find our way back inside to find out."

"I can't get up." Jake moaned. "You'll have to leave me here."

"Don't be stupid," said Vetta, peering over Lucas's shoulder. "We can't leave you."

"She's right," said Shirley. "We leave you in this alleyway, Jake, and you'll get eaten."

Jake grasped his shin and hissed. "That's gonna happen anyway. Least you lot might have a chance."

Simon kicked one of the dead aswangs and then spat on it. "You said killing one of these things would help us, but we just killed two and nothing has changed. We're still trapped in this place, and Julian hasn't shown his face. He's just going to leave us here to rot, isn't he?"

"Whatever plan Julian had, he's abandoned it," said Lucas. "He has no reason to do anything but leave us here to die. I underestimated his power—thought he would be forced to deal with us eventually. There's no reason for him to do anything. He could make it so every second in this place seems like a thousand years."

"Then there's no way out," said Shirley. Without seeming to notice, she actually took a seat on top of one of the aswang's corpses and began rubbing her calves again.

Lucas studied the iron nail still in his hand and tried to understand what Julian had been doing with it. Had Julian known Christ? *Was* he Christ himself?

No, Lucas could not believe that. Julian was not the man he remembered on the cross. That peaceful man had died with a smile on his face, all grudges abandoned. Jesus had willingly shouldered not only the sins of humanity, but also that of the Devil.

Lucas remembered.

Lock In

"Can I ever be forgiven?"

Jesus peered down at Lucifer and smiled. "No, cousin, you cannot be forgiven."

Lucifer collapsed forward, fingers sinking into the bloody sand. "Then it is as I thought."

"No," said Jesus. "It is not. You cannot be forgiven for the things you have done, for they are too wicked, the beast you've become, too tainted."

"So why should I seek the light if it is forever beyond my grasp?"

Jesus fell silent, and it seemed he might finally have slipped away, but then he opened his eyes wide, as if reinvigorated. "Today I die," he said. "You may die with me, Lucifer. Let the beast shrivel away to nothing, and in this very sand beneath our feet, give rise to something else. Seek not forgiveness but rebirth. Ask not for forgiveness, but for redemption. To be forgiven is to erase all that you have done, but to be redeemed is to outweigh your sins with virtue and kindness. You ask if you can be forgiven when you should be asking if you can be redeemed. The answer to that question is yes!"

Lucifer looked up at Jesus. "You think I can simply *change*? To act as though the past never happened?"

"The past has ended, Lucifer. Yesterday died and tomorrow waits to be born. The future is an unwoven tapestry. Stop seeking forgiveness, and instead, become something that requires no forgiveness. It has been your choice to remain outside the light. Come back and feel its warmth."

Lucifer rose gradually, hooves sinking into the mud. Slowly they changed back into human feet—feet he vowed to never again be cloven. He lifted his chin and looked to the skies, the warm rain falling into his eyes. "I renounce myself as The Devil and turn away from all that I was. I cast sin from my shoulders in hope that I may lift others on my back."

Jesus smiled wide. "Yes, cousin. I see you. Your spirit glows."

"I seek not forgiveness but redemption. Forgiveness is given, redemption is earned."

"Yes..."

"I accept you, Jesus, as my saviour." He reached out to the man, needing to touch him, to embrace him.

But Jesus was dead. His eyes had closed. His head hung forwards.

Lucifer cried out, a pitiful moan from deep within his chest. "No, no! I can fix you. I can fix this!" He placed his hands around the ragged wound in Jesus's ribs and tried to pull back the man's death. But nothing happened. Jesus would not return, no matter how hard he tried. Gone forever, and already his absence felt like a great sucking hole in the world.

What have I done?

Lucifer slumped to the ground, broken. What would become of him now? How could he atone for ridding humanity of its saviour? A task unachievable even to an immortal like him.

So wrapped up in his grief was he, that he did not sense the presence behind him until the man stood right at his side speaking. "Why do you weep, angel? Is this not what you desired? It is done. Jesus is in a better place; where he belongs. Disaster has been averted."

Lucifer looked up to see the man he'd met several days ago above Jerusalem's market. The hook-nosed man had a rodent-like aura, and his deep-rooted avarice had called out to him like a beacon in the darkness. Greed was a useful tool to The Devil, and he had used it to control this man. "What do you want, human?"

The man frowned, hooked-nose twitching. "I want my reward."

"What reward?"

"You said if I delivered Jesus to the Romans, I could have my heart's desire. I did as you asked. Are you an angel, or are you not?"

Lucifer looked at Jesus on the cross, so peaceful and still. Gone forever. This man wanted a reward for this betrayal, this travesty? He had forsaken his friend and mentor for personal gain.

No... that wasn't entirely true. Lucifer had manipulated this man—played on his fears and honed their sharpness until they were daggers pointed at Jesus's heart. This man wasn't entirely to blame. But nor was he deserving of any reward.

"The deal you made was with a creature that no longer exists."

"What are you talking about? We made a deal! I had Jesus *killed* for you! I thought they would just imprison him. He was my *friend*."

"You made a deal with The Devil. Don't complain if you get burned."

The man stumbled. His dusky skin turned pale. "T-The Devil? You said you were an angel."

"What is The Devil if not the greatest of all angels? We committed the foulest of sins today, human. Commit yourself to better acts tomorrow and find your way back to the light. It is what I shall do."

There were tears in the man's eyes as he peered at Jesus's hanging body and seemed to realise what he'd done. "So, this was all for nothing?" he said breathlessly. "You told me Jesus would bring strife to my homeland and its people. I thought I was doing what was *right*. I wanted only to serve Heaven."

"I tricked you. I am sorry."

"No! No, this cannot be. I am not a tool of Satan." The man started pawing at Jesus's corpse desperately, trying to shake him awake. "Jesus, I am sorry. I have committed a foulness in the ignorance that I was doing good. I believed The Devil's lies, as you taught me not to. Please! Please forgive me."

"He's gone," said Lucifer, moving to help the man. He had caused this. Killed one man and ruined another.

"Stay back, Satan!" The man flung an arm out at Lucifer,

then turned back and started clawing at the nail in Jesus's left wrist, trying to work it free. The metal was tightly wedged, held fast by blood and splinters, and it took several moments of mad pulling before it started to give a little.

"Leave it," said Lucifer.

The man waggled the nail harder, trying to pull it loose. "No!"

"Leave it!" Lucifer repeated. He had seen enough and could not allow this man's grief to tarnish Jesus's dignity.

The man yanked again, and the nail came free. Jesus slumped diagonally as his left arm suddenly loosed.

Furious, Lucifer tried to grab the hysterical man, but found himself, instead, slashed with the iron nail. He cried out, clutching his cheek as it released black smoke. The iron had burned him, but the blood of God's only son had exacerbated the injury. His eyes pulsed with hot fury, darkness rising within him. Lucifer almost lost control of the beast inside him altogether but pledged to see it gone forever. His eyes stopped pulsing, and the darkness went back inside.

The man gasped, and shrank back in terror, but then he seemed to conquer his fear and leapt at Lucifer again. This time, Lucifer dodged aside and let his attacker fall to the bloody sand on his hands and knees. "Do not be foolish, mortal. I am trying to save you this night."

"Give me what I am owed." He got up and lunged at Lucifer again. "Give me power so that I may undo this."

Once again, Lucifer stepped aside. "You cannot harm me, mortal. And you cannot *undo* this. We are both to blame. We must live with it."

The man snarled. "I shall ruin you, Satan." He lunged

again, but this time, Lucifer remained in place and caught the man's fists, holding him in place firmly.

"You want what was promised? You want power? Fine, here it is. You shall live forever to see the consequences of your actions. Like me, you shall have eternity for which to atone. I sentence you to eternal life, Judas Iscariot. Do not waste it."

Judas wept.

⊥

"I KNOW WHO JULIAN IS," SAID LUCAS, STARING AT THE TWO dead aswangs. Surprisingly, he retained the memory of who one of the creatures had been in life—an Egyptian peasant named Antep. She had drowned herself in the Nile after famine had killed all three of her infant children. The tragedy was that the famine would have taken her too, releasing her soul to Heaven, but instead, she committed suicide and ended up in Lucifer's sadistic care. It was unjust.

Lucas understood now Hell's true purpose. God had not cast Lucifer into the pits to punish the wicked. He had cast him into the pits to rehabilitate lost souls back into the light. God had intended Lucifer to gain his own redemption along the way.

He had missed the point all along.

God, how I missed the point.

"Who is Julian then?" asked Shirley. "I'm dying to know."

Lucas took a breath. "He's Judas Iscariot."

Shirley spluttered. "You mean, the fella what betrayed Jesus? *That* Judas?"

Lucas nodded. "I tricked him into betraying Jesus, then broke a deal I made with him. He must have been plotting revenge all this time—two-thousand years—but I abdicated Hell's throne the very same day I cursed him to eternal life. He's been unable to locate me this whole time, until I returned to Hell and activated his ensnaring spell."

Jake had made it up into a sitting position against the wall and rubbed his shin above his broken ankle; he seemed slightly amused despite the obvious pain. "You cursed Judas to eternal life? Doesn't sound like much of a curse to me, man. I'd go for a dose of that."

Lucas sighed. "Trust me, living forever is a curse above all others. Everything and *everyone* you care about crumbles to dust, but you go on. Always, you go on, no matter the state of the world. Happy memories don't last, but regrets pile up and hang around your neck forever. Judas betrayed Jesus Christ, and he has had to carry that burden for over two-thousand years. A burden I placed upon him, with no chance to ever find peace and be done with it."

"Still," said Jake, "he's kind of being a little pussy about the whole thing. He could have done anything in all this time, but instead, he chose to run a pub and wait two-thousand years to get some payback. Seems like the guy should have moved on."

Simon kicked one of the aswangs again. He seemed to enjoy kicking things. Perhaps it served to remind him the monsters could be killed. "Judas Iscariot. Ha! All the shite from the bible... It's all true then?"

"To a certain extent." Lucas wasn't a big fan of the bible. It gave people ideals they could never live up to. A better book would have helped mankind to understand its true nature and live, not in sin and shame, but in acceptance of itself. You never saw a sad monkey.

"Let's just say the bible was inspired by true events," he allowed, "as were most other holy scriptures from a variety of religions. Judas is not the man he's been made out to be in the religious texts though. He was a proud man, a patriot, and he loved Jesus with all his heart. He believed in the message Jesus was preaching, but there were many who opposed it. Judas feared grave repercussions if Jesus continued on his path, and I convinced him that a rebellion against Roman rule was coming—one that would cause death and suffering on a massive scale. By offering Jesus up to the Jewish elders and the Romans, Judas thought he was saving thousands of lives. He thought he was doing God's work. He thought I was an angel."

Simon grunted at Lucas. "You're a real arsehole, you know that?"

"Yes, I do. I've tried to be better since the day Jesus was put to death. His final act on earth was to ease my suffering and show me a better path, but I failed to show Judas compassion when he came to me broken and vulnerable."

"Maybe you should say sorry," said Vetta.

It sounded absurd, yet Lucas shrugged and walked down the alleyway in the direction of the shops. "I can try, can't I?"

"Where are you going?" Jake shouted after him, clambering up the wall to stand on one leg.

"I'm going to find Judas and apologise."

Jake hopped after him, crushed ankle dangling in the air. "What? You think that will work? We're past apologies, surely?"

"Judas deserves my contrition, whether he accepts it or

not, and I need to unburden myself. Cursing him was my final wicked act as The Devil, and one I have never repented for. I vowed to change my ways the day Jesus died, but Judas caught me while I was still shedding the last of my scales. He didn't deserve what I did to him."

Shirley, Vetta, and Simon got moving and caught up with Lucas and Jake. They grabbed Jake and helped him along, and they exited the alleyway together. The pub was still wrapped in vines, and at the bottom of the hill the aswangs still congregated.

"The buggers are still there," said Shirley, turning back towards the alleyway.

Lucas grabbed her arm. "No. We have to deal with this. Just... stay here. I'm going down to face them. If they attack me, run back into the alleyway, but I need Judas to see you all standing up here. He needs to see the innocent people he is dragging into this vendetta."

The aswangs writhed in a mass, jostling and snapping for position, a pack fighting for dominance. Each wanted to be first in line to devour Lucas as he approached. Where had the two dead ones been in the hierarchy? Was Judas their alpha?

As he reached the bottom of the hill, the aswangs hissed at Lucas like snakes, making him put his hands up. "Easy there! I want your pack leader for a parley."

They didn't understand him of course. Any ember of humanity had long ago been extinguished. Their hisses increased pitch, eyes blazing with savage hatred. Lucas stood his ground and tried to ignore the sloshing in his guts.

"JUDAS!" he bellowed at the grey sky. "Come out and face me. What I did to you was wrong, and I am here to answer for it, but let us end this without any more innocent bloodshed."

The aswangs bristled, desperate to attack, but held back, perhaps, by their confusion. It took a lot to remain standing in front of them, but Lucas was prepared to be ripped apart if it put a stop to this. Willing to die for a bunch of humans he'd only just met. Was he crazy for thinking that way? He'd been alive forever, and perhaps this was the end, but for some reason, he didn't completely dread it.

He looked back up the hill at the others—at Vetta—then turned back and took another step towards the aswangs, close enough that they could snatch his life away if they chose.

"JUDAS! Stop being a coward and face me!"

"A coward? You goad me into committing mankind's greatest sin and label me a coward?"

Lucas reeled to find Judas standing directly behind him. The man seemed different now—taller, prouder, and darker of skin. His hair was no longer red, but half-burnt charcoal. Lucas recognised him as the man he had cursed upon Calvary Hill.

"I am sorry, Judas. Whatever ills have befallen you are my doing. Let us speak as old men and find accord. What do you wish of me to make this right?"

"I wish you to suffer eternally, Satan, as I have."

Lucas tried to empathise with the man's anger, but he couldn't understand why he was so unbending. What did he *want*? Surely not just revenge.

"What I did to you was wrong, Judas, yet you have had an eternity to do anything you wished. Why have you turned your immortality solely towards hating me?"

"You said I should atone for the death of Jesus. Is destroying The Devil not a great act of Good?"

"Yes," he admitted. "If The Devil still existed."

Judas shook his head and smirked as if some great prank had been played on him. His hooked nose twitched. "Yes, of course, you're human now. Such irony. Do you know, I tried to end my life after what you made me do?"

Lucas shook his head. "I did not."

"Well, I did. Hanged myself from a *cercis* tree in a lonely field miles from anywhere. I couldn't live with the knowledge that I had done the Devil's bidding and thought to end my guilt with the snap of my neck. I leapt from the bough, and my neck broke like a twig, but I dangled there *alive*. My splintered neck caused me to lose my mind to agony, but my body refused to die. I hanged there for eleven days—unable to breathe, in utter misery from a broken neck, yet completely alive. I watched the sun set and the moon rise. For eleven mercilessly long days I hanged, unable to do anything but consider what I had done. Then Jesus came to me.

"At first, I thought I imagined him—he appeared on the horizon, miles away—but slowly he got closer, strolling through the fields towards me until I knew he was real. He delivered me from my noose and healed my neck as I lay there broken on the ground. Then he kissed me and left. I was too tired to go after him, so I lay there until the sun went down for the twelfth time. What did that kiss mean, Satan? I have spent two-thousand years pondering the answer."

"The kiss was Jesus forgiving you," said Lucas. "He understood why you betrayed him. I think you were always supposed to. As The Devil, I used to think I was a master of manipulating men, but my actions towards you were exactly what God wanted of me. Release your guilt, Judas. It is undeserved."

Judas snarled. "What difference will it make if I feel guilty or not? You have cursed me to forever dwell outside of Heaven and Hell. What is the point of anything if it leads to nothing?"

"There *is* a point, Judas. Our lives may be without end, but there are billions of souls we can affect for the better. Let our existence matter for *them*."

"The man we murdered on a cross would have agreed with you, as would I—long ago. I was a good man, and you turned me into a monster. I… I killed God's son. There is no redemption for that."

"Yet, we are both here with choices to make. You don't have to do this, Judas. Those people up there on that hill are innocent. Just because we committed a great sin in the past, doesn't mean we have to fill our futures with the same. We can live better lives. Tomorrow can be different"

"I am tired of tomorrows, Satan." Judas looked up the hill towards Vetta and the others. "You care about them?"

"I… Yes, I care about them. I care about all of God's creations, including you. They are innocent!"

"God has abandoned us all."

"No," said Lucas. "There is more to things than you understand. You may have lived forever, Judas, but you are a mere ant on the ground. You cannot see what the eagles see."

Judas glared into Lucas's eyes. "I know that existence needs to change. This one is full of pain and suffering. I have witnessed it all for thousands of years, and I can stand it no longer."

Lucas grabbed the man's arm. "Let me help you, Judas. I did this to you. Let me make it right."

Judas raged and threw off Lucas's hand. The aswangs hissed and snapped angrily, forming up on both sides of the two men.

"You were supposed to die upon my altar, Satan—a gift to the Red Lord. Your celestial soul was to power His entry into this world and earn my ascension. I was to be released, free to serve the new ruler of a glorious existence. Twice now you have prevented me from gaining my deserved reward. I want what's coming to me!"

Lucas frowned. "You speak of the Red Lord? Why is that name so familiar?"

"It should be! You have opposed him for too long now, and His patience wears thin. Your celestial soul would have provided Him the power to invade directly, but you have caused Him inconvenience yet again. A human soul is worthless to Him. But after waiting so long to end you, revenge is worth pursuing merely for its own ends."

Suddenly, things made sense to Lucas. Gladri hadn't made him human to punish him, but to prevent Judas from sacrificing his celestial soul and bringing forth this Red Lord. Heaven had foreseen a threat and prevented it. That Lucas had been caught in the middle was sheer bad luck—not a heavenly vendetta against him. The relief actually brought a smile to his face.

"You've been defeated, Judas. Heaven knew what you were planning, and they turned me human to stop you. Your plans are ruined, so stop this right now, and I shall do all I can to help you."

Judas allowed his anger to simmer for a moment, and without his righteous sneer he seemed vulnerable. "There is no help you could give me. I betrayed God's own son. I have spent two-thousand years awash with sin. Its embrace is too tight now to ever be clean."

"You can come back from this, Judas. Be something else. Change!"

Judas looked at Lucas now, not with anger but sadness. "You sound like a man I once knew. But why is it so wrong to just be who I *am*? I vow to you, Satan, I shall not stop until I have reduced your soul to ash. I shall leave you in this place forever, unable to die, unable to feel anything but misery and regret. It is what you deserve, and the only justice I shall get. First, I must ensure you suffer here alone. Welcome to Hell, Satan, and its name is solitude."

Lucas didn't understand, but then he saw the aswangs take off up the hill. Towards the pub. He shouted at the top of his lungs, "Run! Get away from here."

Vetta and the others panicked as they saw the aswangs coming for them. They turned back towards the alleyway, but thorny vines shot up from the ground and blocked their path.

They were trapped.

Judas grinned unkindly at Lucas, hands rubbing together with glee. "You should never have left my pub, Satan. Out here, you are truly powerless."

Lucas raced up the hill, knowing he would never make it there in time.

⊥

LUCAS RACED TOWARDS THE PUB. VINES ERUPTED IN HIS PATH and whipped at him, thorns slicing his face and snagging his clothing. He fought his way free of them again and again, but it slowed his progress to a crawl.

Vetta screamed in terror as the aswangs set upon her. Simon yelled for help, his machismo faltering as he faced certain death. Nearby, Shirley fought to keep Jake upright on his wounded leg. They were all going to die.

Lucas tripped and fell into a bunch of grasping vines. He tried to get free, but this time he couldn't. "Judas! Stop this! I beg of you!"

Judas strolled among the vines, hands clasped in front of his waist. "Did you take pity on me, Satan?"

"No, I didn't. But you can be *better* than me. These people have done nothing to you. They are innocent. She's a good person, damn it."

Judas looked back at Lucas curiously now. "You said *she*? Who do you speak of specifically, Satan? The crone or the strumpet? Hmmm, I see little chance of it being the former. Could it be? Is The Devil smitten with a lowly human? Does your newly beating heart yearn for love?"

The aswangs stopped their assault and surrounded Vetta and the others, corralling them in front of the pub. Vetta looked down at Lucas, fear in her eyes. Lucas reached out to her, wishing she were closer—close enough that he could grab her and keep her safe. More vines sprouted from the ground and held him in place, forcing him to watch the events to come.

"Why are you doing this?" Shirley shouted at Judas. "We have done nothing, you-you... you arsehole!"

Judas smirked at Shirley, as if her fear were an aphrodisiac. "Welcome to God's paradise, where the innocent suffer, and the wicked play."

"Please, mate," said Jake. "Just let us go, yeah? This is between you and Lucas—The Devil or whatever."

"Alas, The Devil seemingly no longer exists." Judas said it sadly, as though he had been hoping for some grand battle instead of this worthless challenge he had been presented with.

Simon spat at Judas. "Screw you!"

Judas ignored the insult and strolled towards Vetta. He examined her as if she were a trinket. "Are you the pretty little thing who has cast her spell upon The Devil himself?"

"Lucas is not The Devil," she said defiantly. "He is good man. Better than you."

Lucas tried to speak, but a vine encircled his throat and choked the words out of him. Judas seemed amused by Vetta, and he reached out and brushed her cheek fondly. She flinched and turned her head, but her disgust made Judas chuckle.

"Do you know how many young girls I've defiled in two millennia? Too many to count, I assure you, but few were as beautiful as you. It's true, isn't it? You have a kindness most do not—I felt it when I was inside of you." He seemed to relish that memory, and it made him shudder. "It is the innocent, like you, my sweet, who suffer most at God's indifference. Proof that something better is needed."

"Just kill me," she said, forcing herself to stare her abuser in the eye. "I am not afraid of you."

Judas paused and let a leering grin creep across his face. "Oh no, you have more value to me than simply killing you. Come, let us take the tour of this place. You may leave your innocence behind, you won't need it where we're going."

Vetta moaned as Judas reached out and grabbed the

back of her head. He forced his lips against hers, grinding a kiss into her face.

Lucas fought, the vines holding him, but there was no chance of getting to her in time. It made him realise how his former powers had been a quick fix for everything. Without them, he was useless, and forced to see the consequences of his actions play out.

More vines burst from the ground and spiralled around Judas and Vetta as they embraced. Soon it became impossible to see them through all the thorns and leaves.

Lucas fought a vine away from his throat. "Vetta!"

The vines around Judas and Vetta retracted violently back into the ground, like they were being yanked from underneath. The thorns tangled around Judas and Vetta and pulled them downward—the pavement opening up and devouring them. The ground snapped back into place and they were gone.

She was gone.

Vetta...

Lucas got an arm free and clawed at more vines around his throat. He bellowed after Julian, but his words went ignored. The only reply he received were the hungry snarls of the aswangs as they set upon the others.

The people he had been trying to protect.

Shirley went down first, blood arcing from a wide gash in the side of her neck. Jake collapsed on his bad leg as the older woman fell away from him. Simon fell too, stumbling onto his knees as an aswang slashed his side open.

The aswangs were excited, scuttling about like hissing spiders, hungry for more blood.

No! No, I can't let this happen! Lucas ripped one of his arms free of the vines and managed to yank the iron nail out of his pocket. Panicked, he sliced into the vines erratically, and they started to singe and burn away at the slightest touch, like butter being sliced with a red-hot knife. The vines slackened, and Lucas got his legs free, restrained now only by his left arm. He fumbled with the nail, trying to get a better grip on it as his palms began to sweat.

It slipped through his grasp.

"No!"

The iron nail tumbled down the hill for several feet before coming to rest on the pavement. Lucas strained at the vines wrapped around his wrist, but without the nail, he couldn't get free of them. It lay only inches away from him, but he could not reach it. More vines broke from the ground and began to ensnare him anew. They dragged him backwards, even further away from the only weapon he had.

The screams at the top of the hill taunted him.

I can't do this! I can't be human. It's too difficult. I'm too powerless.

"Here!" came a voice. "Take it!"

Lucas looked up to see Shaun standing a few feet farther down the hill. At first, he couldn't believe it, but then Shaun was shouting and thrusting something at him —the iron nail. He had picked it off the ground from where Lucas had dropped it.

God bless that man.

Lucas snatched the nail from Shaun and set about slicing the vines around his wrist. Finally free, he clambered up the hill towards the pub. The aswangs hissed at him, but he launched himself right into the centre of their mass, burying the iron nail into the eye of the first one to attack him. The creature howled in misery as smoke billowed from its skull, and the other aswangs backed off immediately.

Their eyes blazed with anger. And fear.

Lucas waved the nail at them threateningly, warding off the ravenous pack. They seemed to understand that the dull lump of iron in his hand could mortally wound them. Even after an eternity of torment, aswangs could still fear death. "Now get!" he shouted at them. "Get!"

The aswangs retreated, not turning their backs but skittering away with their eyes glaring at Lucas. This wasn't over.

Once it was safe, Lucas twirled to face the others. Jake was bleeding all over, but he managed to drag himself over to Shirley and place his hands on her neck wound. He tried to stop the bleeding, but it seeped between his fingers as Shirley stared wide-eyed up at the sky. She coughed and spluttered. Simon slumped on the ground behind her, blinking slowly and muttering to himself. He was in shock.

"This is all wrong," said Lucas. "You shouldn't suffer for what I have done."

Shaun came up beside him. "You have to help them, Lucas."

"I can't." He knelt beside Jake who was still desperately trying to help Shirley. The woman was done for, and she knew it—the panic was clear in her eyes. Lucas wiped some of the blood from her face and smiled. "Don't be scared, love. I've seen Heaven, and it's real. Only love and understanding awaits you. Eric will join you there before you know it."

Shirley smiled at the mention of her husband's name. Lucas might lack omnipotence now, but he could tell that, behind Shirley's jokes, was an absolute love for this man,

Eric. Her panic was at the thought of never getting to see him again—at never getting to say goodbye—but now that he had dispelled that fear, she could go on her way in peace. All fear left her eyes. Her body went still. The bleeding from her neck eased.

She died.

Jake was weeping, hands trembling in pools of Shirley's blood.

"It's okay," said Lucas, putting a hand on his back. "You can let go now." But Jake didn't let go. He held his hands in place as though he couldn't dare remove them. Lucas had to pull his hands away forcibly. "It's okay, lad. It's finished."

Jake finally let go. He slumped onto his side, broken and distraught.

"Help me!" Simon called from a few feet away. Shaun was already at the big man's side—his face a sickly pale as he looked at his friend. Simon's wounds were mortal, but not immediate. A great slab of his guts protruded from beneath his ribs, but most of the bleeding was internal. Slow and painful.

"H-Help me, man," he grunted again, mouth thick with blood and saliva. It stained his beard.

"I can't help you," Lucas told him, cursing Julian for taking both Shirley and this brave man. "I'm sorry."

Simon shook his head, grunting in pain. "No, I mean *help me to my feet.*"

"Oh!" Lucas thought about telling the man to stay down and take it easy, but at this point, there was no further harm he could do to himself. So, he carefully pulled the big man to his feet, and steadied him against the wall of the pub. The vines there rattled as if annoyed, but Simon ignored their scathing thorns. Lucas was impressed, the man hadn't passed out from his wounds.

Shaun started to apologise to Simon, weeping at his own words. "I left! I'm so sorry. I—"

Simon pushed off the wall and stunned Shaun with a huge punch to the jaw. Shaun twirled majestically before collapsing to the ground with a *thud.* He was unconscious for about thirty-seconds before Lucas was able to help him back to his feet. It took another thirty-seconds after that to get him focusing straight. He rubbed at his jaw and moaned. "Please, Si, just listen to me."

"I get it," said Simon. "You were scared. You ran. But you came back. We're even."

Shaun stared at him disbelievingly. "Seriously?"

Simon shrugged, then winced as another inch of his insides slipped out. He held them in place with a thick palm. "You can't help not being brave in the face of danger, Shaun. You let us all down, but you didn't ask for any of this shit to happen to you. We're all victims here, whatever happens."

Shaun had tears in his eyes. He nodded to his friend's ribs. "You're hurt bad!"

"No shit!" Simon turned to Lucas. "Tell it to me straight, man. Am I going to make it out of this one?"

Lucas wished Simon hadn't asked that question because answering it was hard. "I'm sorry. I don't think so, big man."

Simon didn't give any reaction, but Shaun blubbered. "Calm down," Simon said, nudging him with his elbow. "You can have my car."

Shaun tittered beneath his sobs. "I don't want your sodding car. I want my mate."

"Nah, you're better off. Things were getting weird anyway, two middle-aged men shacked up together. Just take my car and don't look back." He looked at Lucas again. "So, what's next? I have a bit more fuel left in the tank, and I want to put it to good use."

Lucas had already thought about what to do next. He clutched the iron nail tightly in his fist and stepped up to the vines entangling the pub. He cut one of them, and the entire length withdrew, uncovering part of the front door. "We go inside and have a drink," he said. "Then we decide how we're going to crucify that sonuvabitch, Judas."

Blackout

Entering the pub was like coming home. The warmth of the fires washed over them, and the air itself smelled of life. They were closer to true reality, and the effects of Hell wore off quickly. Their limbs were no longer heavy, and their stomachs were no longer famished. Despite that, when Lucas tried to heal their wounds, he could not. Somehow, whatever power he had latched onto was gone—or maybe just expended. Julian's grip on this place was getting tighter, and soon the dead atmosphere from outside would creep inside. Then there would be no way of ever making it back.

Lucas realised now why the aswangs had snatched Max from the outside—they couldn't enter the reality of the pub. They must remain outside of it, close to Hell. That meant they were safe inside for a little while, and Lucas intended to make the most of it.

They poured themselves a drink and sat down at the bar. Simon grabbed an entire bottle of whiskey while Shaun and Jake split a bottle of Vodka. Lucas visited the beer taps, but then decided to grab a bottle of orange juice instead. He sipped it at the bar.

"What happened to Vetta?" asked Jake, as if he could read the worry on Lucas's mind.

"Judas took her. To torment me."

"What's he going to do to her?"

Lucas had a fair idea. "Twist her into something awful and taunt me with her suffering—the most unspeakable things he can think of probably. He wanted my celestial soul, but my endless suffering will do. He has nothing else to strive for. Two-thousand years can make a person pretty bored."

Jake downed his vodka and placed his tumbler on the bar. Shaun filled it back up again dutifully and then nodded to Lucas. "You sure you don't want a proper drink, man?"

Lucas shook his head. "Not right now. That stuff has been keeping me from thinking clearly."

"Yep," said Jake as he downed his second vodka. "It'll do that alright"

Lucas studied the lad for a moment, deciding he quite liked him after all. The wickedness he had sensed last night seemed to have truly gone, and while Jake wasn't without sin, it was easier to see the good in him now. "You've done some pretty bad things, Jake."

His expression grew serious. "I know."

"Are you really any different, or will you go right back to being a violent thug if you get out of this in one piece? Because I gotta tell you, I'm not much interested in saving the life of a lad who goes around beating people up and assaulting women."

Jake raised an eyebrow and stared into his glass. “Don’t think anyone is getting saved here, do you?”

Lucas sighed. “Okay, you have a point there. Let’s just say then, that I don’t much fancy dying alongside a thug who hurts people for fun. Is that still you?”

The question prompted a moment’s thought from Jake, and he seemed to experience several emotions before he answered. “I know I’m bad—a worthless piece of shit—but I never wanted to be that way. It just kind of happened. I did a couple of bad things as a kid without even thinking about what I was doing, then the shame would make me drink and get high until I did more bad shit, and the cycle just kept repeating. It was like being on a ride, except this one would never stop and let me off—just kept spinning me in the same circles. Before I knew it, I was a total mess. Most mornings, I wake up hoping it will be the day someone pulls a knife out and cuts my throat. Guess the day finally came.”

He put his glass out for Shaun to pour him another measure. This time though, he didn’t immediately down the contents once poured. “What I did to Vetta... I didn’t think I was as messed up as that. I’ve slunk lower than I realised.”

“You have a daughter,” said Lucas, not entirely mollified by the lad’s tale of woe, for it was all too common an excuse. “How could you try to hurt Vetta when you have—”

Jack pulled a face. “What you talking about? I don’t have a daughter.” He seemed utterly confused.

Lucas was confused too. “The photograph in your wallet. The young girl?”

Shaun and Simon glanced up from the bar and winced

as if Lucas had said something he shouldn't have. Jake also seemed conflicted by the conversation.

"Oh, yeah." He reached into his pocket and put the photograph of the young girl on the bar. "That's my sister, Chloe. She died crossing the road when she was nine. Guy who ran her down was a family friend, if you can believe it. Accident ruined his life as well as ending Chloe's. He never forgave himself. Both my parents threw themselves into work after it happened. They practically started living at the restaurant they owned, which is when my deadbeat uncle started looking after me. Shit went after that. They went downhill the exact moment Chloe decided not to look both ways. Fucking sucks."

"How old were *you*?" asked Lucas, tummy fluttering as he pictured a poor child being mowed down. Death didn't usually affect him in the pit of his stomach like this. Was this what they called *empathy*?

He didn't care for it.

"I was twelve," said Jake. "I was looking after her the day she died, but I ran across the road with my mates to try and shake her loose. She chased after me, calling my name so I would wait for her." He swallowed audibly and then grunted. "Still remember the sound of her voice even after all these years."

Lucas had seen none of this history last night when he'd read Jake's aura at the bar. The shame had been too deep rooted in the lad to sense it from a brief contact. "I'm sorry, Jake. Last night I judged you a monster, but I forgot that most monsters are made. I wish I could have helped you deal with your guilt. Instead, I've doomed you."

"It's okay." Jake shrugged and pushed his vodka away. "At least I get to die clean and sober. Well, *almost* sober. I was drowning until you healed me today. It's nice to come up for air before I meet my maker, you know?"

"I'm sorry what I said about you earlier," said Simon. His words were slurred from the copious amounts of whiskey in his system, and probably the fact he was fading fast from his mortal gut-wound. "I said no one liked working with you, but that isn't true. We all liked you, Jake. It just dragged us down seeing you screw up so badly all the time. It was obvious you were in pain, but no matter what anyone said, you just wanted to drink and get high. Then you would pick a fight with anyone who tried to help you. We all wanted to be your friend, but you made it too hard. Max went through something similar after he lost his dad to cancer, but he got his shit together eventually. I guess we got tired of waiting for you to do the same."

Jake nodded. "I get it, man. No need to apologise. I'm sorry."

Shaun raised his glass and nodded. "Forgiven."

Jake smiled weakly, but it didn't take a mind reader to know it meant a lot to him. He turned to Lucas and lifted his glass in a salute. "You too, man. No hard feelings. We all know you never meant for any of this."

Lucas was stunned. "Are you joking? I've almost certainly got you all killed."

Simon shrugged. "If it wasn't you, it would have been something else." He took a deep swig from his whiskey bottle. "The booze probably."

"I have a weak heart," said Shaun. "Tell you the truth, I probably wouldn't have made my fiftieth birthday anyway."

Simon stared at his friend bug-eyed. "What? You never told me that!"

"What would be the point? I didn't like thinking about

it, and you would only have fussed. It's why I never settled down. Always felt like I'd be short-changing whatever family I might have. My dad had the same thing, took him at forty-four. *I'm* forty-four."

"You should have told me," said Simon, obviously hurt. He didn't dwell on it too long, though, and eventually gave Shaun a playful shove. "You always were a sodding weakling."

They all laughed, but after they were done, they enjoyed the silence for a while. Each of them likely had a fair amount of self-reflection to do before they faced whatever came next. The worst part of it all was that Lucas didn't blame Judas for wanting revenge.

I deserve this. It's time The Devil got his due.

What he did blame Judas for was terrorising Vetta. And for that, *he* should be the one to pay.

But what can I do? Judas is the one with all the power.

Yet, power could be a downfall. Lucas had once been in a position of power, standing before Michael in the throne room of Heaven. His arrogance had reduced that power to nothing. It had been his downfall. Judas was arrogant too, he knew it. The man reeked of pride. There was a chance, only slight, that Judas's massive advantage could be his downfall too.

There was a chance.

And Lucas would take it.

┴

LUCAS WAS THINKING ABOUT VETTA WHEN HIS ELBOWS BEGAN to sink through the bar. He jumped back off his stool and startled everyone.

Jake looked around in fright. "What is it?"

"T-The bar. It changed!"

Shaun frowned. "What are you talking about?" He rapped his knuckles on the bar, making a *rap-tap-tap* sound.

Lucas crept back to where he'd been sitting and reached out his hand, pressing down with his fingertips. They sunk into the wood, and everyone gasped. He pulled them back out again and liquid dripped from his nails.

Jake slid off his stool, balancing on his one good leg. "What the hell, man?"

"The bar is melting," slurred Simon, head slumped on his arms. "Great!"

Shaun grabbed Jake before the lad toppled over. "What's it mean? What's happening?"

Lucas studied the bar, watching it melt before his eyes. It shimmered like paint mixing with water. "It means the end is coming. Judas is pushing his spell further—erasing the tether to the real world this bar represents. Once it's gone, this reality will be sealed off forever, and I'll probably be stuck here alone until the world ends."

"Or until we stop Julian, right?" said Jake. "You said we were going to crucify him!"

Shaun didn't seem to think that was a good way to spend his final moments, and he was shaking his head adamantly. His slick-backed hair was now all over the place, and the grey was less disguised. "Look at what happened to us when we tried to fight him, and there's another ten aswangs out there somewhere—at least!"

Lucas sighed. "Best thing for you now is to enjoy what time you have left, and hope you earned your way into a better place. Judas won't waste energy keeping you here—and for that, you should be grateful."

"I don't want to die," said Shaun, clutching himself. "Even if I go to Heaven. I... I don't want to die."

Jake peered down at the floor with the most anxious of expressions. It was obvious what he was thinking. He had not lived a good life. He expected to go downward. "I wish I could tell you Heaven awaits, lad," Lucas told him, "but I don't have all the facts. All I can say is that intentions count for a lot. It's worse to commit sin knowingly than to do so through weakness and ignorance. Face your end with dignity and accept whatever comes."

Jake nodded, but looked utterly terrified. He had every right to be.

A barstool toppled over as one of its legs melted away. Bottles tumbled off the shelves and smashed on the floor—part glass, part liquid. The whiskey in Simon's bottle began to dissolve.

Shaun started wringing his hands. "Is it going to hurt?"

"Death is always painful," said Lucas. "But so is life."

The pub's door sprung open and the aswang's howling filled the interior. Judas would not wait for the spell to consume them, nor give Lucas any chance of escape. He was sending in his troops early to finish the job. Whatever fun Judas had been having was over.

Lucas turned to the others. "You ready to face your deaths? The way a man meets his maker is important. You take that with you."

Simon slithered off his stool, right before it toppled over and melted. "I'm dead already," he said, smashing his knuckles into his palm, "and kind of pissed off about it, so yeah—bring it on!"

Shaun was trembling. "Times like these, I really wish I were brave."

"You're standing here," said Lucas. "You *are* brave."

"Ever seen a one-legged man in an ass-kicking contest?" said Jake, hopping on the spot. "You're about to see something really special, guys."

Lucas glared at the open doorway, at the grey nothingness beyond. The aswangs would come inside any minute and tear them all to shreds. There was no way to fight back, they had already given all they had. Judas would keep Lucas alive, but the others were about to die. Lucas had started life as the most glorious of angels, but he was going to end up as doomed as any soul rotting in Hell—like the millions he himself had once condemned. Had he ever truly contemplated what an eternity of agony was like? How had he ever believed such a sentence was deserved?

Because I'm selfish. Remorseless.

No, I'm not. I'm human.

The ceiling began to drip. The bar began collapsing in on itself. The windows clouded over and began to run like hot glue.

Lucas thought he'd left The Devil behind on Cavalry Hill, but such a being could not be buried. He would always be The Devil. He would always be Lucifer. But he had to admit, right now, Lucifer would be a great help. The Devil would not have put up with Julian's games for a single second. That guy was a badass—the very same mofo Julian had been trying to summon for two-thousand years, not the meek human-shadow of a once-great being.

Summon... Julian tried to summon *The Devil.*

"I know what to do!" said Lucas, turning to the others excitedly. "I know how to get us out of this!"

Jake stopped hopping and balanced on the spot with his arms out. "What? How?"

"You all need to bleed. Right now."

Shaun winced and grabbed his tattooed arms. "Come up with a better idea."

"Just do what I say, and I can save us! I need a glass that hasn't melted yet, and I need something sharp enough to cut ourselves on. Deeply."

The pub vibrated. Floorboards grew tacky beneath their feet. The aswangs howled outside, waiting for earthly reality to fade away enough to let them in.

"We don't have time for a treasure hunt," said Shaun, running his hands through his sweaty hair. "We need to run."

"Run where?" said Jake.

"It won't take long," said Lucas. "Just do what I say."

They gathered the items he'd requested and put them on the bar. To cut themselves, Jake had smashed a vodka bottle. The neck was dissolving, but the broken body was still sharp. A pint glass sat beside it.

"Hold out your arms," Lucas ordered, picking up the bottle neck. "Over the bar."

They all did as he commanded, but they trembled and looked worried. They all knew this was going to hurt, but the aswangs were right outside. What else were they going to do?

"What are you planning to do?" Jake asked.

"I'm going to bleed you all and make a circle on the bar."

"Not sure I have much blood left," said Simon, looking decidedly pale.

Jake frowned. "Why are you going to bleed us?"

"So I can summon The Devil."

"But... but you *are* The Devil."

"No, I'm just a human being. The Devil is a part of me that was ripped away last night, but it's something too powerful to be destroyed. My celestial soul still exists somewhere, and I need to reclaim it. Gladri took away my powers, but he must have placed them somewhere. In Heaven or Hell, I can summon The Devil forth. I am going to have myself possessed."

"By yourself?" asked Simon, looking like he would laugh if his guts weren't spilling out.

Lucas shrugged. "It sounds stupid when you put it like that!" He looked towards the door. The first of the aswangs had begun to sidle into the pub, spindly legs spread out, head close to the ground. "But stupid is all we've got. Ready?"

They all nodded, so Lucas slashed each of their forearms with the broken bottle and caught their blood in a pint glass. Once it was half full, he poured the blood on the bar in a rough circle.

"What do we do now?" asked Jake, glancing skittishly at the doorway. The aswangs had begun creeping inside, the fresh blood exciting them as they panted like dogs.

"Stand back and pray," said Lucas.

Shaun grunted. "That's helpful"

"No, I mean it. *Pray*. To Lucifer Almighty, Ruler of Hell, and greatest of God's adversaries. You know He is real, so believe in Him and pray. Leave the rest to me."

The aswangs stalked closer, taking their time, confused by what was going on in front of them. They had expected fear, but instead, they met indifference. The humans in the bar were paying them no attention. Lucas recited the Lord's Prayer backwards—an affront to God—and prepared to speak the ancient words that would summon forth The Devil. He could do this. He could cast another spell.

But his mind was blank.

No, no, no! Come on, think!

He had been so sure he could do this that he hadn't checked his mind to make sure the words were there. His memory told him there was a spell that could help them, but he didn't know the words. Like asking for directions and someone telling you your destination was 'nearby,' but giving nothing else to go on.

"What are you waiting for?" Jake demanded, wobbling on his leg as the floor melted beneath him.

"I... I don't remember the words. I... can't think how to begin the summoning."

Shaun spluttered. "What? Then how... Shit! We're screwed."

"Yeah," said Lucas, watching the aswangs close in. "Sorry about that!"

The aswangs surrounded them.

┴

THE BEGGAR MOVED THROUGH THE CROWD EASILY, AS ALL beggars do. His stench preceded him and parted the huddled masses seeking to avoid his pestilence. The boils on his face wept and burned, but these people bore no compassion for him. Suffering was a background event to a city like this—a sickly beggar no different to a dead rat baking in the sun. It allowed the beggar to be invisible. Even as people stared at him in disgust, they failed to truly see him. If they did, they would see more than just a beggar.

They would see damnation itself.

Lucifer trudged along Jerusalem's cobbles, threading his way between market stalls and crumbling stone walls. Jerusalem might have been a glorious jewel in the desert from afar, but it was coated in filth and decay up close. Place your cheek against the ground, and you could smell the piss. Turn your gaze to the sky, and you would see the vultures. Wherever man congregated, effluence flowed, and in Jerusalem, many were just passing through—they did not care for this place as they did their homes.

Yet it was an impressive city still. The Herodian Temple rose up nearby, proceeded by its vast stone courtyard. Long-nose Jews filled it like teeming ants, while Roman watchmen stood without its borders keeping watchful eye. Tension filled the air—a powdery unease that threatened to combust. Too many religions in one place, too many people of too many types. Jerusalem was a needle point on which the entire world would soon pierce itself deeply. Lucifer grinned beneath his hood.

Ahead, the narrow streets widened into a meeting place. The bustling crowds here solidified into an enraptured mob, all fighting to get to the front. The man who held their attention was named Jesus, but he was not who the beggar had come to see this day.

Instead, he sidled into a nearby alleyway where he startled a sleeping dog and caused a washer woman to rush indoors at the sight of him. Was he really so hideous? Or merely a reflection of the hideousness in others? The lack of compassion for a sickly old beggar was the true horror here.

A minute's walk took him to a stairwell leading up to a terrace. Barefooted, he took the cold steps carefully, not wanting to rush this moment he had been anticipating so long. Oh, how he loved to corrupt the pious, the patriotic. The faithful.

On the terrace, several men sat drinking wine and ale while watching the street below. They observed Jesus, that man in the market square who spoke so quietly and yet so powerfully. The enraptured crowd grew every second, and the terrace drinkers were awestruck by what they were seeing. One man, however, seemed to watch events with a heavy heart.

It was to this man the beggar gravitated.

"A gift to us all," he said, gaining the troubled man's attention.

The man flinched at the sight of him but did not shoo him away. "Yes, Jesus is the wisest of all men."

The beggar grinned. "A *messiah*, one might say."

"No! Never *that*. Jesus is just a man."

"Some say otherwise. I heard Jews in the temple refer to him as King—a title sure to send many a Roman to despair."

The man scrutinised the beggar, hooked nose pointing out from above a pair of plump, dry lips. In many ways, he resembled a rat or a mole. "Jesus would be the last to proclaim himself such a thing. Trust me, I know him as brother."

The beggar feigned surprise. "You serve this man from Galilee? One of his acolytes?"

"I am no *acolyte*, beggar. I count Jesus as friend and mentor, but not master. As I said, he is the wisest of all men. Those below are smart to listen."

The beggar admired the splendour of the man's fine clothing for a moment, and the luxurious gems on his hands. A good man, perhaps, but one tempted by shiny things. "You clearly love this man, so why do you appear so weary of thought? What weighs upon your troubled mind, friend?"

"I am not your *friend,* beggar. You forget yourself to speak to one such as I. Leave this place, lest the guards arrive and toss you down the steps."

"Your mentor would preach acceptance of all men. Tolerance. Compassion."

This seemed to trouble the man even more. "Jesus is not correct in all things, as no wise man should be, else there would be no capacity for further learning."

"You are a wise man yourself, Judas."

The man's dark eyes narrowed. "How do you know my name? You are but a simple beggar, and I only recently arrived in this city."

"I know you well, Judas Iscariot. You are a patriot, a pragmatic man who puts the needs of the whole above those of the few. An admirable man that has not escaped the attention of Heaven."

"You do not speak for Heaven, beggar."

Lucifer let his disguise disintegrate. The other drinker on the terrace did not notice him, for it was his will not to be seen. Even as he allowed himself to glow with a beautiful light, only Judas looked upon him. The man was astonished—more so when Lucifer spoke in a voice that obliterated all other sound. "I speak with the full authority of Heaven, human. I am one of the Three, highest of all angels."

Lucifer struggled not to ruin his act with a sneer as he thought about Heaven and all its condescensions. His brothers dare cast him down into this pit, to leave him festering amongst worms and maggots? He would see Heaven burn. This meek human before him was merely a stepping stone towards that end. "You would do well to heed me, Judas Iscariot."

Judas trembled. "Y-You come from Heaven? W-What would you have of me, angel?"

"To turn your life to glorious purpose. God needs an instrument, a faithful soul to prevent an upcoming calamity."

Judas went pale. His neck bulged as if he might gag. "Say it is not so. What is this calamity of which you speak?"

A jar of honeyed-ale perched on the wall of the terrace, and Lucifer took it now as an act to calm the man, to make himself appear more corporeal and less unearthly. He had not partaken of alcohol before, yet he found the taste quite... *agreeable*. He smiled with delight and pointed the expression at Judas. "Do you love this man, Jesus?"

Judas nodded. "Dearly."

"And how would Jesus feel if he brought about disaster and death?"

"It would destroy him. Nothing could be further from his desires."

Lucifer nodded, making his eyes appear considerate. "Then you must save Jesus from himself. His words of love and understanding are doomed to elicit the opposite response. The Romans bristle at his presence already, for they have no tolerance of demagogues. The memory of Clodius is a wound not yet healed."

Judas huffed. "The Roman Empire was founded by demagogues. Caesar himself was the biggest of all."

"Demagogues are merely a tool used to hone the blades of violent men. Rome would rather put Jesus to the sword than see him incite rebellion from the forums and marketplaces."

"And what of their great Cicero?" Judas argued. "He is a man revered for causing unrest in the forums."

"A Roman long dead and tolerated only for his friendship with Caesar. The Empire is young and prone to impetuous whims, Judas Iscariot. Tiberius is more powerful than any man who has lived, yet he wields that power dispassionately. He does not want it, and his officials do as they please."

Lucifer peered down at Jesus in the marketplace—Jesus of Nazareth, Jesus of Galilee, King of the Jews—and found himself unexpectedly impressed. The small man was gentle and unassuming, lighter skinned than most, and longer haired than all. He had a way about him—a presence—that drew the eye and kept it there, but the thought that he might be the son of God...

Pah!

"All actions have consequence, Judas Iscariot, and history itself is shaped by the smallest of men. Jesus invites folly. Heaven has foreseen it, as it sees all things. The lost lambs in the market listen to Jesus's honeyed words hoping for change, but all they shall receive is more of the same—poverty and bloodshed."

He upturned the mug of ale over the wall and let it splash against the stone. It ran just like blood. "It was even worse before Rome civilised the world," he went on. "What savages will people become if left to their own devices once again? Accept Rome with all its flaws, for it is the thing that keeps mankind from the Abyss. Your mentor shall inflame, when he wishes to save. He is *misguided*. Not a sin, but a danger indeed."

Judas had tears in his eyes, and he stared intently at the man below who he so obviously loved dearly. "Can it be true? Jesus wishes to save us all, but is he tempting fate? He is one man angering the might of an indomitable empire, an empire that I believe keeps our chaotic world from darkness. I fear what will become of my countrymen if we are left abandoned of Rome's embrace."

Lucifer smiled, knowing he was witnessing the agonising twist of a man's soul. "I find no pleasure in saying this, Judas, but your mentor does not serve God, only himself."

"A lie! Jesus is beyond his own selfish desires."

Lucifer glared, eyes turning red. "Do not deign to raise your voice at me, mortal! Jerusalem is set to ruin, and the empire shall shed blood to create a river. These people shall not be saved by Jesus of Nazareth—they will be his unwitting victims. You know this to be true, child, for you are of the light of Heaven. Do not let your love for one man make you turn your back on all others."

Judas trembled, watching the ale leak down the wall. "I fear I do not know my own mind. My heart rends."

Lucifer reached out and grabbed the man by the shoulder and locked eyes with him. "You know what is right, child. In your heart, you know! Your mentor is already being heralded as King of the Jews, and Rome does not tolerate monarchs not of its own making. The prefect has only to raise one finger and his centurions will raze the Herodian Temple to the ground."

"The prefect is an even-handed man."

"Yet a servant to the empire and its people. He cannot tolerate Jesus's disruption any longer, and your mentor's voice stretches farther every day. *Quiet* the man if you love him. Move Jesus along before his welcome is forever overstretched."

"Jesus does not listen to me. I have asked him many times to leave, to move westward back to Galilee. He refuses."

"You state him to be a selfless man, yet he is one who does not listen to a trusted friend?"

"He listens to his conscience, and the will of the Lord."

Lucifer shook his head, almost mockingly. "The words of many an aspiring king. Soon he shall proclaim himself Jesus *Rex*."

Judas grew angry. "What would you have of me, angel? You have made argument, now state desire!"

"Heaven desires nothing but for men to flourish and for peace to reign. If you desire the same, you shall find a way to muzzle Jesus. If he will not leave, then force his words to silence some other way. But act quickly, before it is too late."

"I… I cannot betray a man I love."

"Then you betray your very nation, and all the innocent souls within. Silence Jesus, and you shall see the world reach a new dawn of enlightenment. Fail, and it shall plunge into an everlasting darkness."

"Jesus is too wise. He will know if I act against him."

Lucifer grunted. "You fear a peaceful man? Fine, a token of Heaven's appreciation to aid you." He waved a hand over Judas. A trickle of light spilled from his fingertips, but nothing else.

"W-what did you just do to me?"

"I have given you a gift, the ability to act without detection. Your behaviour shall illicit no attention, making you part of the background. People will see you yet struggle to remember you. You exist within a veil, a face in a cloud of smoke. Once Jesus is a threat no longer, I shall lift the veil and reward you with unending good fortune and a place awaiting you in Heaven. Whatever your heart's desire shall be yours."

Judas grew red in the cheeks, greed glinting in his eyes. As pious as this man might be, he could not suppress the avarice that defined his inner self. "I shall find a way to stop Jesus," he muttered. "You have my word. I just don't want him to get hurt."

"Be the pragmatist we are counting on you to be, Judas." Lucifer had begun to growl, losing patience. "Is the suffering of one man not worth enduring, if it saves the agony of thousands? Do what you must and know that Heaven shall forgive all."

Judas swallowed and then nodded. "I shall do what needs to be done. I swear it."

"Good. Heaven will be watching."

"W-What if I need to speak with you again. What if..."

Lucifer growled louder, then reminded himself he was supposed to be kind and merciful. He had twisted this man to his will, and now things were dragging on intolerably. "Why would you need to speak with me again, mortal?"

"J-Just... I might need help in my task. Something might go wrong. I would just feel better if—"

"Fine, so be it," Lucifer had to force himself to smile instead of wrenching this insolent mortal's insides. "If you have need of me again, child, just speak these words..."

†

"I KNOW THE WORDS," SAID LUCAS, MEMORIES FLOODING BACK to him in a rush. "I remember!"

"Then hurry up and say them," said Jake, hopping frantically on one foot. "'Cus we're about to die."

The aswangs closed in. Simon stunned the first by lobbing what was left of his melting whiskey bottle at them.

Lucas spoke the words quickly—the words he'd told Judas Iscariot two-thousand years ago. That was how Judas had known the spell to summon him from Hell. He had been trying to snare Lucifer for two millennia, not knowing the creature was no more, and yet his endless patience had paid off. Lucas had returned to Hell and activated the spell.

Now it was time to cast it again.

Jake cried out as an aswang leapt up and snatched his arm in its jaws. It started shaking him like a pit bull.

Simon collapsed against the bar, too weak to fight—on borrowed time already. Shaun panicked and skittered about like a fly trapped inside a glass.

Lucas spoke the final words and turned to the aswangs with utter hatred in his eyes. Hatred at what he had created. "Time someone taught you mangy mutts how to heel!"

He smashed his fist down in the centre of the bloody circle on the bar. The pub exploded with light. Everything not nailed down went hurtling against the walls—aswangs and people included. The beasts tumbled backwards, head over limbs, and crashed against the furniture. Simon, Jake, and Shaun fell into a pile, grabbing hold of one another for support. And, amongst it all, stood Lucas.

The Devil.

"BOW DOWN BEASTS FOR IT IS I WHO MADE YOU! BOW DOWN!"

The aswangs recovered to their feet, but the moment

they set eyes on Lucas, they cowered. One of them urinated.

"Whoa!" said Jake, slumped up against the bar. "He's like the aswang whisperer."

Lucas stepped towards the aswangs, making them tremble. "Prostrate yourselves before your master or suffer everlasting agonies." The aswangs dropped onto their bellies. "Now begone! BEGONE!"

The aswangs got up and scurried for the door like a fire had been lit behind them. Lucas watched them go, and then faced his companions with a contented smirk upon his face. He couldn't help but enjoy their expressions of awe. Never before had he felt so powerful, for only after being absent of strength did he realise how much of it coursed through his veins.

He marched towards the bar, and the others scooted out of his way on their butts. "It's okay," he told them with a smirk. "I'm still me. Just a tad over-excited."

"T-That was pretty awesome," said Jake. "Are we safe now? Is it over?"

"Not yet. I still have to take care of Judas, but this time he's the one in the shit-barrel."

The pub had stopped dissolving. Lucas focused for a second and everything reformed and solidified. The pub was now under his control, and so would everything else be shortly, for he was The Devil, and Hell was his home.

He knelt down beside Jake and examined the lad's ankle. His arm was pretty torn up too, flesh hanging off.

"Y-You're... smoking," said Jake.

Shaun pointed a trembling finger. "And your... your *feet*!"

Lucas glanced down and saw his feet were now hooves,

something he'd once vowed would never again happen. "Oh, sorry about that, fellas," he said, willing the hooves away. He concentrated on stopping the oily black smoke coming from his skin too, and it soon went away.

With his body once again under full control, he placed a hand on Jake's ankle and smiled at the lad. "About time we took care of this, I think."

Jake's eyes widened. "You can fix it?"

"It's already fixed."

Jake looked down at his healthy ankle and whooped with joy. "The man does it again. Wow, that feels better."

Shaun grabbed Lucas and dragged him to his feet. He was still panicked, even with the fight now over. "You have to help, Si," he said. "You need to help him right now!"

Simon had slumped over onto his side, mouth open as if humming to himself. The truth was he was breathing his last breaths. Lucas looked at Shaun and saw more fear on the man's face than since this whole thing began—he was more terrified of living without his best friend than he was of dying a painful death.

"Hold on," said Lucas, kneeling over Simon and pressing his hands into the deep wound beneath his ribs. The blood was clumping—thick with organ-matter and flesh. Simon's life was all but gone. Most of him had already slipped away.

You aren't going anywhere, big guy!

Lucas concentrated, not on the power Gladri had left him with, but on the power he had always possessed. He pulled forth his link to Heaven, Hell, and the spaces between, and made sure that the bed they had waiting for Simon was no longer available. A few seconds was all it took, but it was still a relief when Simon opened his eyes and gasped.

"Cock it!" the big man shouted after he caught his breath. "Shite, shite, shite. Damn… That was one weird-ass trip."

"I brought you back from the brink," said Lucas. "I'll send you my bill after all this is done."

"Yeah, and I'll send you mine for dragging me into this crap in the first place."

"Call it even?"

"Yep."

Lucas stood, and when he reached out to the bar, a bottle of beer flew out of the fridge and landed in his hand. He bit off the cap and swigged the whole thing down. Wiping his mouth and gasping with satisfaction, he studied the three fit and healthy men standing before him and told them to prepare themselves. Shit was about to get real.

Jake folded his arms and stood straight—full of vigour. "So, we finally gonna take it to Judas now?"

Lucas grinned, then amused them by doing a tiny jig. "Fellas, there are two things old Lucas does extremely well. One is supping fine ale. The other is making life miserable for eejits like Judas."

Shaun frowned. "Why is he Irish now?"

Jake chuckled and told him, "Oh, that means he's a badass again."

Lucas leapt in the air and clicked his heels. It was time to go and save Vetta.

Second Wind

"Judas doesn't hate me for giving him eternal life," explained Lucas. "He hates me because I cursed him to live a life of irrelevance. It was supposed to be temporary, a way for him to betray Jesus without being suspected, but when I... *changed my ways*, I forgot to remove the curse. I condemned him to an eternity of mediocrity. No matter how much he's worked, or how much knowledge he's gained, people will never take much notice. His accomplishments will never be appreciated. He's probably never made a single friend who's seen him beyond a mere acquaintance. His entire, endless existence has been mundane and without end. I promised him a place in Heaven, but I have kept him from it for two millennia. I made Judas so unmemorable that I forgot all about him and the spell I cast."

Simon began laughing. "Wait, you're telling us you cursed this guy to an eternity of blandness because you... you just forgot about him?"

Lucas found himself chuckling too, and then couldn't stop. "Ha! How much it must have chafed his sack seeing his name in Christian lights, when in reality, he was alive and crying out for attention. Judas is a name known to all, yet not a soul gives a flick about the real deal."

Jake joined the laughter now, but he also seemed confused. "So why did he decide to run a pub?"

Lucas shrugged. "A bartender watches while everyone else enjoys themselves—making friends, finding love. A bartender is part of the background."

Shaun shook his head, smiling but fighting against it. "We should stop laughing. It's terrible. The poor guy has suffered so bad!"

Jake frowned at him. "*Who* has?"

It took a moment for them to get the joke, but then they all bellowed.

"Just some guy behind the bar," said Simon.

"Some guy who has Vetta," said Lucas, bringing things back down to a level. "I don't know about you fellas, but I like that wee lass. And I owe her."

Jake nodded. "You're not the only one."

Lucas knew what Jake was referring to and wondered if he ever could make it right. "We've lost some fine people today," he said, "but that is the price of being alive. Death is a gobshite lurking around every corner, but while it visits some too soon, for others it is well overdue. It's time to put right a wrong. Judas deserves his death, so what say we fellas go give it to him?"

"Hell yeah," said Jake, pumping the air with his fist. "I always assumed I'd end up in Hell, but I never thought I'd be fighting myself out of it alongside The Devil."

Simon grinned. "And I never thought The Devil would be so small."

"Aye," Lucas admitted. "But I have a cock for days!"

"Remind me not to piss next to you," said Shaun. "So, what do you need us to do, boss?"

"I need you," said Lucas, "to stay here."

Everyone groaned. Jake the loudest. "What? Are you serious?"

Lucas grinned. "Just kidding. Here, accept these gifts." He clicked his fingers and all of a sudden, they were all holding solid silver swords. Their jaws dropped in astonishment as the weapons materialised in their hands from the air itself. Jake swiped his sword left to right, then beamed at Lucas to show his satisfaction. "Sweet."

Lucas frowned for a moment—something wasn't quite right. He clicked his fingers one more time and replaced the sword in Simon's hand with a golden axe. "There, that's better. Now you have the whole vVikingViking-vibe going for you."

Simon chuckled and raised the sharp axe up onto his shoulder. With his bald head and bushy beard, he really did resemble a burly Norseman.

"Wait," said Shaun, clutching his own sword awkwardly, like he wondered whether to use it as a weapon or a walking stick. "Things can't be this easy, can they? We're just going to stride out of the pub and start hacking our way to victory? Why can't you just end the spell and let us go home?"

Lucas sighed. There was always one buzz-kill at a party. "The weapons are just for effect, matey. Truthfully, I'm going to be doing most of the heavy lifting, but if anything tries to take a bite out of ya, use the sword. Silver and gold are very effective at slicing demons. You all ready?"

They nodded.

Lucas led them to the pub's front door. What they saw outside surprised them, even Lucas. The shops and pavement had disappeared, replaced by a vast desert of endless dunes.

"That wasn't there earlier," said Jake. "I'm almost certain."

Lucas's eyes narrowed. Judas was not without power of his own, and he was using it to try and retain his control over their reality. On the horizon of this vast desert sat a twinkling jewel, and Lucas knew exactly what it was.

"You fellas ever been to Jerusalem?" he asked.

"No," said Shaun. "Why?"

"Because it looks like that's where Judas wants us to face him. Come on, we have a walk ahead of us."

They set off out of the pub into the desert. The earlier cold had been replaced by an unbearable heat, but Lucas did not let it affect his companions. He summoned a cooling breeze that washed over them as they walked. The effect was, overall, quite pleasant. Hell could be a nice place if you forced it to be.

"You said that Judas was human," said Jake as they trudged up the first dune. "How can a human do all this?"

Lucas shrugged. "Trinkets, spells, rituals. Some of the most powerful beings on Earth are human. Judas has been alive a long time—who knows what knickknacks he's managed to accrue. That, plus I essentially made him unkillable two-thousand years ago."

Jake pulled a face. "And you can't just... smack the bitch

down? I mean, you're The Devil again, right? Can't you make this all go away?"

"Magic is an odd thing, lad. It has rules. You can counter a spell, but you can't erase it unless you find the source. Judas gains power from something, but until we find out what it is, I can't stop his nonsense. The plan is to face him, then squeeze his testicles until he weeps the truth."

The breeze around them suddenly increased, buffeting their clothes. As they headed up a shifting dune, a gusting wind caused them to lose their footing. They stumbled and used their weapons to anchor themselves in the sand. Lucas stared over the top of the dune and saw Julian's latest trick. "Heads down," he shouted. "It's about to start raining cats and dogs."

The storm came in an eye-blink, tossing rain and sleet at them, and hurling high speed winds right in their faces. The weather was so dense that Lucas lost sight of the others and found himself hopelessly disorientated. The hail struck his eyes and forced them closed.

Judas wasn't beaten yet—perhaps he was just getting started.

Bring it on!

"Lucas," Shaun called out. "I can't see you. Help!"

"I got you, man," said Simon, obviously finding his friend amongst the hail.

"I'm over here," called Jake. "Shit, man, this is proper English weather."

Lucas laughed. Judas would not break them with a hail storm. Lightning struck two feet from his foot, and the black clouds suggested a second strike was coming. He threw up an arm and redirected the bolt just in time so that it struck ten feet away, turning the sand black.

"He's throwing lightning!" Shaun cried, his courage wavering. "Why do things keep getting worse?"

"Keep moving," said Lucas. "I'll keep you lads breathing, I promise."

More lightning dropped from the sky, but Lucas deflected it all. He could not see his companions, but the more he focused, the more the storm began to ease and the rain to depart. Slowly, the weather cleared and revealed the others to be standing a mere dozen feet away, yet they had been invisible in the storm. Lucas went over and patted them warmly on the back.

"See, your uncle Lucas has everything in hand. Judas will need to try a lot harder than that."

A skittering sound alerted them, and they turned to see a sheet of multi-coloured desert moving towards them. An army of fat scorpions approached, their mass forming a constantly moving kaleidoscope of colours and size that rushed towards them in a wave. Their tails stung the air excitedly. Their claws pinched at the sand.

Shaun held his sword up, but it trembled like an electric toothbrush. "A-Are those scorpions?"

Lucas reached out a hand and summoned a massive golden warhammer with beautiful engravings. The scorpions moved fast and would be on them any minute, but he was looking forward to a fight.

"Judas has an affinity with creatures unseen," he said. "A scorpion exists beneath our perception until its stinger is already buried in our flesh. Let's crush the cheeky critters and send the man a message."

The sword in Shaun's hands was still trembling, but he slowly got it steady. "B-But there are thousands of them."

"Aye!" Lucas nodded. "Shouldn't take us too long."

┼

LUCAS LED THE DEFENCE, DROPPING HIS MASSIVE WARHAMMER down onto the dunes like the stomp of an elephant. Sand and pieces of crushed scorpion spat up into the air. He forced his will into the weapon and created a shock wave ten feet wide with every hit. Hundreds of scorpions exploded.

Jake and the others set about with their own weapons. Simon sweeping his axe laterally like a pendulum and scooping up dozens of scorpions before flinging them into the air, Jake and Shaun stabbing their swords at the ground like they were picking up litter.

A thousand more scorpions erupted from the sands. Judas's power was awesome, but it must also be draining. The man couldn't keep this up for long, surely. No link to Hell was that vast.

Jake shouted as a scorpion made it onto his trouser leg. Lucas reached out and clicked his fingers, breaking the scorpion's back. He did the same thing several more times as more arachnids made it inside their defences. Before long, it sounded like he was keeping time to a rapid polka. *Click-snap-click-snap-click-snap.*

"There are too many of them," cried Shaun, stamping his foot down and swinging his sword. He had a scorpion hanging off his arm, embedded by its stinger, but he didn't seem to notice.

Lucas tried to count the remaining critters and lost

count at seven-thousand. "You're right," he said. "We need to run. You fellas get a head start. I'll buy you some time."

"We'll try not to leave you for dust," said Jake, grabbing the others and retreating. They made it to the top of the dune, then picked up speed as they careened downhill.

The scorpions tried to give chase, but Lucas opened up a pit in the sand that swallowed them up. He lost focus for a second, and dozens of scorpions skittered up his legs and started stinging him. Their poison was useless against him, but their piercing stingers still served as a distraction.

He clapped his hands together and the dune around him exploded, sand leaping up into the air and forming a cyclone. Next, he waved his arms and the cyclone widened and moved away. It sucked up scorpions by the hundreds and tossed them high into the air. There were far too many to catch them all, but he had broken their ranks and left them in straggling groups.

He'd done enough.

With a grunt, Lucas let his warhammer tumble from his hands. It evaporated before it hit the ground. Then he turned and fled, spotting his three companions in the distance. They had made considerable progress, but with his regained power, Lucas slid across the desert with ease and caught up to them in moments.

Simon grunted. "You took care of things?"

Lucas spoke slowly, weakened by all the energy he had just expelled. "Yes, everything is... hunky dory."

"You okay, man?" asked Jake, looking concerned.

"Yeah, just a tad tuckered out. Don't fret about me, lad. Come, let's keep moving."

Jerusalem lay near now and Lucas concentrated on reducing the distance between them and it, rolling up the desert before them, but his success was marginal. He needed to take some time to rejuvenate. Even The Devil did not possess endless resources.

"How did Judas bring an entire city here?" asked Shaun, marvelling at the high walls and towering domes coming into view.

"It's not really Jerusalem," explained Lucas. "It's a conjuration, something Judas has constructed from memory. He obviously feels it's home. That will give him power, make it easier for him to... to focus." He lost his breath, something that shouldn't have been an issue for a celestial being. He felt odd. Wrong.

Jake grabbed him before he fell down. "What's wrong with you, man? You don't look right."

Simon pointed to Lucas's arm. More of that black smoke flowed from his flesh, snaking out from his sleeves. This time he wasn't exuding dark power, he was *losing* it. "I... I feel weak. Something is..."

Simon grabbed Lucas and started patting him down. To their astonishment, the big man found a scorpion hiding under Lucas's right sleeve. The critter was hanging on by its stinger which was buried in the space above his elbow. Simon yanked it away and was about to toss it when Lucas shouted at him to halt.

"Give it to me."

Simon handed Lucas the scorpion. It thrashed and whipped its tail, but the stinger had broken away when it was removed. Lucas examined the squirming creature for a second, then crushed it in his fist. He cursed and threw the husk into the sand where it leaked a dark grey substance. "Iron," he said, shaking his burning hand. "Feck it!"

"What does that mean?" asked Shaun. "Iron hurts you, like the nail hurt the aswangs?"

"Iron hurts anything not born of the Earth. Hey, Simon, do a fella a favour and remove the nail from my pocket. Last thing I need is that spilling free and burning me a good 'un. I don't even know what Jesus's blood would do to me right now." Simon reached obligingly into Lucas's pocket and rooted about for the nail. Lucas wriggled. "Easy there, fella!"

Simon eventually found and retrieved the nail, stuffing it into his own jeans. "Okay, got it."

"Look after it. It's important, somehow."

Simon nodded. They were about to get going again when Lucas stumbled unexpectedly onto his knees. A piercing agony exploded in his chest. Jake had to grab him and hold him upright until the pain subsided.

"What's happening?" Shaun demanded. He pointed his sword at Lucas, which felt slightly unfair.

Lucas collapsed forward and placed his hands in the sand. "The... the iron. It's in my veins... corrupting me. It's making me weak. My powers..."

"Shite on a banana," said Simon. "We're screwed all over again then?"

Lucas forced himself back to his feet, although he almost fell again. He reached out a trembling hand. "I'm not toothless yet."

The others frowned, not knowing what he was doing, and at first, Lucas feared that nothing would happen, but then the sands began to tremble. He fought the pain in his chest and focused on the way ahead. He focused on Jerusalem. He willed a path to take shape. Ahead, to either side of him, the sands began to pile up into towering dunes, leaving a low, compacted pathway between them. A pair of sandy cliffs formed a mile long.

Jake gasped. "Whoa!"

"We don't have long until I'm too weak to piss," said Lucas. "So, I thought I'd make the going a little easier. Come on!"

They hurried along, enjoying the solid ground beneath their feet after having endured the shifting sands of the dunes. The sandy cliffs cast shadows over them, keeping them cool from the scorching heat Judas tried to cast down on them. A good thing, because Lucas was too drained to cast a breeze on them anymore.

"Those scorpions are still after us," said Shaun, looking back nervously. The kaleidoscope of colour was a mile behind them, but gaining.

"Aye," said Lucas, watching the roiling mass. It was going to be a challenge keeping ahead of the little buggers, and any more of their poison would be the end of him. It took extra impetus to get a move on. "Eyes front, fellas. The unholy land awaits."

⊥

THEY MADE IT TO THE HIGH SANDSTONE WALLS OF JERUSALEM just as the sun was setting. It wasn't truly the sun, but it seemed this fake reality liked to obey certain rules. The scorpions were right behind them now, having gained ground over the last thirty-minutes. A cast-iron gate barred their way, and Lucas was certain it was not a feature of the original city. Nothing he could do would affect it. He couldn't place so much as a fingertip upon it. Another dose of iron would cripple him.

"Is this the only way in?" asked Jake, peering up at the thirty-foot gate.

"No," said Lucas. "I'm sure Judas built a side entrance for us to use."

Shaun looked hopeful. "Really?"

"What do you think, ye great sow. This is the way in. This is the way we go."

"How?" asked Simon. He grabbed the bars and rattled the gate, but it barely moved. "I'm getting fed up of locked doors. The ones in the pub were bad enough."

Shaun was staring back at the arachnid army fast-approaching. "The scorpions will be here any minute."

Lucas closed his eyes to think. He wanted a beer, but perhaps he could do without one for now. Surely, he could put a good plan together without getting rat-arsed. He could try the *Open Sesame* spell again, but with the gate being made of iron, he wasn't sure it would work. And they wouldn't have time to try a second spell. The scorpions would be on them any minute, and this time there would be no escape. He could already feel the last of his powers draining, and if another of those little buggers stung him, he would be useless.

"You have an idea, right?" asked Shaun, fidgeting nervously. He tapped his sword against his leg in a quick rhythm.

Lucas tried to think. His powerful mind was his once again, and he was able to rapidly view the entirety of human history as if it were a single moment in time. It told him what was needed. "Stand back lads, I'm about to rock your world."

Lucas summoned the sands once more, but this time, instead of parting, they came crashing down on top of the scorpions, burying them fifty feet deep. The crushing weight would grind them to dust. Airborne sand struck the four men in the face, making them shield their eyes.

Lucas kept his focus as best he could, willing reality to bend to his command. The sands rolled beneath them, desert piling up against the walls and gate. Jake, Simon, and Shaun panicked, afraid they would get buried, but Lucas ensured their feet stayed above ground. He protected them.

The sand beneath them rose, billions of grains collecting and clumping together. The earth itself lifted them on its back—exalted beings hoisted towards Heaven.

"Is now a good time to say I don't like heights?" said Simon, looking a little less tough than usual. They were now forty feet in the air, above the gate, and looking down at the swirling desert below.

"Why didn't you say so, fella? Allow me to get us down." Lucas waved his arms, and the sand spilled over the stone walls, dropping them back down towards the city. Several times they almost fell, but Lucas kept them all steady. Simon cried out the entire time, but somehow, he managed to make it sound manly.

Jake and Shaun simply stared, shocked into silence. The desert rebuilt itself within the city walls, depositing them safely on the ground. There, they waited for several minutes until the world settled. Only then did they allow themselves to take a step into the city. Lucas, however, remained where he was.

Jake looked at him. "You coming, man?"

"Yeah, just give me a... a minute." He sat down on the ground, worried he would fall otherwise. The world around him was blurry, and more black smoke trailed from his flesh. He feared he might not be able to go on. He was not regenerating quickly enough—if at all. "I... I just need to rest."

"Don't think that's going to be an option," said Simon. "Judas must know we're here. We're sitting ducks."

Jake was looking around in awe. "So, this is really Jerusalem? Jesus was born here?"

"Jesus was born in Bethlehem," Lucas muttered. "*Eejit!*"

Simon nudged Shaun. "Come on, let's give him a hand." They got Lucas under the arms, and together they were able to get him back on his feet. He shuddered with weakness. "Just one step at a time," Simon told him. "We can still finish this."

"Aye, but no more cabaret from me, I'm afraid. I'm all tapped out."

"We'll find another way," said Simon. "At least now we have a chance of facing Judas. We'll get Vetta back, together."

"And out of here in one piece," said Shaun. "That's a priority too, right?"

Lucas nodded, out of breath. "Aye."

A replica of Jerusalem lay before them, modelled in exquisite detail. Every brick, tile, and wooden beam was immaculate. The market awnings fluttered in the wind, wares displayed beneath them. Spires and domes cast shadows in a thousand directions.

There was, however, one thing very wrong with this Jerusalem—it was deserted. Seeing the ancient city devoid of people was eerie. Jerusalem was a beacon of humanity, a place people gravitated towards endlessly, so to see it lying abandoned like this was all wrong. Jerusalem had never been empty. It had never been abandoned.

"Where do we go?" asked Jake. "This place is huge."

"Over there." Lucas pointed. "We're heading to the main marketplace. I have a feeling that's where we'll find Judas.

┴

THE CITY WAS STILL DESERTED WHEN THEY MADE IT TO THE marketplace, but now a haze had descended upon them—a fine mist making it hard to see. The cobbled walkways glistened with moisture, but they were not slippery. It was all an illusion.

Jake had a mournful smile on his face as he took in the sights. He seemed to be thinking of something happy, but that happy memory contained sadness. "Me and Chloe used to lie in our bunk beds when we were little and talk about all the places we would visit when we were older. She always wanted to go to Disney World, and I always wanted to go to Australia to see the kangaroos." He shook his head and huffed. "She would be so angry that the first time I've been outside of England is a make-believe version of Jerusalem."

"Have you never even been to Spain?" Shaun asked incredulously. "I had you pegged for the Magaluf type."

Jake shrugged and seemed embarrassed. "I always spend my money the moment it hits my pocket. Tough to get away when you have a drug habit. Besides, who the hell would go with me?"

"Who were the two you attacked me with last night?" asked Lucas. He was still feeling weak, but he was now able to walk on his own at least.

"Just a couple of lads who buy gear from my Uncle. I

told them I would sort them out if they helped me give you a kicking."

Lucas rolled his eyes. "What fine gentlemen."

"No, they're total scumbags. If I get a second chance after this, I'll get as far away from them as I can."

Shaun looked at Jake for a moment, then nodded thoughtfully. "You know what, kid. We get out of this, and I'll take that trip to Australia with you. Who knows how much time I have left with *my* dicky heart. Might as well start enjoying myself while I can."

Simon gave Shaun a playful tap on the arm. "You got some secret savings stashed away I don't know about?"

He shrugged. "I can do the backpacking thing. I don't eat a lot, and I've slept in worse places than Australia!"

"I suppose you have. Okay, lads. I'm in. We get out of this alive and the three of us will trek to the land down under." Simon looked at Lucas. "How about you, Lucas?"

Lucas chuckled. "What? Me go to Australia? No, thanks, I had enough heat in Hell. Plus, they have that whole thing about barbecues. What is so great about burnt food covered in mosquitoes? The beer tastes like gnat's piss too."

"What's got into you?" Jake frowned.

Lucas leaned up against a wooden cart full of fox pelts. "Sorry, fellas. Old Lucas is just feeling a mite under the weather. It's got him worried."

Shaun looked worried. "You don't think we can take down Judas?"

"I don't know. That scorpion really did a number on me. Not sure how many matches I have left to strike. I'm about to find out, either way."

The others frowned at him, so he pointed to the passage he had spotted between two rows of buildings. "That's where Judas will be waiting for me. There's some steps leading up to a terrace. We met there before. I need to go alone."

Simon obviously thought it was a bad idea, and his beard bristled in disagreement. "Alone? Why would we make it easy for him? We should all rush him and beat the little rat to a pulp."

"While I love a pugnacious fella like yourself, Simon, it's the wrong move. We go up there looking for a fight then that's all we'll get. If I go up alone, perhaps I can end this thing without more misery. I still have some power, but I'm weak. Maybe I'll pull something out of the bag without things getting nasty. I do my best thinking on my feet anyway, so let me try and end this by myself before we press the big red button."

"Are you sure?" asked Jake. "This isn't just your fight anymore, man. That son of a bitch killed Max and Annie, and Gheorgie. And he took Vetta."

Lucas patted the lad on the shoulder and smiled. "You're really not quite the arse you started out as, Jake—and I have a soft spot for bad boys gone good, almost as much as good girls gone bad—but I know what I'm doing. If I'm not back in five minutes, wait another five. If I'm not back after that, start drinking. Another five and you might actually have to do something."

The three men agreed to take cover behind a small pavilion where Jesus Christ had once preached to the masses. Lucas remembered seeing the man as if it were only yesterday. On that day, he had watched from the terrace and plotted Jesus's downfall. He had wanted to get God's attention.

Lucas stepped into the passageway between buildings

and moved down the cobbled street. Ahead and to his right, were the steps that would lead up to the terrace. It seemed Judas had a penchant for the past—as most eternal beings did. The more time that went by for an immortal being, the harder it became to remain comfortable with existence.

Even Lucas had found the 21st Century difficult to endure. In ancient times, men had been easy to understand. Their actions were out in the open. Now people lived their lives through technology, their thoughts expressed via code and emoticons—things he could not read instinctively. It was hard for an ancient being to find a place in an ever-evolving world.

Perhaps that was why Judas had chosen this place and time. It was the last time he felt secure, his final days before The Devil had cursed his life away. The last days before he betrayed his friend, Jesus. This whole city stunk of regret and anger.

Lucas started up the stone steps. They, like the marketplace, were moist and covered in haze, but his footing was secure as he ascended, and he soon found himself on that familiar terrace. This time, however, the tables and chairs were unused, and only a single man stood looking down at the city below.

It's time to finish this, Judas, in the place where it all began.

Judas was standing in the same spot he had been when Lucifer had approached him disguised as a beggar. Now, Lucas didn't have a disguise, or even any idea of who he was. After thousands of years, he was still lost and confused. Jesus had been right about him.

"I've come to make this right, Judas," Lucas said. "I have to try one last time."

Judas turned around slowly, a smile upon his face. "I go

by Julian these days. Seems we've both grown tired of our past selves."

"Aye, you're right there. The creature that cursed you died beneath Jesus on the cross. I'm sorry I didn't repent in time to offer you mercy and compassion. Everything that has befallen you—the *evil* you have committed—it is all my fault. Put the blame on me, and I shall carry it. Change, and there might still be hope for your eternal soul."

"Eternity needs an end," said Judas. He didn't seem confrontational anymore, just fed up—sad, even. "I have lived two-thousand years—too long for a man. I haven't felt an ounce of joy since last we met upon this terrace. Seeing you again has finally given me purpose and joy again. I *feel* something. Where have you been hiding all this time, Satan?"

"I left Hell and vowed never to return. Your spell was pointed at the wrong place. It doesn't matter, your plans are ruined. There is no point in things getting any uglier. Come back to the light, Julian. It is never too late. Release Vetta and allow us all to leave this place."

Julian swallowed, and took a long look at the abandoned city below. "Sometimes things begin after they are already too late, and they can never be reset. My entire existence has been a sword hanging over your neck, Satan, and now all that is left is for me to swing."

"So why haven't you? What's stopping you?"

"I'm afraid. Afraid of seeing what's left once I finally take my revenge upon you. For two-thousand years it has been the only thing that has sustained me. Once I kill you, I fear I shall be truly empty."

"So, don't kill me."

"That is not a choice I can make, Satan. The Red Lord's

favour may be beyond my reach, but your death will be enough. Enough for me." He threw out a hand, almost lazily, and a tangle of thorns erupted and spewed forth. Out of instinct, Lucas phased out of the way and reappeared three feet to the left. The act made Judas's eyes go wide. "Y-You claimed to be human! What has happened since last we spoke?"

Lucas hadn't wanted to show his hand, so he played it down. He should have pretended to be completely powerless and lulled Judas into a false sense of security until it was time to strike. That plan was down the shitter now, so he would have to keep on his toes. "Heaven left me with a slim vestige of power. A mistake, perhaps."

Judas threw another tangle of thorns, and this time Lucas chose only to duck. He tried to make it seem like he was too weak to phase out a second time, and he huffed and panted. Perhaps Judas would get overconfident if he thought all Lucas had were a few tricks and half a battery.

"Maybe now you might present half a challenge," said Judas with a sneer. "Unlike before."

"Wait!" Lucas put his hand up. "Just wait! Vengeance will not change what you have lived through, Julian. It will not change you! Your fate will be the same unless you choose a different path. Your past does not have to define your future."

Judas licked his lips and lowered his hands for a moment. "You think I can be forgiven?"

"No, but you can be redeemed."

"*You* are my redemption, Satan. You made me kill the son of God. You have ruined lives by the thousands. I do their memories justice by ending you."

Lucas nodded. "You're right. Why am I even fighting

you? I have an eternity of sin to pay for, and I have evaded justice too long. If killing me will heal you in some way..." he got down on his knees. "Then so be it. I am sorry, Judas. Truly."

"My name is *Julian*!" He grabbed Lucas's skull and began to squeeze, cracking bone and compressing brain matter. Lucas almost welcomed the crushing oblivion, despite being terrified of it. He was beaten, not just physically, but spiritually, and if it had to end now, then that was okay. All that he had been put through since meeting Gladri in that alleyway...

Enough. I just want it to stop. Have I not suffered enough?

His eyes bulged from the pressure. His skull began to cave in. Black smoke billowed from his wounds.

Judas removed his hands and stepped back in shock. "You bleed darkness."

Lucas was woozy, and he crumpled forwards onto his hands. "All things bleed."

"You are *not* human. You... Did you deceive me once more? Did you convince me you were human when you have remained The Devil all along?"

"N-no..." Lucas's head buzzed. His vision filled with black smoke. Despite his weakness, he could feel his skull re-knitting itself and healing. You couldn't kill The Devil by crushing his skull it seemed.

"You are not human," said Judas, the cogs visibly whirring in his head. "Yes, it is true."

Lucas began to panic, not liking the look in the other man's eye. "No, I am not. I am—"

Judas struck the words from his mouth, backhanding him across the face. He placed a foot on Lucas's chest and pinned him to the ground. "I shall have your celestial soul after all, it seems. The Red Lord will change the very fabric of existence with me as his faithful servant. Yes, it shall be glorious. Any last words, Satan?"

"Yes," said Lucas, struggling with the foot pressing down on his chest. "I forgive you. And so does Jesus."

Lucas used the last of his strength to send out a message to Heaven that he prayed would get there.

The message read: HELP ME!

Last shot

Jake didn't like sitting around waiting like this. Thinking had always been his curse, and the more he thought, the more he hated himself. His mind had a talent for conjuring shame and remorse, and it was that talent which had led him to quell such emotions with drugs and alcohol. It was so long now that he couldn't tell if he had started out that way and took drugs, or if he took drugs and became that way.

All the same, he was sober now—and it hurt! It hurt because his mind recalled things in crystal clarity that he had spent years trying to suppress. The stream of misery began with the sight of his little sister snapping under the wheels of a speeding Volvo. Her eyes somehow locking onto his as her body slid across the gravelly road, leaving bloody streaks behind her. Then his mind reeled off all the innocent people he had intimidated and attacked, for slights as small as bumping into him at the pool table. The tale of misery ended with the attempted rape of a young girl outside a Chinese takeaway.

The memory of what he had done to Vetta was no longer murky. How could he ever make up for that? For everything? If he had never been born, the world would have been a better place. The euphoria of Lucas bringing him back from certain death had worn off, and now he was ready to die—eager even. It was what he deserved. It was what he wanted.

Anything but sitting here *thinking.*

He had to help Vetta.

Simon and Shaun were sitting on the ground beside Jake, but they didn't talk, just stared at the ground. That was why Jake was the only one who noticed when there was a shift in the strange haze blanketing the air. The mist seemed to part, to move away—particularly from the raised stone circle in front of them.

"Hey," he nudged Simon. "Hey guys, look!"

The other two men looked up, then immediately leapt to their feet. The dark cloud above the stone circle began to mold into shape before them.

Perhaps they should have run, but since meeting Lucas—The Devil pretending to be a cheeky Irishman with a soft heart, or some other trippy shit like that—they had been in constant danger. It was starting to feel normal, and there was little point in running in a place built entirely to screw with them. So, whatever was happening, they were ready to just get it over with.

The black cloud continued to take shape, slowly forming into the shape of a man. Then the darkness started to lighten, and the cloud possessed detail. Suddenly, a man stood before them with long brown hair and gentle features. He told them his name was Jesus, and that he was there to pass on a message. Lucas needed their help. They needed to hurry.

As soon as the image had formed, it unformed and returned to black smoke—and then disappeared altogether. The strange haze came back to fill the void it left.

"Was that really Jesus?" Shaun asked, blinking rapidly. "Jesus sodding Christ?"

"Don't think his middle name was *sodding*," said Simon.

"I don't know what that was," said Jake, wondering if it was one of Judas's games, "but I believe Lucas needs our help. Come on, let's go find him."

They went to make a move, but Shaun stayed where he was until Simon frowned at him. "What's wrong?"

"What if we *don't* help Lucas," he said. "If Judas kills him, maybe this will all be over. We're just caught in the middle of this thing, right?"

Simon actually seemed to think about it, astonishing Jake who assumed Simon was all up for giving Judas a beat down. Despite his reservations though, he didn't state agreement with Shaun. "Come on, man. We can't turn our backs on Lucas."

"Why not?" Shaun became animated, and Jake knew it was because he could sense his argument wasn't a lost cause. "Lucas is The Devil," he said. "I think we're on the wrong team. Even those monsters—the aswangs—are victims of his. Did you see them obey him like faithful dogs? We could just let this whole thing play out. Maybe it's the only shot we have left."

Simon looked at Jake and shrugged his beefy shoulder. "Man has a point. We've been following Lucas's lead this whole time, and it's done nothing but get people killed. Maybe we should have been working against him this whole time. If this is a good versus evil thing, surely The Devil is the bad guy?"

Jake hated that he saw the logic, but something in his gut told him it was all twisted. Lucas had been trying to protect them. And whether he had screwed it all up or not, intentions mattered. They had promised him their support, and he was relying on them, and Jake had enough of letting people down. He had done it his entire life and couldn't anymore.

"Look guys, I know I'm a screw up, but I have a feeling about this. Lucas fixed me, not just my wounds, but *me.* He gave me a chance to be free of all the poison in my past, and that doesn't sound like something an evil monster would do. I don't know much about Heaven and Hell, right and wrong, but I know that Lucas fixed me after Judas gutted me. Judas killed our friends, not Lucas, and I think, if we don't help him now, something really bad will happen."

Simon looked at Shaun and sighed, as if waiting for a counter-argument, but Jake didn't give anyone a chance to speak against him. "All of us have had second chances," he said softly. "None of us are the people we once were. Doesn't Lucas deserve a chance to change too?"

"Fine," said Simon, a little irritated, but nodding his head. "We've already wasted enough time. Let's get this done. Jerusalem isn't as pretty as I would have hoped anyway."

Jake chuckled. "It kind of stinks too. Lucas headed into that alleyway over there. He mentioned some steps. Let's go."

They took off at full-speed in a hurry to help The Devil.

What they hadn't counted on was the aswangs being back in the game. The hellish creatures were lined up in front of the alleyway, blocking their way to Lucas. Side by side, they seemed like an unholy football team, spindly limbs tapping the ground like studs, swollen skulls like helmets. Their dank black hair hung in front of them like towels.

Jake clutched his sword, checking it was still in his hand and hadn't evaporated when Lucas had left. Simon strengthened his grip on his axe over his shoulder and jutted out his beard. He really did resemble a Viking like Lucas had said. Shaun, with his tattoos and greying black hair, looked more like an emo vampire. Jake was the kid of the group. They made quite the bunch.

"Least this time we're armed with more than pool cues," said Shaun, readying his sword more confidently than he had against the scorpions.

"Looks like they forgot who their master is," said Jake.

"You gonna run again, man?" Simon asked Shaun. "I'd just rather know about it now."

Shaun hefted his sword, left and right. "I guess I'm done running. No matter how hard I try, it doesn't get me anywhere. I'm ready to go down swinging."

"Good man," said Simon. "Now let's get to work."

Like highland warriors, they charged the aswangs, outnumbered three to one, but roaring triumphantly at the top of their lungs. Jake plunged his sword straight into the breast of the biggest aswang he could see, and Shaun did the same next to him. Their silver blades withdrew from beast flesh easily—as light as a feather—and they continued slashing all around. Simon swung his massive axe and yelled obscenities at the aswangs. Jake grinned. It was the best fight he'd ever been in, and for once, he hadn't started it.

They just had to avoid getting ripped apart long enough to help Lucas. No problem, right?

⊥

LUCAS TRIED TO CRAWL AWAY, BUT JUDAS KICKED HIM INTO the air. The man had grown, power radiating from every inch of him. What was the source of his power? Where did Judas get his strength?

"How does that iron feel inside of you, Lucifer? Does it burn? It has reduced you to a mewing kitten. It was only supposed to bind you in place, but you lied about being human. You are still a creature deathly allergic."

"Stop this, Judas. The Red Lord seeks only to sunder God's creation. He cares not for the likes of you."

Judas shrugged. "No different to God then. What do I have to lose by serving another? Even if he breaks his deal and casts me down, I am no worse off than before. I've made deals with The Devil already, you'll remember. You condemned me, Satan, and God allowed it. My loyalty to Him was discarded."

"Loyalty?" Lucas laughed, even though he was writhing along on his belly like a crushed worm. "You killed God's only son."

"Enough! My life's only regret is that I betrayed Jesus. After his death, no action—good or bad—held relevance. Until now! Now, I shall change the course of human history, as I did once before. This time I shall not do so unwittingly."

Lucas crawled away but could do little else. He had used what strength remained sending out a plea to Heaven. It had been several minutes now, and help was yet to appear. Jake and the others hadn't come either. Were they still waiting for him? Or had they cut and run? He wouldn't blame them if that were the case, but if Judas managed to bring the Red Lord to Earth, they were all done for.

Perhaps that isn't such a bad thing. Change can be for the best. The world may already be too broken.

Lucas felt blasphemous for thinking it, but maybe God going into hiding had been the wrong decision. Mankind had failed to thrive in his absence. It only grew angrier at the injustice and cruelty inherent in its own nature. A new regime might not be so bad. Was humanity worth so much suffering?

Lucas was numb, but the delicate caress of Vetta's nails on his back replayed itself in his mind. The thought of her, and of all the other decent men and women he had witnessed throughout history, filled him with sadness. Sadness that human life was so fleeting. And what about the children? For the love of God, someone needed to think about the feckin' children.

Mankind is worth fighting for. I will fight for it.

Lucas climbed to his feet stiffly, pained all over. Judas stepped out of his way to give him some space, but it was obviously only so he could enjoy knocking him down all over again. He wasn't planning to rush this fight, and you had to give the fella props, Judas was delivering an ass-kicking to The Devil himself.

Lucas wiped his mouth, spitting black smoke instead of blood, then he smirked at Judas. "You know why I picked you? Why I knew you would be the one to betray Jesus? Because you're too arrogant to serve another. You betrayed Jesus because you envied what he had. You wanted people to bow down before *you* and not him, but the truth is that you're a bag of hot wind that no one gives two shits about. My curse only expanded what was already there—a conceited bore incapable of inspiring so much as a twig. You won't serve the Red Lord, Judas. You're only capable of serving yourself."

Judas sneered and grabbed Lucas with his bare hands, which was a mistake. Even without his powers, Lucas could still knee a fella in the clackers—and he caught Judas a beauty. The man folded like an accordion and struck his head on the low stone wall. It was enough to daze him. And while Lucas was unsteady, he knew enough to follow-through on his attack by throwing himself on top of Judas and raining down fists and elbows.

He quickly drew blood from above Judas's left eyebrow, and it buoyed him, for it proved that Judas was still just a man. Part rodent, maybe, but still just a man.

Judas cried out and tried to shield himself, a cowardly weakling unable to do anything but bleed. Yet, he was still wily enough to grab something from his belt and throw it in Lucas's face. The dust was heavy, more like grit than dander, and when it entered Lucas's eyes, it filled his head with screaming.

Judas kicked him away and got to his feet.

"Iron filings!" Judas cackled victoriously. "I have been preparing to fight The Devil for two-thousand years. You think a simple pummelling would be enough to stop me? You are doomed, Satan. This whole existence is doomed. It is finished."

Lucas could barely see. The blurry shape of Judas came towards him, but it was like looking through murky water. There was a red glow coming from somewhere, and inside that crimson light, Lucas sensed the presence of something truly terrible. Something utterly monstrous. A giant, crushing all before it into dust. A beast he had faced before. Recently, during his time in Hell.

The Red Lord.

One of the Three.

"Master, I serve you!" Judas bellowed in victory. "Accept my gift and come forth. Enter God's domain so that you may crush it, and in the ashes, rise."

Lucas jolted as fish hooks pierced his insides. He felt himself being pulled while held in place at the same time, wrenching his entire body. His vision swirled, and the world became a mess of sound and colour. His mind felt as though it was slipping away, and then coming back briefly before slipping away again. His soul burned.

His soul was being wrenched away and devoured. The Red Lord was coming forth, using Lucas as a hook to hold on to. Soon there would be nothing left of him. The world became dark, and he felt himself falling, losing himself. Everything was fading away. It felt like sleeping.

And all that was left was the sound of voices.

Only voices.

┼

JAKE MADE IT UP THE STAIRS FIRST, LIMPING SLIGHTLY FROM A gash on his thigh, but he immediately skidded to a halt when he reached the terrace. Shaun hit the back of him, then Simon bulldozed both men forward—but Jake barely noticed as his vision focused on what he was seeing.

Judas stood over Lucas, a great sphere of bright red light hovering between his hands. Inside the sphere was something terrible, something indescribable, something in no way of this earth—and it was tearing Lucas apart from the inside.

Lucas slumped on his knees, stone still as a stream of shining gold light spilled out of him and disappeared into the glowing red sphere. At his back, translucent wings shimmered, not really there, more like a memory replaying.

The Irishman had no idea they had arrived on the terrace to help, and luckily, neither did Judas.

"I told you," said Jake, whispering. "Some bad shit is going down. We need to stop this!"

"How do we know that thing isn't God?" said Shaun, wavering as he clutched an aswang bite-wound on his hip. "Maybe Lucas is being pulled back to Hell where he belongs."

Simon shook his head—the only one of them without an injury from their recent battle with the aswangs below. "Shaun, wake up, man! Whatever that thing is, it ain't God. Come on!"

Shaun let out a long, reluctant sigh. Then nodded. The three of them raced to help Lucas, almost like there had been an unspoken command that all of them had heard. Simon was quickest, and he shoulder-tackled Judas against the low stone wall. Jake and Shaun followed up by kicking the man on the ground. It felt low, booting a prone target, but if they let Judas get up, who knew what crazy shit he would unleash on them—the guy straight-up magicked a city into being.

The glowing red sphere had petered out as soon as Simon tackled Judas, and Lucas now slumped to the floor as if released by invisible ropes. Whatever had been happening to him was stopped, for now.

"This is for Max, you piece of shit!" shouted Shaun as he stomped Judas into mud.

"Where is Vetta?" Jake demanded, delivering a kick of his own.

Simon roared. "And this is for wasting my lunch break, asshole."

Judas threw out a hand desperately, not even looking up to see where they were. A flash of light dazzled them, and then began to burn. It sent them stumbling backwards, and Judas was able to get to his feet. He was bleeding all over but sneering irritably.

"You fools!" he cried. "I am Judas Iscariot. I have walked the Earth since civilisation was in its infancy. You think I can be beaten by a mob of grease monkeys!"

"Hey," said Jake, punching Judas in the face and stunning the arrogant sod. "That's *ex*-grease monkey to you!"

Judas slumped back against the low stone wall, clutching his long nose that was now bleeding. His hands were trembling, and he went to throw one out towards them.

"No, you don't," said Shaun, smacking Judas around the head and sending him back into a daze. "I've seen enough magic tricks for a lifetime."

"Fools!" Judas muttered. "You cannot defy me."

"We'll see about that," said Simon, grabbing Judas and hoisting him up onto his shoulder like a doll. "Time to fly."

With an effortless shrug of his shoulders, he tossed Judas over the low stone wall to the cobbles below. They heard the man's neck snap even from up on the terrace, and when they looked down, they saw Judas's body sprawled among the scattered corpses of a dozen butchered aswangs

—their weapons were still buried somewhere amongst all that demonic flesh.

Jake ran over to Lucas. The Irishman was no longer transfixed, but he was in a bad way—a hella bad way. "Lucas, we did it! Si threw that bitch right over the side."

Lucas gave a weak smile. "Serves the wee feck right."

"He's dead," said Shaun. "So, what do we do now? How do we get out of here?"

Lucas closed his eyes and moaned. Jake realised they were crowding him. "Give him some space, man. He's messed up."

"I... I'm dying," said Lucas.

Jake frowned. "No way."

"My body is breaking down. I thought it was the iron-poisoning from the scorpions, but it's not. My body is decaying because it's human."

"But you're *not* human anymore. You got your mojo back. You're the freakin' Devil."

Lucas reached out so that they could help him sit. "No... I didn't *become* The Devil. I summoned my celestial spirit into a human vessel, and it's been rotting away since. Why didn't I think what I was doing? I'm done for, but it's what I deserve. After what I did to Vetta..." He felt tears spill down his cheeks. "I don't have long left. Please, help me up." They got him standing. "Show me Judas."

Jake nodded. "Alright, man."

They helped him over to the low stone wall of the terrace, and Simon pointed to the streets below. "I dumped the bastard right over the wall. Right down... W-What the shite?"

There was no longer a body on the cobblestones below.

Lucas exhaled through his nose and gripped the wall

unsteadily. "It is as I fear. Judas cannot be killed. If he were dead, this place would cease to be, and we would have Vetta back. Jerusalem still stands, and thus, so does Judas. I have to die now before it's too late."

"What are you talking about?" Simon grabbed Lucas and stared at him. "What do you have to die for?"

"I am weak—too weak—and yet my celestial soul still resides within this human vessel. If Judas recovers and tries to take it from me again, I will be powerless to resist him. We cannot let him succeed. If the Red Lord—"

"Okay," said Simon. "We get it! End of existence and all that. You need to die to prevent the world becoming a dodgy Brad Pitt movie." The big man suddenly shrunk, appearing meek and exhausted. "What do you need us to do, Lucas?"

"Just help me up onto the wall."

None of them spoke. They just did what they were asked. Simon lifted Lucas from one side, while Jake got the other. Shaun placed a hand on his back to keep him steady. Lucas looked down at the harsh cobbles below—ready to end it all.

┼

So, this is it, THOUGHT LUCAS AS HE STARED DOWN AT THE hard cobbles below. This was to be his end, dashed to pieces next to where Jesus had once taught love and compassion. Lucas would die in the same city God's son had. Jerusalem was a place of death.

And rebirth.

He was human now. Would he die with a cleansed human soul, welcomed back into Heaven? Or would God let his soul perish forever? Lucas would accept either outcome, for both were more than he deserved. The Red Lord's assault on God was all his fault.

When Lucifer had incited civil war in Heaven, he had weakened the forces of Good substantially. All those angels killed, all the chaos and madness. It had given the Red Lord the opening he needed to breach God's protective barriers and start devouring the Earths.

One of the Three.

Lucifer and Michael's youngest brother. Crimolok. The Red Lord.

All knowledge of Crimolok had been erased from Heaven, dispelled from the mind of every angel, and yet... and yet it had all come rushing back to him in an instant.

Heavenly knowledge summoned forth into a human brain. Somehow, the crossed wires of whatever he now was had caused a glitch, and Crimolok's memory had returned. Finally, the Red Lord had a face.

And it was ruination and despair.

The worst Evil ever created.

The last born. The last of the Three.

It was a relief that he wouldn't be around to see the battles ahead. His part was over.

"It's been a pleasure," Lucas said to the three men who had helped him up onto the wall. "I hope you fellas find a way outta this. Sorry, I dragged you into my mess."

"Wait," said Shaun, eyes flickering with panic. "We might end up stuck here? For how long?"

Lucas shrugged. "Maybe forever, but hey, at least you have each other."

For once, Shaun didn't complain, he just stared at the city beyond, silently mortified. Lucas didn't really expect them to be trapped there forever. Judas would kill them before long, and whatever happened to them after was up to Heaven. As was the case with all men who die.

Lucas wished he got a chance to save Vetta, or at least say he was sorry. Unfinished business was an ill thing to take along with you.

A wind rose, caressing his face as he peered over the city of Jerusalem. It was a pleasant sensation to end on, and he was about to close his eyes to enjoy it, when he noticed the wind had brought something with it.

A blue feather.

It was out of place in the desert, more suited to a tropical bird than an arid one, but he was certain it was real, not a figment of his imagination. It seemed to direct itself directly towards him, fluttering determinedly on the wind.

Lucas snatched the feather out of the air and studied it. It looked so familiar. It *felt* familiar.

"Want us to push you?" Simon asked.

Lucas turned, thoughts flooding his mind. "What? No, just wait a second!" He held the feather up to them. "I think I have an idea—feck!"

The stone bricks beneath Lucas's feet crumbled, and he found himself floundering on the edge. He reached out his arms to grab someone, but it was too late. Simon and Jake snatched at him in vain as he tumbled backwards. He couldn't see the cobbles rising up to meet him as he fell, but he sure as hell felt them when his body shattered into pieces.

Passing Out

Jake, Simon, and Shaun were kneeling next to Lucas, and Vetta was there too! She hung upside down from the same inverted Crucifix Jake had, but she was held in place by iron cuffs instead of nails. When she saw Lucas, she screamed for him to help her—but he couldn't. He was slumped on his knees with the others either side of him, and all he could do was blink. He remembered falling—his body shattering on the cobbles. So where was he now? What was happening?

Fires burned from torches around the room. Iron pillars rose in each corner. It was the shrine room Judas had set up at the back of the pub. Somehow, Lucas and the others had ended up there.

Judas appeared in the centre of the room, cheeks ruddy, expression smug. "To think, you were once the master of deception," said Judas, seemingly delighted by this turn of events.

The man was unhurt, while Lucas felt like he had fallen

from a rooftop and shattered his bones against the cobbles. It had just been an illusion though, hadn't it? Jerusalem had been an illusion. His plummet to death had not really happened—even if it had felt like it.

"The terrace," he said, understanding he'd been tricked. "The terrace was this shrine room, wasn't it? You disguised it to trick me!"

Judas smirked. "But of course! I knew you had your celestial soul back the very moment you cast the spell in my bar. I had to get you in here to complete my ritual. It was almost done before these imbeciles interfered."

"*You're* an imbecile," Jake muttered under his breath.

Lucas struggled against his bonds. "I'm just borrowing The Devil. I'm still human."

"Even better. The soul will be even easier to take from you. I conjured Jerusalem to give you something to fight against, to wear yourself out while under the illusion you were making progress. By the time you made it up to the terrace, you were already exhausted and unable to put up a fight. Now you're hanging on by a mere thread. Let us cut that final string."

"You'll end existence if you allow the Red Lord to wipe out humanity! I know him. He is without compassion."

Judas rolled his eyes, more like a teenager than a bi-millennial. "Existence is relative. One is as good as another, and my situation can only improve."

Lucas shook his head, worried that blood was leaking from his nose and mouth instead of black smoke. He struggled with his bonds again, but he was tethered to an iron loop in the floor in front of him. His wrists were shackled together in his lap, and his hands bulged into fists as he tried to wrench them free.

"Billions will die, Judas. Don't you care? You cursed yourself by killing one man. What do you think killing an entire world will do to you?"

Judas plucked a hooked knife from inside his coat and tapped it against Vetta's exposed stomach. It was the same knife he'd gutted Jake with. "Do you know something I have learned over the last two-thousand years, Satan? I learned that the rules don't matter if you change them. I played by God's rules and was condemned. Rather than continue trying to succeed at a rigged game, I shall simply play something else. Something with a different set of rules."

"Oh, shut the hell up," Simon shouted. "You sodding moron."

Judas turned, stunned. "I beg your pardon?"

Simon appeared disgusted—even shackled to the ground and in peril. He glared at Judas as if the man were nobody. "All I've heard you do is blame other people for your own shite decisions. Boohoo, so you killed Jesus. Nobody forced you to. Nobody forced you to do anything these last two-thousand years."

"He did!" Judas pointed at Lucas. "He forced me to do the things I have done!"

"No, he never did! He fed you a con, and you fell for it. What you're really mad about is how gullible you were. Get over it already."

There was silence in the cramped space, and even Vetta stopped sobbing on the crucifix. Judas acted as though he'd been punched. It took several moments for him to gather himself. Once he had, his expression turned dark, and he marched over to his captives with the knife held in front of him.

Simon lifted his chin and squared his shoulders, getting as upright as he could on his knees. "Slit my throat, I don't give a shite. Won't change the fact that you're a whining moron! So, why don't you go and suck my big hairy—"

Judas slashed his hooked knife through the air, killing the words coming out of Simon's mouth. The sharp blade met flesh and tore through throat muscle like soft cheese. Blood spurted into the air and soaked them all.

Simon's eyes went wide. His lips trembled. And then he wept. "No!"

Shaun collapsed awkwardly onto his side, restricted by the bonds around his wrist. His eyes were stuck in a wide-open stare as his sliced throat gushed blood. He gurgled and tried to speak, but before he got close to forming a single word, his life passed away, and he went still—eyes wide open. The grey streaks in his hair turned red.

"You bastard!" Simon bellowed at Judas, raging against his bonds. "I'm gonna kill you!"

Lucas closed his eyes and prayed. He prayed to God to please forgive him for just one moment and help these people. Couldn't Heaven put grudges aside just this once and lend a hand?

Please! If not directly, then at least—

His thoughts tumbled away as he felt a cool breeze wash over him. There was a presence in the room, something large taking up the empty spaces. Lucas opened his eyes and saw something beautiful standing before him. Heavenly Aura washed over everything as Gladri materialised in the centre of the room—massive wings brushing against the ceiling.

Lucas couldn't believe it. His prayer had been answered—but how? How did Gladri know to find him here?

Lucas looked down at his clenched fists and slowly let them fall open. Inside his left hand lay a crumpled blue feather. The one that Gladri had shed last night and had somehow floated into the illusion of Jerusalem. A miracle?

Probably not. But I'll take it.

Gladri threw out a slender, velvet-skinned hand and sent Judas flying across the room. He struck the wall and immediately fell unconscious. A vile-smelling black cloud evaporated from his body. Lucas knew, at once, that Gladri had just removed the curse Lucifer had cast two-thousand years ago on Cavalry Hill.

Judas's immortality had just been surgically removed.

Gladri turned to Lucas and cast a rage upon him fierce enough to light the room. The torches around the perimeter flared. "Lucifer, you fool! I took away your soul for a reason, yet you reclaim it within a day! You reclaim it even after learning of this fiend's intention to devour it."

Lucas tried to pull his hands free from the cuffs. They were metal, but he didn't think they were iron. "I… I needed to help these people."

Gladri looked around, eyes settling on Shaun bleeding on the floor. "Human lives are not worth jeopardising all of existence. If the Red Lord succeeds, there will be *no* human life. You are a selfish fool, Lucifer."

Lucas nodded. He was done arguing with Heaven, had finally learned his lesson. "You're right, Gladri. My whole existence has been one of self-service. Even trying to be good, I was really just serving myself. I've never sacrificed. I've never given a part of myself to help another. Until today. So please, forgive my foolishness, and just help them. Help them!"

Gladri sighed, an action that sent a gust of wind through the small room. "Fine!"

The angel moved throughout the room, waving his slender, delicate hands indifferently. Simon and Jake were suddenly free of their bonds. They got up, rubbing at their wrists. Simon rushed over to Shaun and shook his friend.

"That one is already gone," Gladri told him.

"You're an angel," said Simon. "Fix him!"

Gladri glared at Simon, intolerant of being commanded by a mortal. He looked more demon than angel. "And drag him away from Heaven? This man was your friend—is that what you want for him? He has earned his reward, but you would take it from him?"

Simon peered at Shaun, then slowly lifted his wet eyes back to Gladri. "He... He's in Heaven?"

"I can recall him, if you wish?"

Simon shook his head. "No... No." He smiled slightly, then crossed Shaun's arms across his chest and stroked his cheek. "Let him rest."

Next, Gladri turned to Lucas, but Lucas waved him away. "No, help her!" He pointed at Vetta. "Help her!"

"Not yet, Lucifer. There is something you have that no longer belongs to you." Gladri threw out an arm, making Lucas scream as black flame burned out of him. His celestial soul fed him once more, and his insides felt lighter. "You endangered us all," barked Gladri. "Do not seek to reclaim your past again. It is gone from you forever. Do you understand?"

Lucas couldn't catch his breath to speak, but he nodded. He wanted Heaven to know he was done fighting. He would accept whatever fate he had coming and be thankful for it

—just so long as Heaven helped him right now. "Vetta! P-Please."

Looking increasingly irritated, Gladri turned to Vetta and waved his hand. She didn't fall free from the crucifix as intended, however, and Gladri frowned. "I cannot free her, brother. Her bonds are of iron."

"Then unshackle me and *I'll* help her! I'm human. I can touch iron." Lucas strained at his bonds. Now that he was no longer possessed by a celestial presence, his human flesh was recuperating rapidly. He was getting back his strength.

"You're not merely human, Lucifer," said Gladri. "Is all not yet clear? Are you truly so blind?"

"W-What?" Lucas paused, torn between saving Vetta and hearing a grand truth that Gladri seemed poised to reveal. "J-Just untie me," he said. "We'll deal with the denouement later! First, I have to rescue the girl."

Gladri chuckled and shook his head. "As petulant as always but have it your way."

Gladri raised an arm to Lucas, intending to free his bonds, but before his hand got halfway up, the angel shuddered and bucked. Something flashed across his beautiful white throat and golden light spilled out like hot blood. Gladri's glacial eyes pulsed, showing more emotion than they had since the dawn of time. Something was wrong.

Judas stepped out from behind Gladri, holding the hooked knife in his hand. Lucas realised then that it had been forged from folded steel and iron with a vein of silver running along its edge—a weapon forged to take down angels and demons. You couldn't kill an angel with a knife, but the iron was enough to devastate Gladri temporarily, and silver acted as an amplifier.

The angel froze in place, shuddering in pain while Heavenly Aura leaked out through his sliced throat. Simon and Jake helped each other up and rushed at Judas, but Judas shoved them casually away with a blast of air from his palm.

Then he conjured the red sphere again.

Gladri's chest cracked apart in a vortex of golden light. The light drained out into the red sphere. Inside the orb, something terrible fed—the mouth of a worm suckling at a rotten breast.

Lucas screamed. "No! Judas, stop!"

Judas sneered at Lucas, with black and oily malice swirling in his eyes. "It is already done."

More golden light flowed out of Gladri and into the red sphere. Judas stood there, smiling, looking about himself like he expected something to happen. There was a sudden *snap* as the sphere yanked the last of the golden light from Gladri and closed like a blinking eye.

Judas appeared confused, and when nothing else seemed to happen, his sneer fell to confusion. "W-What is happening?" he muttered. "Red Lord, I have given you what you wanted. It is done! Come forth and consume this place!"

While this was happening, Jake crawled stealthily over to Lucas, and then started yanking at his bonds. Between the two of them, they were able to pull the cuffs open, and Lucas got free.

Jake was hurt, winded badly, but he managed to stand. Lucas got up beside him and patted the lad on the back. They needed to let Judas know they were back in the game.

Lucas laughed at the man in a mocking tone. "If you think

the soul of a Heavenly bureaucrat like Gladri is worth the same as mine, you're a fool, Judas. I am Lucifer, one of The Three. I was the second angel born into existence. I am closer to God than all but the two brothers born with me. My celestial soul is caviar. Gladri's was popcorn chicken! You big feckin' eejit!"

Judas was at a loss, but he soon recovered. Two-thousand years of set backs had given the man a talent for reacting.

He strode towards Lucas, hands already summoning dark energy at his sides. Lucas moved to meet him, his own hands no longer able to wield power, but ready to wage war in whatever way they could.

But Judas was too fast. Lucas was no match for his power.

Judas threw up a hand and froze Lucas in place, compacting his bones with the minutest movement of his fingers. "I could break you right now!" He sneered, spittle flying from his lips. "Whether or not the Red Lord is sated, he is fed, and more powerful than ever before. He will reward my loyalty, and even more so once I remove you from the battles to come. First though, I shall see agony leak from you until you are a puddle on the floor. This is my moment, Satan. This is my redemption."

Lucas tried to move, but he couldn't. It was like when Gladri had held him in place outside in the alleyway. Gladri had frozen him to enact a punishment. Judas was doing so to exact revenge. Even after two-thousand years, it all just boiled down to one simple thing—hatred. The strongest of all human emotions.

But Judas moved away from Lucas, leaving him frozen. He turned his sights toward Vetta, a salacious glint in his eye. She was hanging upside down, sinews bulging in her neck—a tied lamb about to be slaughtered.

Lucas was too frozen to scream.

But Vetta wasn't. She screamed without end.

Judas smashed her in the face with his knee, then placed the edge of his hooked blade against her belly. He drew it playfully along her flesh, scratching but not cutting. As he spoke, he kept his gleeful stare on Lucas.

"Before I *end* you, Satan, I shall make you watch while I disembowel every one of these pathetic maggots you have tried to save. I shall show you what impotence truly feels like. Starting with her."

Lucas fought to move. He used every muscle fibre to try and get free, refusing to be controlled by a monster like Judas—a monster he had made—but the spell cast upon him was unbelievably strong. Desperately, he searched for that light, that energy, which had allowed him to heal Jake. Gladri had said he was more than merely human. He needed to find out what that meant.

It was time to finally find out who he was.

Judas lifted the knife and poised it over Vetta's navel. She squirmed and begged, but it only made Judas's grin wider. He licked his lips as he lifted the blade high above his head. There, he let it linger for a moment, sharp edge catching the light from the shrine room's torches. Then, without word, he plunged the knife downward, towards Vetta's navel.

Vetta screamed. Lucas fought, concentrated, prayed. But he couldn't move. Not even an inch.

No!

Jake threw himself against Judas and knocked the man aside. The wicked blade had been about to sink deep into

Vetta's flesh, but it missed and struck thin air. Judas had been taken by surprise, which allowed Jake to get in a punch, knocking the man down on his ass.

"It's wrong to hurt a lady," Jake growled. "Trust me, I know!"

Judas howled as Jake kicked him in the ribs. The lad had transformed back into the thug that had attacked Lucas and Vetta last night, but this time, his moral compass was pointed in the right direction. His fury was righteous. Jake raised his fist again and prepared to knock Judas's lights out. But Judas clambered to his knees and threw himself forwards, clinching with Jake like a winded boxer. Air exploded from Jake's cheeks as Judas's shoulder knocked the wind out of his sails. He beat at the man's back, but his blows were weak.

Lucas felt a slight movement in his neck, the hold on him lessening as Judas's focus turned elsewhere. Jake had got in some licks, but now he was stumbling about like a blind man and out of the fight.

At first it was unclear why he was stunned, but then he turned to reveal the hooked blade sticking out of his stomach. Judas placed a hand around the handle and yanked it free, pulling coils of Jake's intestine with it. It was the second time he had gutted the lad.

Jake got down on the floor, almost leisurely, and stared into space. Judas stood over the lad and glowered. "You dare put your hands on me, boy! A wastrel like you? I'll spread your entrails across my bar and use your skull as a urinal."

Jake put a hand up somehow despite his injuries. He was fading fast, skin already pale, but his eyes were wide and alert.

"Wait! You're right. I'm a... a mess. But only because this world has screwed me over again and again. My whole life has been a misery because of rules I can't follow. You think I care about God, or angels? I got dragged into this shit. Just like I've been dragged into other people's shit since the moment I was born. It makes me so... so *fucking* angry. Help me."

Judas appeared disgusted. "I'll slice your throat and all your pain will go away."

"No, don't let me die, man. I want to fight for your cause. I don't care about this screwed up world any more than you do. You say God is the reason for all of the crap and misery, then I want to see a change too. Let me help you hit restart on this motherfucker. It's going to be lonely otherwise."

Judas seemed incredulous. "You just attacked me, you maggot! You expect me to recruit you?"

Jake took a moment too long and Judas went to cut him. He put his hands out just in time to dissuade the man again. "No! Please, man, just..." he nodded at Vetta—still upside down on the crucifix. "I... I got a thing for the Pole tart. I didn't want to see her get hurt. That doesn't mean I'm with this asshole!" He gestured to Lucas. "I acted to save *her*, not to stop *you*."

Judas raised an eyebrow and seemed to think. He looked at Vetta with a suspicious squint. The scrunching up of his face made his unpleasant face even uglier. "I could give her to you, you know? I could heal you and make her your slave forever. My power is vast. You would not believe it."

Jake grinned lecherously, although in obvious pain—his intestines lay in his lap. That he was still lucid was an act of pure determination, and perhaps the effects of the cut being so surgically clean. "If you help me, man, you'll have already given me more than anyone else ever has. I'll have your back for life; I swear it. Every powerful person needs followers. Give me the Pole tart, and I'll be your soldier."

"You monster," shouted Vetta. "I would never be with you, Jake."

Judas glanced at Vetta and seemed amused. When he turned to Jake again, he was full on smiling. "I shall see the world destroyed, boy. Would you truly betray everything you've ever cared about?"

Jake winced, starting to succumb to the pain of his mortal wounds. "God took the last thing I cared about when he let my sister die."

Lucas swore at the lad. His invisible bonds continued to loosen as he fought with them, but he had to be careful not to reveal that he was getting free. Yet, he couldn't help but scream at the lad, which betrayed that he had regained the ability to speak.

"Jake, you bastard! You had a chance to be better than this!"

Judas stopped smiling and became serious. He folded his arms, bloody knife pointed in the air. "Hmmm, yes... Satan used an act of betrayal to condemn Jesus to death. It seems fitting he should be undone by betrayal himself. I shall heal you, Jake, but if you make a single move towards me, I shall place you in a white-hot cell and keep you burning there for eternity. Take my hand."

Judas reached out to Jake, and Jake, in trembling agony, reached out and accepted it. His wounds began to heal—as quickly as when Lucas had fixed him. He miraculously made it up to his knees, keeping hold of Judas's hand and shaking it vigorously. "Thank you, man. You won't regret this."

Judas sneered. "I never regret anything."

"We'll see!" Jake's tone changed. He yanked Judas's hand and pulled the man off balance. The exertion caused his guts to spill out again, his body not yet fully healed by Judas, but he did not let go. He kept yanking Judas off balance.

"Now, Si. Do it now!"

"What is the meaning of—" Judas fought to get his hand back, but before he could free himself, Simon appeared behind him and drove the iron nail from Jesus's cross into his neck. The big man had been keeping hold of it ever since Lucas asked him too outside the gates of Jerusalem, and he hadn't forgotten its power.

Judas was human, and therefore unaffected by the iron itself, but the wound in his neck was deep, and he was losing blood fast. He swiped out with his hooked blade but didn't seem to have a target. Simon whacked the man's arm with his big fist and sent the knife clattering to the ground.

Now Judas was dazed and unarmed.

Lucas finally broke free and raced over to help. He was about to strike Judas, his fists wound up and ready to unleash hell, but instead, he stopped and froze on the spot again. This time it was by his own doing.

No more blood. This has to stop.

"Judas, you're finished. The Red Lord hasn't arrived, and you're mortally wounded. You might have a lot of power, but you're not immortal anymore. Gladri removed the curse I placed on you two-thousand years ago. You're dying. So stop fighting; it's time to talk."

Judas clutched at his bleeding neck, hissing in pain. His

words were thick with saliva. "I will not make the mistake of... of listening to The Devil again. Just finish me off, you vile creature."

Lucas took a step back, hands out in front of him. "I don't want to see you die, Judas. I wronged you—and if you truly believe it will bring you peace, then pick up that blade and cut my throat. I won't fight you."

Jake and Simon looked at each other in horror, but Lucas hoped it wouldn't come to that. It wasn't a bluff—he would really go through with it—but more like faith in things turning out okay. They had to.

"Or you can finally let go of all your anger and try to find peace. I've been where you are, Judas. You blame other people for your crimes, and you are indeed a victim of the past, but what happens tomorrow is down to you. Forgive me, Judas, and I shall forgive you."

"Are you crazy?" said Simon, standing with the iron nail ready to stab. "After all this guy has done? Max, Annie... *Shaun*!"

Lucas sighed at Simon. "Will spilling his blood change anything? If Judas decides to be different, he could one day do some good. If he dies, then death is all he will have ever given the world."

Judas was shaking his head like he couldn't believe what he was hearing. It seemed to be dawning on him that he was actually dying and that the blood coming out of him was real. As much as he seemed afraid, he also seemed relieved, like a cancer had been removed from his soul.

His words were venomous, and yet they seemed to lack any genuine bite. "Are you mad?" he whispered. "Just kill me and be done with it! This world is not a place for mercy.

If you don't end me here, then I vow to end *you* one day, Satan. The Red Lord—"

"Is just another master you don't want, Judas. When we met, you were a good man who wanted to protect this world. Be that man again. Earn the salvation I took from you and be proud of who you are once again. Only then can you truly beat me and overcome what I did to you."

Judas was weakening, physically and emotionally. He collapsed onto his side, heaving and gasping. He waved a hand, and the shackles around Vetta's legs and wrists popped open. She tumbled to the ground awkwardly, arms and legs tangled. With that done, Judas closed his eyes and moaned. "Just... get it... over with."

"Let me heal you," said Lucas. "Let me take away your pain. We can let Judas die, but Julian can live on."

"No! No, I... I want to die. I want it to be done. Hell finally awaits me."

Lucas knelt over him. "It doesn't have to be that way. You have one last life to live, and you could make it count. You could outweigh all the bad with a single lifetime of Good. It only takes one man to change the world for the better. Just look what Jesus achieved. Be his student again and spread his teachings as he wished you to."

Judas huffed and gave a pained laugh. Bloody drool slung from his mouth. "You compare me to Jesus?"

"Jesus was just a man. You can be just a man too."

Judas nodded, eyes drooping. "Yes, I... I would like that very much."

"Then just say yes!"

Judas was falling unconscious, cheek against the ground. "Y-Yes. Yes!"

Lucas reached out his hands, knowing he could heal

this man—not just his bodily wounds, but also the ones inflicted on his mind. The power was still within him, he could feel it. He was more than merely human. All this pain and suffering could be put right.

In the corner of his eye, Lucas spotted Vetta crawling on her hands and knees. She retrieved something from the ground and began hurrying towards Judas. Something glinted in the firelight.

Lucas threw his hands up at Vetta and shouted. "Vetta, no! Don't do it!"

But it was too late.

┼

JUDAS JOLTED, THE VEINS IN HIS NECK BULGING AS HIS OWN hooked knife plunged deep into his heart. Vetta had attacked him from behind, wrapping her arm around his shoulder and striking at his chest while he lay on the ground. She was a wild animal as she yanked the knife free so she could plunge it in a second time. And then a third. Eventually she was stabbing a corpse—over and over again.

Lucas reached out to her, hands trembling as he worried she might suddenly turn the blade on him, intentionally or not. "Vetta, love, it's over. You killed him as dead as he's gonna get."

Vetta's eyes bore into Lucas, feral and animalistic. She looked like a beautiful, frightening demon. Simon appeared beside her, placing a thick hand around her wrist. He did so gently, and slowly, so that Vetta eventually let go of the knife still jutting out of Judas's chest. Then, all at once, she collapsed into herself, sobbing and shaking in Simon's meaty arms.

Lucas watched as Judas slowly lurched forwards onto his face, and the sound of his skull clonking against the ground made him wince. So much blood. So much death. Not just now, but throughout human existence. Why had God made something so wonderful, only to obfuscate it with pain?

Lucas was determined to find the answer.

But not today. Not now.

Gladri lay on the floor, still alive, but his vast wings decaying to dust. Yet, despite his approaching death, the angel stared up at the ceiling calmly, contemplatively. Lucas dragged himself over to his brother with tears in his eyes.

"Gladri, you live still?"

"A while longer it would seem. Long enough to contemplate my failures, brother."

Lucas shook his head. "You have none."

"The Red Lord grows fat on my soul. What is left of me is soon to expire."

"Your soul lives before me, Gladri. It speaks to me."

Gladri blinked. "Not the part that matters. Soon I shall slip away to air and dust," he sighed, "but you must live on, Lucifer."

Lucas blinked and more tears cut down his cheeks. "I am sorry. It should be me lying in your place. I... I caused all this. When I went to war against Heaven, I gave Crimolok the opportunity he needed to invade. This all started thousands of years ago."

"Who do you speak of, brother?"

Lucas shook his head. "It doesn't matter. This is all my fault. I should be the one to suffer."

Gladri spoke his next words in a tone of amusement. "No, brother. It is *you* who must live on. *You* who is important. Dark days lie ahead, and it is to you this world will turn. Hold back the coming oblivion."

"What are you talking about?" Lucas demanded. "You cursed me to be human to keep me from interfering. Heaven wished me to be impotent. Now you say I must act?"

Gladri closed his eyes, a peaceful smile on his thin, silvery lips. His wings were now mere cinders ebbing away to nothing, which left him looking like a tall and slender man with unnaturally pale skin. "Not impotent, brother—merely *different*. You have been given humanity as a punishment, yes, but also to help you with what lies ahead. Only humanity can protect humanity. Shield this world from harm, or all shall fall to ruin. The abyss awaits, but we must avoid it at all costs. *Hastam in Caelum.*"

The Latin phrase sent ice through Lucas's veins. Had he misheard? "Brother, what did you just say?"

"Strike where you are needed, Lucifer. Wield God's wrath as if it were your own. Do this, and redemption shall be yours."

Lucas's mind was awash with thoughts buzzing like a cloud of locusts. What Gladri was saying could not be true. Heaven sought to twist his fate yet again, but this time, he was willing to play along. He needed to put things right. That was the only way he could ever hope to atone. He placed a hand against Gladri's alabaster cheek. The angel was ice-cold. "My name is Lucas, brother. If Heaven seeks my help, it can bloody well ask me for it properly."

Gladri bucked, life at an end, but his gasps turned to laughter. "Impudence! Has endless penance done nothing to change you?"

"Not a jot!" Lucas grinned, but was also firm in his defiance. "I am the same as I have ever been."

"Then perhaps this world has half a chance. So be it, Lucas. Heaven begs your assistance. Help us... Please."

Lucas had been waiting for this moment for thousands of years. His eternity finally had an end in sight and time held meaning once more. Actions mattered. Tomorrow mattered. What he did now could finally make a difference. Heaven was finally willing to accept him as ally instead of adversary.

He smiled at Gladri and kissed his forehead. "Sorry, brother, I won't help Heaven." Gladri sputtered, but Lucas kept on. "But I will help these people. I will fight for them, for this world. For humanity."

Gladri's sputtering stopped, and he gradually settled, and then smiled. "That shall have to be enough then. Good luck, brother. May your days ahead be brighter than those behind you."

"And yours, brother. Enjoy your peace."

Gladri was dead. His wings disappeared, and his body began to crumble. Soon it would be as if he had never existed—a being old beyond imagination, gone in moments. Simon and Vetta sat in a huddle by the wall, watching in awe.

Sensing things were over, Simon spoke. "If... if Gladri had his soul taken, how was he still here to talk to you?"

Lucas watched his brother fade away to dust, and then looked up at his remaining companions. "Angels have a celestial soul born of Heaven and an inner-soul born of themselves. You cannot remove an inner-soul, for it is their identity. No one can take away who you are. It was Gladri's power and essence that the Red Lord consumed—not *who* he was but *what* he was. The Red Lord is my younger brother, Heaven's forgotten abomination, and he is more powerful now than ever. My task of taking him down will likely be impossible, but I will try. Feck it, I will give it all I got."

"Why is it *your* job?" said Simon. "How could you hope to fight that thing we saw in the red sphere? It was terrible. Why do *you* have to fight it?"

"Because I'm Heaven's Spear. And because I caused this. When I led a war against God, I weakened Heaven and distracted God from more powerful enemies. Billions have died since that day. I had no idea the damage I was causing."

Vetta managed to find her voice. Some of the wildness had fled from her eyes, and she seemed less panicked. There was blood on her hands that she had been staring at. "What does this thing mean? Heaven Spear?"

Lucas shook his head, hardly believing what Gladri had called him—but the angel had been clear. "I am the second coming," he said, awe-struck by the very notion. "Jesus Christ was the *Messiah*—humanity's saviour. I am *Hastam in Caelum*—humanity's protector. It means existence has reached its conclusion, and whatever happens next is unknown. Fate is whatever we make for ourselves now, and we'll have to fight for every day."

Simon knelt back down beside Shaun. Blood pooled all around him, but Simon didn't seem to care as it soaked his jeans. He looked up at Lucas. "Was the angel telling the truth about Shaun going to Heaven?"

Lucas nodded. "Angels can't lie—or rather, they *can* but would never dare to."

"You were an angel," said Vetta. "You lie."

"Aye, and that's why I don't have wings anymore."

Vetta moved over to Jake then and looked at him. His guts were poking out beneath his blood-soaked shirt, and his eyes were stuck wide open. "He saved me," she said. "At the end, he saved me."

Simon sat with his arms draped over the top of his knees and seemed solemn. "I'm glad he got to go out on a good note. Gives me something to remember him by."

"Very few souls are born bad," Lucas told them. "Jake was just the end result of bad decisions and worse luck. His life could have turned out a million different ways. I hope what he did at the end gave him a clean slate with Heaven."

"I hope so too," said Vetta, and then turned away from his body. She moved over to Lucas and asked him, "What now? How we leave this place?"

"Through the door." Lucas pointed. At the edge of the shrine room now lay a normal wooden door with a brass handle. Whatever charms Judas had placed on the room had been extinguished. The torches had gone, and instead, a light bulb swung overhead. No one had noticed the change.

Simon staggered over to the door. "Can't wait to go home and get my arse in the shower. Then I have to figure out a way to explain..." He looked back at his dead friends. "Everything."

Vetta followed Simon, and Lucas saw no reason to stay either, so they headed out the door, relieved to find themselves in a normal looking back-office of a pub. Their relief continued when they made it out from behind the bar and found everything looking normal in the lounge. Unremarkable. Ordinary.

"Nice knowing you," said Simon, picking up speed as he

headed for the pub's front entrance. He grabbed the handle so hastily he almost missed, but then he gave it a hearty yank and pulled open the door as his face turned upwards towards the sun.

The streets of Jerusalem met them.

It wasn't over yet.

The Morning After

Simon took one look outside before turning around and shaking his head. It was unclear whether he was angry or broken. Vetta remained beside Lucas, staring out at the desert city.

"I thought it was finished," she said.

Her words stung Lucas, not because they were unkind, but because they seemed so disappointed in him. After all they had been through, he still hadn't been able to end this. "Judas is dead," he said, "but the spell he cast isn't. What am I missing? What source of power is so deep that it remains in place even after the wielder has died? It must be something truly ancient, something tied directly to Hell—or Heaven. Maybe..."

His mind began to put the pieces together. It was so obvious. Of course, there was only one object that could have given Judas such vast and endless power. An object tied to God himself—by way of his son.

The nail.

Lucas whirled on Simon who was now sitting at the bar. "Big guy! You still have that chunk of iron on you?"

Simon frowned, not understanding, but then seeming to twig. "You mean the nail? Yeah, I still have it. I'm hardly going to let go of the one thing that has got us through most of this shit. It's right here..." He pulled it out and placed it on the bar. "In my pocket.

Lucas approached slowly, now more in awe of the nail than ever. This small chunk of iron had Jesus's blood on it. God's only human son. It was ugly and twisted, and yet so beautiful. "I think this might just be the most powerful thing in existence. The reason Judas was so powerful was because he harnessed a link to Heaven, not Hell as I assumed. To harness Heaven on Earth is to possess a power equal to angels."

Simon nudged the nail towards Lucas. "You're welcome to it. Just use it to get us out of this, and then I would like to win the lottery."

"I would like to win lottery too," said Vetta, and she didn't seem to be joking.

Lucas took the nail, sure now that he could feel it buzzing with power. "Maybe, let's just start with getting us out of this first, yeah?"

Vetta looked worried. She had her arms folded as she spoke to him. "So, what do we do? You can use the nail to get us home, yes?"

Lucas looked at the nail in his hand and was forced to shrug his shoulders. "Judas used it to create a false reality. That's pretty powerful mojo, even for someone as old as me. I need to try and remove the binding."

"How?" asked Simon.

"Only God knows—and he ain't talking. Suppose old Lucas will just have to wing it! Silence please, folks."

Vetta and Simon didn't talk, they just watched Lucas intently. Lucas asked for theatrics only to distract himself from the gravity of the situation. If he failed to remove the spell, they would be trapped there until they starved to death.

He squeezed the nail in his fist and concentrated—sought that stream of power that had helped him before, that narrow link to Heaven Gladri had left him with. The same link Jesus Christ had once been able to harness? Were they truly the same, two sides of a single coin?

No, Jesus was here to spread peace.

I am here to fight a war. Heaven's Spear. I need to put a stop to this. There is too much work ahead of me to be delayed.

Lucas opened his eyes again. He wasn't sure if anything had happened, but he had felt... *something.*

Vetta touched his arm and made him flinch. "Lucas, look!"

The pub's rear exit was rattling. The front door slammed shut and made them yell.

"That don't feel good," said Simon, getting up from his stool and looking back and forth.

Vetta moaned. "Please, I just want to go home. I want to speak to my mama."

Lucas reached out and took her hand. He squeezed it tightly, as much for his own sake as hers. "I'll get you there, lass. I promise."

The door shook again as a massive blow struck against it. Something was coming in. The three of them backed up against one another and prepared for a fight—a fight they had been praying would not come. The nightmare was not yet over.

The door flung open. Something stepped inside. Two figures.

Large, imposing.

Smiling.

Vetta saw her friends and raced over to them, throwing her arms around them and squealing. Lucas recognised the two men immediately as part of the friendly group he had drunk with last night. The one not hugging Vetta seemed embarrassed, and he blushed as he spoke. "I hear talking inside, but door is stuck. I kick. I do not mean to break."

Simon was beaming. "Nothing wrong with a bit of force, mate. We've been trapped inside here a while. It's been the lock-in from hell."

Lucas realised he was smiling too. He wasn't sure he would ever get used to his body doing things on its own without his conscious directives, but right now, it felt good. Unfamiliar emotions rushed through him, but for once, he didn't want them to go away.

He went and shook the hands of the two Polish fellas and told them how glad he was to see them again. "Can I get you fellas a drink?" he said, looking past them to see the busy chip shop outside. Its queue went right out the door.

They were home again.

And Lucas was going to do whatever he had to do to protect it.

⊥

IT WAS A WEEK LATER WHEN LUCAS SAW VETTA AGAIN. SHE came into the pub—recently renamed *the Black Spear*—and spotted him standing behind the bar. The shock on her face took several seconds to wear off before she approached. "L-Lucas, I didn't think I would ever see you again."

He was polishing a glass, but he placed it down on the bar to speak to her. He wasn't quite sure what to do with his hands, so he put them in his pockets. "Aye, it's a little harder for me to get around these days, so thought I would stay put. Heard there was a pub without an owner, so decided to try my hand this side of the bar for a change."

She frowned. "You buy bar?"

He shrugged. "Place is still registered to a one *Julian Elms*, but as long as I keep the paperwork up to date, and the taxes on this place paid, I'm sure no one is going to have much reason to fuss. Tell you the truth, I didn't know where else to go. Can I get you a drink?"

Vetta sat on a stool and nodded. "Vodka, please. So, you are just barman now?"

"As noble a calling as any, lass."

"But you are *special*. You are supposed to be fighting bad things, yes? When we finally break Julian's spell, you say you have work to do. I thought I would never... You stayed here!"

Lucas saw the hurt in her eyes. He should have reached out to her already. "I've been planning to get in touch, lass, I promise you. Just needed to get my house in order first—or my bar, such as it is. Every day I have wanted to knock on your door and tell you I'm here, but..." He sighed. "Vetta, lass, I don't want you involved in the shit-storm coming my way. I've hurt you enough already."

While he'd been talking, he had poured her vodka. She took it from him and clutched it tightly. Her hand was shaking slightly, and she glared at him. "World is ending, yes? Big war with Heaven, angels, monsters, God, lots of craziness, yes?"

"Aye, lass, you could say that."

"Then I am involved whether I like or not! Everyone is involved. If war is coming, then how can you fight it alone?"

"Because it's my job, lass. I don't have a choice. You do."

She shook her head, then swept an arm over the busy room. Business was good, but that's not what she was indicating. "These people don't know what is coming. I do. I know. You took away my blindness when you dragged me into your fight with Judas. I cannot go back to being blind."

Lucas studied her face and realised it wasn't as delicate or as pretty as before. She was harder. Tougher. In fact, she was stronger than he gave her credit for. She had peered into Hell and had not closed her eyes. It was wrong to shut her out. He chewed at his lip for a second, then sighed. "Want a job?"

Vetta flinched. "What?"

"Lucas needs himself a wench behind the bar. He can't bring the fellas in on his own."

"That's... sexist."

"Aye, but I'm from an older generation where that kind of thing is alright. You in?"

"I... yes, I would like job. I start now?"

"No time like the present. Get yourself behind the taps, lass, and old Lucas will show you the ropes."

Vetta got up from her stool and headed for the hatch. Before she made it behind the bar, she was knocked aside by a figure in a hoodie. The stranger moved quickly and made it over to Lucas before anyone could stop him. Beneath the hoodie, two burning-red eyes glared. Gnarled fingertips reached for Lucas, silver-tipped and razor-sharp. One slash at his throat would be the end.

"Ah shite!" Lucas said, readying himself to feel the pain.

Before the stranger could swipe at Lucas, his attacker flew sideways into the bar. A large man appeared from the staff door behind the bar and grabbed the hooded figure by the neck, slamming his head into the bar several times before letting his motionless body slump to the ground.

Then Simon turned to the pub's drinkers and put a large hand up in the air. "Nothing to see here, folks. Just some idiot we barred last night. Looks like he took it personally."

The drinkers were wide-eyed, but they gradually went back to their conversations. Simon and Lucas stood behind the bar, staring down at the unconscious stranger at their feet. Vetta hurried through the hatch to join them. "Simon!" she said, confused.

"Oh, yeah, right," said Lucas. "Simon's been helping me get set up here."

The big man shrugged at Vetta. "Shaun's gone. I needed something to do with my nights."

"You saved my backside there," said Lucas. "Don't go thinking you're due a raise though."

Simon tapped the unconscious stranger with his boot. "Who is he?"

Lucas sighed. "Just the first of many. The war has already begun."

"He doesn't look human," said Vetta, not looking afraid by Lucas's comment.

Lucas noted the silver fingernails. "This here, is an agent of the Black Strand. A tad unprofessional by their standards, but they must have thought I'd be an easy target.

I'd take offence, but they've done far worse in their time than underestimate me."

"Who are the Black Strand?" asked Simon.

Lucas sniffed. "They're first in line. You both ready for a fight?"

Simon was grinning. "I like to kick things. I'm with you, man."

Vetta nodded reluctantly, but then more assuredly. "Gheorghie was my friend. A monster killed him. I want to stop the monsters."

Lucas gave them a lopsided grin. "Then Team Lucas is complete."

Simon patted him on the back, rocking him against the bar. "We'll work on the name later, boss."

"Aye," said Lucas. "Names are important. We should get it right."

They all stood there, thinking, until someone knocked a knuckle against the bar. "Hey! Can I get a drink here, please, mate? Where the hell is Julian anyway? This place is a fucking circus since he's been gone."

Lucas turned to the customer and gave the young man a grin. There was blood on the bar from the skull Simon had just cracked against it, so he grabbed a rag and began cleaning it. "Oh, Julian had to go on an unexpected trip. Don't expect him back any time soon."

The lad scowled as if he didn't like the answer. Lucas realised then that it was one of the two lads who had attacked him with Jake in the alleyway. "So, who the fuck are you?" he demanded of Lucas. "You look familiar, innit?"

"Lot of people say that." Lucas offered his hand over the bar.

The lad frowned but took it eventually. As soon as their

palms touched, Lucas saw it all—the lad's entire history in the blink of an eye.

"The name's Lucas," he said. "This is my bar. And you, sonny boy, will behave yourself, or end up like your old man shanked in the prison showers." He yanked the lad's hand, pulling him awkwardly over the bar. "Of that, you can be sure, Conner Mullins of Tynsall Avenue."

The lad snatched his hand back and hurried back to his friends, not even waiting for his drink. Lucas turned to face Vetta and Simon, who were staring at him in awe.

"What was that?" asked Simon.

Lucas shrugged. "Seems like Heaven wants me to run a clean bar. Now, how 'bout we have ourselves a wee drink? And let's hope that, at least for tonight, we won't see any more blood on the bar."

That was something they were all happy to drink to.

Same Again

The roadwork on the corner made the high street a death trap. Cars overtook one another on the narrow street and gave no warning of whether or not they were turning into one side street or the next. That the lights did not seem to be working made things even worse.

Ruth needed to get across to the post office, but every time she took a trembling step onto the road, a car seemed to steam right across her path and sent her retreating back onto the pavement. Seventy-six was not an age for mad dashes across the road.

She jabbed an arthritic finger at the silver button beneath the lights, but still they failed to work. At this rate, she would be stuck on this side of the road all day.

"Want a hand, my love?"

Ruth glanced aside to see a handsome young man offering an arm to her. He had a layer of dark black stubble that would have been untidy in her day, but in this age, it was probably what counted for fashionable. His clothes, also, seemed very much the product of today—jeans more like a young girl's leggings than a grown man's trousers, and his suit jacket seemed odd over his plain t-shirt. Yet, his smile was full of warmth, and his eyes sparkled with kindness. Five minutes she had been trying to cross the road, and this was the first person to come to her aid.

"Thank you, young man. Good to know there's still some good souls about."

The man smiled wider, making Ruth blush. Young men did not notice her in such a way anymore. It wasn't a sexual look, but it was a focused stare, one that meant he was seeing her as a vibrant human being and not just an old lady. It was funny how much she missed being noticed by a stranger.

He linked his arm in hers and said, "There are plenty of good souls about, but the modern world keeps everybody's eyes downward. If only something would finally get them looking up again."

And wasn't that the truth. As they took their first steps across the road, she gave a short chuckle. "You didn't have mobile phones and computers in my day. We all sat together around the radio or sat outside our front doors with a cup of tea. This generation is going to end up with square eyes."

The young man laughed, a soft, infectious sound. "You're not wrong. The world changes so quickly, don't you think?"

They carried on across the road, taking things slowly. The young man even put a hand up to keep a white van from running them down. "Hold your horses," he barked protectively.

"You don't know the half of it," she told the man. "The older I get, the more I feel like an alien who landed on another planet. Kind of makes me ready for the grave."

"Don't be maudlin," said the young man with a grin. "If things stayed the same, humanity would have no place to go. It's part of the human spirit to want to move forward. Could any other animal have put itself on the moon?"

Ruth tittered, wishing the edge of the road wasn't getting so near. She was enjoying this brief, yet unexpected conversation. "What animal would be stupid enough to try? There's nothing on the moon but a whole lot of nothing."

They reached the curb, and the man helped her up onto the pavement. He placed an arm on her shoulder and squeezed. "You're not wrong there. Still, you don't know until you try, huh?"

"I suppose you're right there, young man. Thank you for helping me across the road. My name's Ruth. What's yours?"

The young man's attractive smile grew wider than ever, revealing a perfect set of teeth. His eyes twinkled almost mischievously. "Oh, you can just call me the Good Samaritan."

Ruth frowned. Then the young man shoved her in the chest, so hard that she felt a rib crack. She tumbled backwards off the curb and back into the busy road. The side of her head struck the asphalt, and she was dazed.

She didn't hear anyone cry out, or even notice the assault, but she heard the heavy rumbling of a large, angry engine. She turned her head just in time to see the bus's thick tyres grinding towards her. The squeal of brakes was the last thing she heard.

The Good Samaritan strolled away from the bloody scene whistling a merry tune. He had no plans for the day, but he quite fancied himself a beer.

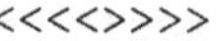

Plea From the Author

Hey, Reader. So you got to the end of my book. I hope that means you enjoyed it. Whether or not you did, I would just like to thank you for giving me your valuable time to try and entertain you. I am truly blessed to have such a fulfilling job, but I only have that job because of people like you; people kind enough to give my books a chance and spend their hard-earned money buying them. For that I am eternally grateful.

If you would like to find out more about my other books then please visit my website for full details. You can find it at:

www.iainrobwright.com.

Also feel free to contact me on Facebook, Twitter, or email (all details on the website), as I would love to hear from you.

If you enjoyed this book and would like to help, then you could think about leaving a review on Amazon, Goodreads, or anywhere else that readers visit. The most important part of how well a book sells is how many positive reviews it has, so if you leave me one then you are directly helping me to continue on this journey as a fulltime writer. Thanks in advance to anyone who does. It means a lot.

Don't miss out on your FREE Iain Rob Wright horror starter pack. Five free bestselling horror novels sent straight to your inbox. No strings attached.

For more information just visit this page:
www.iainrobwright.com

Iain has more than a dozen novels available to purchase right now. To see full descriptions, visit the link below.

- **Animal Kingdom**
- **AZ of Horror**
- **2389**
- **Holes in the Ground** (with J.A.Konrath)
- **Sam**
- **ASBO**
- **The Final Winter**
- **The Housemates**
- **Sea Sick** FREE!
- **Ravage**
- **Savage**
- **The Picture Frame**
- **Wings of Sorrow**
- **The Gates**
- **Legion**
- **Extinction**
- **TAR**
- **House Beneath the Bridge**
- **The Peeling**

Sarah Stone Thriller Series

- **Soft Target** FREE!
- **Hot Zone**
- **End Play**

Iain Rob Wright is one of the UK's most successful horror and suspense writers, with novels including the critically acclaimed, THE FINAL WINTER; the disturbing bestseller, ASBO; and the wicked screamfest, THE HOUSEMATES.

His work is currently being adapted for graphic novels, audio books, and foreign audiences. He is an active member of the Horror Writer Association and a massive animal lover.

www.iainrobwright.com
FEAR ON EVERY PAGE

For more information
www.iainrobwright.com
iain.robert.wright@hotmail.co.uk

Artwork by Books Covered Ltd

Editing by Autumn Speckhardt

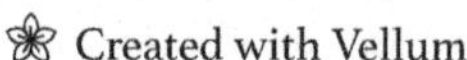